LOST FLIGHT

Dan Bomkamp

Published by
Joel Lovstad-Publishing
2406 Columbus LN.
Madison, WI 53704

Printed in the United States of America

ISBN: 0-9749058-7-9

Other books by Dan Bomkamp
Adventures of Thunderfoot
More Adventures of Thunderfoot
Thanks, Thunderfoot
The Gosey
Voyageur

Cover design by Joel Lovstad-Publishing
Cover photo by Doug Stamm

For Dad

Acknowledgements

I wish to thank several people for their help with this book.

I want to thank Ron and Marguarite Huls, Boscobel Airport, for their advice and help with the information on the planes in this story. I think they thought I was a little daft with some of my questions, but I hope they see that their advice was put to good use.

I want to thank Jean Benson, Muscoda Public Library, for her help in researching the Pleistocene era and the early days of Lake of the Woods. It was a tremendous help.

Thanks, also, to the many good friends with whom, over the years, I made numerous fly-in and houseboat trips to Lake of the Woods in Canada. Those trips gave me many ideas for parts of this book. What a fun way to research.

Great thanks go to my good friend, Doug Stamm. His beautiful photo of a Beaver float plane graces the cover of this book. You can view more of his work at: www.stammphoto.com

And of course, I want to thank my friend and editor, Joel Lovstad for his wonderful copy editing skills and advice on ways to keep the story moving. Finding the right editor can make or break a book. I've found the right one.

LOST FLIGHT

Prolog

Lake of the Woods

The Pleistocene Epoch, 10,000 BC: The world is a cold, dark, frozen place where winter lasts nearly all year. The short summers are barely long enough for the grasses and trees to become green; then it is autumn and winter quickly sets in again. Ice covers nearly all land of the northern continents. Unrelenting mile-thick glaciers grind across the landscape, constantly moving southward, their massive weight and tremendous pressure scouring everything off the face of the land, right down to the bedrock.

Much of the water of earth's oceans is trapped in the glaciers, causing the sea levels to be lower than they have ever been. Land bridges between continents are exposed on the surface for the first time in all of history. Moisture evaporating from the immense sheet of ice forms clouds and fog that continuously swirl across the land; even summer months are cool and dark.

This has been the way of things for tens of thousands of years. But the last great ice age is finally coming to an end. The climate slowly begins to moderate a fraction of a degree at a time. Over the next few centuries temperatures climb in tiny increments and the great sheets of ice begin to melt. It takes many lifetimes, but glaciers that had been forming for 20,000 years now are beginning to shrink, exposing land that had been buried for eons.

The Pleistocene Glacier that covers all of North America begins to melt, and the frozen lands come alive, awakening from the icy sleep of centuries. Over the next several hundred years, the glacier shrinks farther and the frigid water left behind by the melting ice forms a vast inland sea known as Lake Agassiz. It covers much of what will be Canada and the northern United States. (Modern day Lake Winnipeg and Lake Manitoba were once a part of this inland ocean, and its ancient shoreline is still visible in many places across Canada.)

As temperatures continue to rise, the water slowly evaporates. Lake Agassiz shrinks and areas of land start to emerge. These islands continue to grow as the water recedes, turning them into large, dry land masses of the northern continent. Seeds blown on winds and dropped by birds take root in soil left behind by the glaciers. As vegetation appears, it attracts more animals and birds; more seeds are scattered in other areas as creatures inhabit the land. A once barren region is becoming less hostile and more inviting to the beasts, and soon it will be found by man.

About 2,000 BC, people of the Laurel Culture – mound builders – begin to live in the area. Most likely their ancestors had crossed the land bridges when the seas were low. They make and use copper tools and weapons. (Those relics can still be found today in many places in northern forests.) They hunt the abundant animals and fish for food. The forest provides more sources for nourishment – roots and berries – as well as shelter.

But by 1,000 BC, the Laurel people had disappeared. New people – the Blackduck Culture – either drove the Laurels out or assimilated them by interbreeding with them until they were mixed into the new culture. The Blackduck people thrived for hundreds of years. Their numbers grew and some moved farther south to become the roots of the native North American Indians.

A young French explorer, Jacques de Noyon was the first European to venture into this wilderness of lakes and islands in 1688. Although only 20 years old, he was among a brave group of men searching for a passage to the Western Sea, or Pacific Ocean as it would later be called. Many European explorers were convinced that there existed a water passage to the west that would provide a route to the exotic lands of Japan and China. Their interests also included finding a source of furs and other treasures to send back to Europe.

Although Jacques de Noyon didn't find the passage to the Western Sea, he did find amazing wealth during months of exploring this area rich in fur bearing animals beyond his highest expectations. The local Indians were more than willing to trade their furs for the many goods he had brought with him. And little did he know just how big this land was. This giant lake covered nearly 2,000 square miles. Later, more than 14,000 islands and 65,000 miles of shoreline would be discovered.

Large birch trees for building canoes and shelters flourished on the islands. Huge pines provided wood for houses and fires. Wild rice grew in abundance in the shallows of the lake. Ducks, geese, and game animals provided more than ample food. It was truly a remarkable place.

Jacques de Noyon had failed in his attempt to find passage to the Western Sea, but he did discover one of the most amazing natural resources of the world – a land filled with vast natural riches; a land that would someday be a recreational paradise for thousands of outdoor enthusiasts. He called this amazing place *Lac aux Iles* – Lake of the Woods.

Lost Flight

Chapter 1

"Oh boy, Mom's gonna skin me," Matt Tanner thought to himself as his new running shoes sank into the soft mud at the edge of the small pond. He could feel the cold water as it ran down over the tops and between his toes. The water was deep enough to get the cuffs of his jeans wet. He waded in deeper and stopped. Bubbles of gas rose up from the bottom of the marsh. He scrunched up his nose to the strong odor of decaying vegetation. "Well, I'm wet now. I might as well keep going," he said to himself. Crouched in the thick willows bordering the pond, he had snuck up on the little moose calf that was standing in the water up to its knobby knees. Anxious to try out his new digital camera, he hoped to get close enough. He could see the little moose bent over with its head under the water getting a mouthful of green vegetation. Matt stood nearly straight up and readied his camera for a shot. Just as the baby's head came up, water running from the vegetation in its mouth, he snapped the picture. The little moose heard the shutter click and looked his way, but didn't seem alarmed. Matt turned the camera to take a vertical shot and snapped again. This time the moose's ears perked up and it looked hard in his direction, most likely wondering what that strange creature was and why it was making those snapping sounds.

Matt took another step forward to get a better angle. His feet sunk deeper into the gripping mud. As he struggled to keep his balance he heard the hooves of a larger moose coming his way, sloshing the water and rattling through the willows.

"MMMMuuuuuuhh!" she bellowed. "MMMMuuuuuuhh!" It was surely the calf's mother. Matt ducked down and stayed perfectly still. The black shape of the huge animal charged through the brush and willows, snuffing and bellowing. He tried to turn and run, but he had sunk into the mud nearly up to his knees. Try as he might he couldn't pull them free. The willows whipped back and forth as the angry mother moose charged closer.

"Mathew, it's time to go," his mother's voice called out.

"Shhh, Ma. Don't make any noise."

"Matty! Come on, sweetie."

"Ma! Be quiet or she'll hear you," he whispered. He was sure the moose had heard his mom and they would be trampled in the next few seconds. "We've got to run, Ma," he said.

"Mathew, it's time. You've got to get up now. We're going to have breakfast and Brandon is on his way over here."

He heard the reeds rattle right next to him and he felt the warm breath of the angry cow moose on his cheek. He turned his head and looked straight up at the big black moose. With her muzzle just inches away, her black eyes bored into him. He knew he was about to be run over when the animal slowly dissolved and his bedroom came into focus. He rubbed his eyes. His mother was standing over his bed smiling. "You must have been having a scary dream," she said as she brushed the hair away from his forehead. "Who was she?"

"I, uh, jeez! That was a dream? Holy cow, Mom. I thought I was already in Canada," he said grinning sheepishly. "She? She was a mother moose who was charging me."

"Well," his mom said, "I'm glad it was a moose and not some girl you were dreaming about. It won't be long now... just a few days and you'll be there for the whole summer. So get up now. We'll be leaving soon and Brandon will be here to pick you up."

His mind cleared of sleepy cobwebs. Matt realized that the long awaited day was finally here. He jumped up from bed and trotted off to the bathroom. As he took off his pajama top, he looked in the mirror and flexed his biceps. Noticeable was just a hint of muscle forming, and some slight definition of the chest muscles on his otherwise thin frame. He was a long way from being a muscle man, but at least he was getting over that skinny boyish look. He brushed his teeth and then stepped into the shower. The hot water soaked into him, waking him fully. After he toweled off he smeared some jell into his short, light brown hair that some would call dirty blond, and mooshed it around until it had that "slept in" look. As he manipulated the spikes he recalled the previous morning when he hadn't noticed his dad watching him apply a similar treatment until he heard the chuckle from behind. "So that's the way it's *supposed* to look?" his dad had asked. "It looks like a hand grenade went off on top of your head."

Matt just grinned. "Yeah, that's the way it's *supposed* to look, Dad," he said. "Not any worse than those *duck butt* hair cuts you used to have. I've seen those pictures of you when you were my age."

"That's *duck tails*, and they were very stylish," his dad said, playfully slapping him on the butt. Thinking of his dad's good natured ribbing, Matt smiled and gazed into the mirror, pleased with the blue eyed guy looking back at him. In a few months he'd be thirteen – a teenager!

He slipped on some tan cargo shorts, a red Wisconsin Badgers tee shirt, tennis shoes without socks, and headed down the stairs to the kitchen. His parents and their best friends, the Watsons, were about to have breakfast. Their long awaited dream was beginning today.

Chapter 2

Matt ran down the stairs, stopped at the kitchen doorway, and surveyed the scene. His mom and Sandy Watson were making breakfast and his dad and Todd Watson were leaning over a large map spread out on the dining room table. A stack of suitcases and duffle bags were piled by the door to the garage. Everyone was talking, and then the click of toenails drew his attention as his dog, Kirby, overjoyed to see Matt, came skating across the hardwood floor to greet his master. Rubbing up against Matt's legs and wagging his tail wildly, Kirby carried in his mouth his favorite toy – a one legged, stuffed duck named Donald.

"Hey, Kirbo! What's up today?" Matt said as he leaned to greet the dog with generous ear scratching. "I was sleeping real hard this morning. I didn't know you left my bed," he said. The dog almost turned inside out with joy. Matt grabbed Kirby's face and bent close to him. "And how is Donald today?" he asked. Kirby laid the wet duck down so Matt could say good morning to Donald, too. Matt picked up the cloth duck and greeted it. His mom grinned at him. "Talking to a dog I can see, but to a toy duck? Matty, sometimes I wonder about you." Matt grinned and handed Donald to Kirby.

Just as he righted himself, he felt a powerful pair of arms encircle his chest from behind and he was lifted from the floor. He began giggling and wriggling to get free.

"Arrgh, the Grizzl Bear attacks!" He felt a mouth on the back of his neck as "The Grizzl Bear" playfully chewed on his neck. A huge smile spread across his face and he twisted and turned trying to get loose. "Arrgh, Arrgh," came the fierce sound of his attacker. Finally the arms holding him eased their grip and Matt's feet dropped to the floor. He turned and jumped into the outstretched arms of his best friend in the world, Brandon Watson.

"Brand! Dang, I've missed you," he said. He wrapped his arms around Brandon's neck and hugged him. "I haven't seen you for three weeks."

"Hey, Matty. Same here, bud. I've been studying hard at school so I'll pass my exams."

Eighteen-year-old Brandon was in his first year of college. He and Matt's older brother, Mark, had been best friends. But when Mark died in an auto accident two years earlier, Matt and Brandon became like brothers, first sharing their grief, and then sharing the healing that eventually comes with the loss of a loved one.

Matt let go of Brandon and stepped back. "Jeez, Brand. You been working out? You're lookin pretty buff."

Brandon grinned. "Yeah I've been in the gym a little." He eyed Matt up and down, gently squeezed his bicep, and gave pretence that he was impressed. "Looks like you've been working out, too." He grinned some more.

Matt flexed his muscles a little, and then felt foolish that he had done it.

"Come for breakfast, boys," Matt's mom said. They all sat on stools around the island snack bar and dug into the plates of eggs, bacon, and toast. Excitement about their upcoming adventure had everyone talking at once. Kirby made the rounds to each person putting on his "Starved Dog" act and got handouts from everyone.

Chapter 3

There was a lot of chatter as plans formulated for the upcoming weeks. Matt watched Brandon as he ate and talked about school and his exams. Matt idolized Brandon. When he and Mark were friends, Brandon always treated Matt as an equal, not like a little kid, including him in things he and Mark did.

The two families had always been close. Mike Tanner and Todd Watson met in Air Force flight school in the late 1960s and served in Vietnam flying troop carriers and supply planes. During their service together they became good friends and after they left the Air Force, they both looked for jobs as commercial pilots. At first, jobs had been scarce and they had to settle for a few starter positions at small airlines, but they kept applying for better jobs and in time they were both hired at American Airlines.

Occasionally they flew together, but most of the time they were all over the world, each on their own flights. Then, by chance, they both were in London for a layover. Mike invited two of his flight attendants to go out on the town with Todd and him. Matt's mother, Carol and her friend Sandy were those two flight attendants. The rest of the story is pretty obvious. The two pilots and the two flight attendants hit it off, and in the following year, they dated as often as they could, were engaged, and sometime later both couples married.

As "old married men" Todd and Mike grew tired of living in apartments that they were seldom in. They liked the mid-west, Wisconsin especially, and found homes just a block apart in St. Francis, a Milwaukee suburb. A couple of years later, both wives gave birth to sons, Brandon and Mark, just a month apart. Carol and Sandy retired from American to care for their kids, but occasionally filled in on a flight when an emergency arose.

Five years after Mark was born, Mathew came along. When he was old enough to accompany his big brother, Mark took him everywhere. They were very close and spent a lot of time together. Brandon Watson had been Mark's best friend, and they always included Matt in their activities. Since their dads were gone so much, the three boys gravitated to each other for male companionship.

Flying was pre-ordained in Mark and Brandon. They were a little younger than most beginners, but their parents were all in favor of them learning to be pilots. Once they started lessons, Matt always tagged along, and from the hanger of the small airport where they received instruction he watched his two heroes practice.

Mark and Brandon had just celebrated their sixteenth birthdays, and Brandon had just gotten his driver's license. Matt was playing in a soccer game, so he wasn't with them the day they were heading to the airport to take their first solo flights. As they crossed an intersection, a drunk driver ran a stop sign and hit the passenger side of the car broadside. Mark was killed instantly. Miraculously Brandon was barely injured.

Brandon blamed himself. Even though Mark's death was a terrible blow to the two families, everyone knew Brandon had not been at fault. But the boys had been like brothers, and the grief lasted a long time. Matt began relying on Brandon, now in his brother's absence, and it seemed only natural for Brandon to take over the role of best friend and big brother to Matt.

Brandon was engaged in animated conversation with all the parents about the upcoming summer. Matt sat quietly, admiring the nearly six feet tall, well built, movie star handsome lad. He took particular notice of Brandon's hairdo similar to his own – that "hand grenade on the head" look. His sparkling green eyes winked at Matt and he smiled with his wide, easy grin. He was quite fond of the boy, and he knew they would soon be heading into the Canadian wilderness for an adventure filled summer.

"So, Brandon," his dad said. "You and Matt will be coming next Thursday?"

"Yeah," Brandon replied. "My last exam is Tuesday. Matt has school till Wednesday. We'll fly up to Nestor Falls Thursday morning, and then if the other plane and everything is ready, we'll fly into Clearwater Bay that afternoon."

"We'll have all the supplies loaded and tied down for you," Todd said. "We're taking all the perishables with us. All you need to bring is your clothes and your fishing gear."

"And Kirby," Matt added.

Kirby's tail thumped the floor when he heard his name.

“Oh, yeah, I almost forgot about Kirby,” Todd said.

Matt slipped Kirby a slice of bacon. The dog gobbled it up and swallowed it without even chewing. “We need our guard dog to chase away Grizzl Bears, don’t we Kirb?” Matt laughed.

Grateful to be included in the conversation, wiggling with joy, Kirby was on his feet, Donald held gently but firmly in his mouth. He didn’t know what they were talking about, but hearing his name excited him. But he had no way of knowing just how much excitement was in store.

Chapter 4

Watsons' house was all closed up for the summer. Todd had arranged for a neighborhood boy to mow the grass, and Sandy's friend next door would keep an eye on things and water the plants. The newspaper was cancelled and the mail forwarded. Just before they came to Tanners' for breakfast, they set timers to turn on lights in the house at various times. Brandon would be staying at the Tanners' house with Matt until they were both finished with school, so he had his clothes and fishing gear with him, all packed and ready. It was necessary for the grownups to leave now so they could get the resort up and running for the early fishing season.

For the Tanners and Watsons, Clearwater Bay Resort was a dream come true. When Mark and Brandon were both 13 and Matt was only 7, the two families had taken their first fly-in vacation to the resort. They loved it so much that they made reservations for the following year before the end of their week stay.

They found some of the best fishing and relaxation they had ever experienced at Clearwater Bay, situated at the extreme northwest of Lake of the Woods – that huge lake and river system that covers nearly 2,000 square miles of Canadian wilderness, has 14,000 islands and more than 65,000 miles of shoreline. For the next three years they vacationed at Clearwater Bay and became good friends with the elderly owners, Thor and Ida Olson. Besides the good fishing, they enjoyed meeting and making new friends in the main lodge, a huge log structure, where everyone came from their individual cabins to eat their meals in the dining room. It served as a social gathering place, where plenty of fish stories were traded. For the days when rain kept the vacationers off the lake, there were billiards, foosball, card games, and because there was no television signal so far north, movies from a VCR had to suffice.

They didn't go to the resort the year Mark died. It was too hard coming to grips with his death, and the thought of going on vacation just didn't appeal to any of them. But, by the next year, they had recovered enough that they felt they would go again. When they arrived, they noticed how age was taking its toll on

Thor and Ida. They were getting too old to take care of the Lodge and the ten cabins that accommodated guests, and the six outpost cabins that fishermen could fly to for a day or two of remote fishing. Of course, they had hired help, but even with a cook, dock boy, a cleaning girl and a bush pilot that doubled as handy man, it was getting to be more than the two old folks could handle.

One evening while they were chatting by the huge natural rock fireplace in the Lodge, Thor mentioned to Mike and Todd that he had put the place on the market. He wanted to retire. That sparked the idea of buying Clearwater Bay Lodge. Financing the deal wouldn't be a problem. They had made a lot of money during their 20 years as commercial pilots, and had good pensions. The problem was going to be convincing their wives that they should leave their comfortable homes each spring and spend the summer and fall cooking, cleaning, and waiting on other people.

Carol and Sandy realized how excited their boys had become with the idea. They were willing to do their share of the work; Brandon was already a licensed pilot, so he could handle the bush pilot duties. Matt could be the dock boy and help with the rest of the work, too. After several weeks of convincing from their husbands and sons, Carol and Sandy finally agreed they would give it a try. An offer was made, the Olsons accepted, and a short time later, the Tanners and the Watsons owned a Canadian resort. Mike and Todd retired from American Airlines and began preparations by obtaining all the required permits and licenses. And now, after months of planning, the two families were about to embark on their grand new venture.

Chapter 5

Todd and Mike and their wives drove in a rental van to the small airport where they kept their private planes in a hangar. Brandon and Matt followed in Brandon's Jeep. Each family owned a four-seat, single engine Cessna Skyhawk that would haul only a limited amount of luggage and gear. Todd and Mike had flown up earlier and purchased all the groceries and other supplies they would need at the resort, and that was waiting for them at Nestor Falls. So all they were taking with them on this trip was their clothes and personal belongings.

Their newly acquired business came complete with two planes that were also waiting at Nestor Falls. Since everything had to be flown in, they wanted both as full as possible on the initial trip. The grownups were going to fly the big plane, the *DeHavilland Otter*, a large floatplane that can haul ten passengers and a lot of cargo. Though not as speedy as their Cessna, the Otter was a workhorse of a plane.

Once the boys had finished school, Brandon would pilot the other plane, the *DeHavilland Beaver*, from Nestor Falls to the resort. The Beaver, while much smaller than the Otter, was still a very large single engine plane. With a wingspan of 48 feet and an overall length of over 30 feet, it was much bigger than anything he had ever flown. But Todd and Mike were quite confident in the abilities of the young pilot. "He can fly better at eighteen that I could when I was twenty five," Mike had said.

"But that's such a large plane," his mom had protested.

"It doesn't matter, honey. Larger plane, larger engine, it's all relative. Brandon is a good pilot with good, natural flying instincts. I'm not worried a bit about him flying the Beaver." So, that was that. The boys would take the other Cessna from St. Francis to Nestor Falls and then fly the Beaver in to the camp.

They had a great working plan for the summer. With three pilots – Mike, Todd, and Brandon – one of them would pick up fishermen at Nestor Falls with a float plane. That town is right on the bay, so it makes for a perfect transfer point for those who land in regular planes at the air strip. Then they could load their gear into a float plane and be flown to the resort farther into the wilderness. It was a popular trip in the fall for hunters, too.

Brandon more than likely would be the one to fly those who wanted to use the remote camps. The smaller Beaver would work well for that, while the Otter would be used to transport large groups and the heavier cargo from Nestor Falls.

At the airport they drove up next to the waiting Cessna that had been fueled and was ready for them. Mike and Todd transferred the luggage to the plane while the moms hovered and worried about leaving the boys alone. "Now, don't forget," Sandy said. "If something comes up, call Grandpa. He'll help you,"

Brandon nodded. "Yeah, Mom. Don't worry about us. We'll be fine. We'll be up there in less than a week."

"Well, I have to worry. That's my job as a mom," she said as she hugged Brandon goodbye. She hugged Matt, too. "You see to it that Brandon behaves." Matt grinned and nodded.

His dad handed Brandon a folded map that was a copy of the one they had studied the previous night. "Now, just remember… follow the Canadian Pacific Railway north along the east side of the lake. When you get to Kenora, swing to the west and you shouldn't have any trouble finding us. You've been there as many times as we have, so it shouldn't be a problem."

"Don't worry, Dad. I remember it real well."

"Just follow the railway, and don't cut across the lake. With all of those islands, you can get really screwed up and you might end up in Alaska or someplace," Mike laughed.

"We'll be careful, and I'm not worried. I have my navigator right here with me," Brandon said. He put his arm around Matt's shoulders.

Matt grinned and hugged his dad goodbye. "See you in a week," he said.

The boys watched the Cessna taxi down to the end of the runway, get up speed and lift off. It always made Brandon's heart beat a little faster to see a plane lift up, knowing how the forces of physics and the shape of the wings were working to achieve lift. Even though he knew all about the dynamics of flight, it still amazed him each and every time it happened.

"Well, we've got your house all to ourselves for six days," he said to Matt with a big grin.

Matt started dancing around. "Partay! Partay!"

The two boys laughed all the way to the parking lot. They jumped into Brandon's jeep and headed for home, anxious for these next few days to pass quickly, so they, too, could be zipping down that runway on their way to adventure.

Chapter 6

The day passed quickly back at Matt's house. Brandon and Matt both had exams to study for, so Matt worked at his desk in his room and Brandon spread his books out on the dining room table. They had been given strict instructions to eat everything in the refrigerator before they left the following week. Determined to give it their best shot, at dinner time they grilled hamburgers and heated frozen fries in the oven.

That evening Brandon was sitting on the couch reading from one of his text books with his socked feet propped up on the coffee table. Matt sat at the other end of the couch, propped up his feet and stuck his nose into a book of his own. Brandon snuck a glance at the younger boy and marveled at how much he was beginning to act like Mark. Matt had his elbow resting on the arm of the couch, twirling his hair around his finger, just like his big brother used to.

"Brand?" Matt said.

"Yeah, Matty?"

"Do you ever think about Mark?"

"Every day. In fact, I was thinking about him just now."

"What were you thinking?"

Matt slid over next to Brandon, and Brandon laid his arm around the younger boy's shoulders. "I was just thinking that you're so much like Mark. You're beginning to act like him. You're like a second Mark."

Matt looked up at Brandon and smiled. "I miss him," he said quietly.

"I do too, Matty."

They sat in silence with their books open, but neither of them was reading.

"Brand?"

"Yeah?"

"Do you think Mark is in heaven?"

"Yeah, Matty, I think he's up there looking down on us right now."

There was silence for several minutes.

"Brand?"

"Yeah?"

"Will you teach me about flying?"

"You want to learn to fly, too?"

"Yeah. All the other men in our families have learned. I want to learn, too."

Brandon got a far away look in his eyes and smiled. "It seems like just yesterday when Mark and I talked about learning to fly. I remember the first time Mark and I took off in the trainer with our instructor. Jeez, Mark was smiling so wide. I remember that look on his face the first time he took over the yoke and actually steered the plane. He loved flying."

"Was he a good flyer?"

"Oh, yeah. He took to it so easily. He was a natural."

Matt leaned against Brandon. He could hear Brandon's heart beating. Brandon rubbed the boy's arm. "I'll never forget the poem that Mark taught me after that first day we actually flew the plane."

"Tell it to me?"

Brandon's face had a distant smile, as if he was reliving that moment when Mark had recited the poem to him. "It's called High Flight, and it was written by a young American pilot who flew for the Canadian Air Force in 1941," he explained. "He joined the Canadians because he was too young to get in the American Air Force. He wanted to fight in the war and loved to fly, so he was in England training with the Canadians. He wrote this poem on the back of an envelope after he had been on a training flight." Then he began reciting the poem from memory:

"Oh I have slipped the surly bonds of earth
And danced the clouds on laughter silvered wings.
Sunward I've climbed and joined the tumbling mirth
of sun-split clouds and done a hundred things
You have not dreamed of -
wheeled and soared and swung
into the sunlit silence.
Hovering there,

I've chased the shouting wind along and flung
My eager craft through footless halls of air,
Up, up the delirious burning blue,
I've topped the windswept heights with easy grace
Where never lark or even eagle flew
And with silent lifting mind, I've trod
the high untresspassed sanctity of space,
Put out my hand, and touched the face of God."

Neither of them spoke for several minutes. Then Matt broke the silence: "Mark taught you that?"

"Yeah. He said it captured how he felt when he was up there in the air," Brandon replied.

"Is the guy who wrote that still alive?"

"His name is John Gillespie McGee Jr. He was killed in a training accident just a few days after he wrote that poem."

"Will you write it down Brand? I want to learn it."

"Sure."

They sat in silence for a while, and then Brandon noticed that Matt had fallen asleep. He carefully picked up the sleeping boy, carried him to his room, and put him on his bed. He slipped off his socks and pulled a blanket over him. "Good night, Matty," he whispered.

Brandon passed through the bathroom that adjoined Matt's room and Mark's former room where he was going to sleep. As he undressed, he stared at Mark's sophomore picture grinning at him from the desk. "I'm probably the first person to sleep in here since Mark died," he thought to himself. "Hey pal," he said to the picture. "You keep an eye on Matt and me, okay?" He could hear Mark's laughter and see the twinkle in his eye as he drifted off to sleep.

Chapter 7

Brandon felt a breeze on his face as sleep left him. He opened his eyes and was staring at Kirby's black, wet nose, his chin resting on the bed, watching for movement. "Hey, Kirby. What's up?" The dog's tail wagged furiously, adding to the breeze he had already created while watching Brandon sleep. "I suppose you have to go out." Donald was on the bed, and Kirby took the toy in his mouth. His tail knocked against the wall and he whined, galloping back and forth between the open door and the bed.

Brandon sat on the edge of the bed, scratched the dog's ears, and then got up and walked into the bathroom. He did his most urgent business, and then went into Matt's room.

"Hey, Brand," Matt said smiling, still in his bed.

"Hi, Matt. Did I wake you?"

"No. Kirby's tail thumping woke me. I thought somebody was at the door." They both laughed.

Kirby was getting frantic. He had an urgent need for a trip outside. "I'll take Kirby out," Brandon said. "You'd better get up. You have to get to school in less than an hour." He followed behind Kirby, hurrying to the front door.

Brandon slipped on a tee shirt and shorts and went barefoot out into the glorious spring morning. He waited while Kirby ran across the yard, carefully put Donald down on the grass, and then found just the right bush to water. When he was finished checking out all the smells that had accumulated in the yard during the night, he retrieved Donald and headed back to the house.

Brandon could smell bacon frying. He couldn't help but laugh when he saw Matt at the stove frying bacon and eggs wearing only his underwear and an apron tied around his waist. "You're quite the little homemaker, aren't you?" he said.

Matt glanced his way and grinned. "Butter that toast?"

After the breakfast, they showered, dressed, put Kirby into his outside kennel for the day, and then off they went. Brandon dropped Matt off at his middle school on his way to Marquette University where he had an exam that morning at 11 o'clock.

The next days few passed quickly. On the eve of their trip to

Canada, Brandon was on the phone ordering a pizza since they had eaten the refrigerator empty. "Mom will be proud of us," Matt said grinning widely.

They both packed large duffel bags with clothes and readied their fishing rods and tackle boxes. Going to bed early didn't do anything to help them get to sleep, and both of them lay awake for a long time thinking of the adventures that awaited them in the next few months.

"Brand?" Matt called out quietly through the open doors of the bathroom.

"Yeah, Matty."

"You asleep?"

"I'm answering you. What does that tell you?"

Matt laughed. "I can't go to sleep."

"Yeah, me too. Try counting walleyes."

Matt giggled. "Night Brand."

"Night Matty."

The next morning they loaded their clothes and fishing gear into the jeep, along with Kirby, his water and food pans, and a fifty pound bag of dog food. They gave the house key to the house sitter and headed for the airport.

It was hard to tell whether Kirby or Matt was more excited as they both found it difficult to sit still on the short ride. Kirby trotted back and forth across the back seat with Donald clutched tightly in his mouth, and Matt babbled constantly about all the things he planned to do during the summer in Canada. "They've got huge northern pike up there. I'm gonna fish till I catch a twenty pounder! And big walleyes, too!" He rambled on: "I heard there are big lake trout and smallmouth bass and perch like you never saw before..."

"When will you do your work when you're fishing all the time?" Brandon asked smiling.

"I'll get the fishermen out on the lake," Matt replied, "and then, if you don't have to fly anywhere, we can go fishing with one of the boats. In a few weeks we'll know all the hot spots and we can charge for being guides, too."

"You've got it all figured out, don't you, Matty?" Brandon said.

"Yep... Matt's Guide Service. I'll be rich by the end of the summer."

Chapter 8

The Cessna was already sitting along the runway when they arrived at the airport. Brandon had called ahead and asked that it be fueled and made ready for takeoff. He had also filed a flight plan required when crossing into Canadian airspace. The airport manager had sent the flight plan ahead. Brandon and Matt would have to land in International Falls for an inspection and customs check. That, too, was standard procedure when entering Canadian airspace.

"Do you have Kirby's vaccination papers and all of his records?" Brandon asked.

"Yeah, he's good to go. The vet gave me copies of everything he needs for crossing the border. I have it all in my duffle bag."

Kirby thumped his tail.

Brandon pulled the Jeep next to the Cessna and they loaded their gear and the dog food into the luggage compartment. While Matt and Kirby waited, Brandon parked the Jeep in the long term parking area and gave the keys to the manager in the office. He walked across the pavement to the plane, climbed aboard, and stowed their duffle bags and fishing tackle in a pile in the cargo area. He stretched the cargo net across the gear and hooked it on tie-downs on the side and floor of the plane. "There. If we hit some rough air, we won't have fishing poles flying all over the plane. Well, get in and let's get in the air," he said with a huge smile.

Matt lifted Kirby into the back seat and hooked the seatbelt through a special harness that Mike and Todd had made for him. It allowed him to move around, but kept him in the seat and out of harm's way if there was any trouble. Kirby had flown with them many times, and he loved it, so he was wagging and slobbering with wild anticipation. He had carefully deposited Donald on the seat beside him.

"I see Donald is going along, too," Brandon said.

"If we forgot Donald, we'd have to go back and get him. Kirby would have a fit!" Matt laughed.

The two boys belted in and Brandon started the engine. While it warmed up, he put on a headset and motioned to Matt to do the same with another set on his side of the plane. Using the headsets made it much easier to have a conversation. They didn't have to shout over the noise of the engine. Then he eased the throttle ahead and used his feet on the pedals on the floor to steer the plane onto the runway. They made their way to the far end of the runway and turned the plane so it was lined up. Brandon called on the radio: "Tango Echo Three Three Niner, ready for takeoff."

"Uh, Three Three Niner, there is a United Heavy leaving Mitchell Field right now. Keep an eye out for him. He'll be climbing to altitude in your area."

"Roger. I copy that, a United Heavy. I'll watch for him."

"Keep an eye out to the east, also. Lots of O'Hare traffic in that area. Okay, Three Three Niner. You're clear for take off. Have a nice summer, boys."

"Roger that."

Matt looked at Brandon. "What's a Heavy, Brand?"

"A big jumbo jet, Matty. We don't want to get in his way. Keep a sharp look out. If you see any planes, sing out. Okay?"

Matt grinned. "What song do I sing?"

They both laughed. "Well, let's get this old girl up in the air and see how she runs," Brandon said. Matt gave him thumbs up and he pushed the throttle all the way in. The Cessna started at a slow roll and began gathering speed as they raced down the runway. Brandon watched the gauges. All were in the green. As they approached take off speed, Brandon adjusted the rudder to line them up perfectly, and then pulled back on the yoke. The plane lifted off the ground like a bird soaring on a summer breeze. In no time they were nearly one hundred feet off the ground and climbing steadily. Although Matt had flown many times, he held his breath as they lifted off the ground. No matter how many times he flew, he always loved the sensation of the takeoff.

Brandon climbed to an altitude of one thousand feet. He leveled off, and grinning he turned to Matt. "What do you think of that?" he asked.

"Dang, Brand! You do that as well as anyone I've ever been with. Not a single bump." Obviously, he was impressed with his friend's flying ability. Both of the boys kept a sharp eye out for other planes until they were clear of Chicago air space. They held a steady course toward International Falls. Soon the cities gave way to farmland, and not much later, they were passing over dense forest with very few homes and farms. The farther north they flew, the wilder the country appeared below them.

After an hour or so of flying Brandon asked: "Want to take your first lesson?"

"What? Now?"

"Sure. No time like the present. It's a beautiful day. Not much wind and lots of open sky."

A little apprehensive, Matt nodded yes.

"Okay, first, look at the dials," Brandon began his instruction. "See that one? That's the airspeed. Keep that in that green area. If you're going too slow you might stall out."

Matt nodded.

"That middle one is the artificial horizon. It tells you if you're flying level. Try to keep the wings level to line up with the little plane on the dial. And the one next to it is the altimeter. It tells you how high you are."

Matt nodded again.

"That one in the lower left is the ADF – the Automatic Directional Finder, and the one next to it is the Turn Bank indicator. Watch that one when you make a turn. The middle one is the Directional Gyro, and next to it is Rate of Climb. You won't have to worry about them. I'll keep an eye on them. Those other two are radio dials."

"It's a lot to keep in your head all at once," Matt said looking at all the dials.

"You don't have to worry about all that right now. I'm just explaining how it all works. Now look at those pedals by your feet."

Matt looked down and Brandon said, "They control the rudder. That's the thing at the back of the tail that moves back and forth to turn the plane left or right. Push on the left pedal, you go left. Push on the right one and it turns you to the right. Pretty simple, eh?"

Matt nodded again.

The yoke will also turn you. If you turn it right, the plane will tip to the right and you'll turn. That's where you have to look at the Turn Bank Indicator and the Artificial Horizon. You want to keep them close to the middle of the scale. Don't do anything too radical. Once you've made your turn, look at those gauges and they will help you line everything up again. Turn left, same thing, and by pulling it back, you lift the nose of the plane, and pushing it forward drops the nose. It's just like the steering wheel on a car, except this goes up and down, too."

Matt acknowledged that he understood.

"The only other thing is the throttle, and we'll just leave that alone for right now."

"Okay. I think I've got it," Matt said.

"Put your feet on the pedals and take hold of the yoke. Get the feel of it."

Matt did as he was instructed. He could feel the plane respond as he moved the yoke a little to the left. Brandon released his yoke and grinned. "You have control. You're flying, Buddy."

Matt's heart pounded as he held the yoke and felt the plane moving at his touch. His hands were gripping the yoke so tightly that his knuckles turned white.

"Loosen up. It's not going to fall down instantly. It'll almost fly itself. You just have to show it where to go." Brandon smiled as Matt loosened his grip and relaxed a bit.

"Try a slow turn to the left," Brandon said. "Watch the Turn Bank dial so you don't go too steep." Matt turned the yoke to the left and the plane tipped a bit to the left and turned.

"Very good! Now bring it back to the same heading we were on. Just look at your Directional Gyro and make it go back to the same heading." Matt turned the yoke again to the right and moments later they were level and flying in the same direction as they had started.

"Wow! That's the coolest," Matt said grinning.

"You've got the hang of it. I'm going to take a nap. Wake me up when we get to International Falls."

"What? Brand! Wait a minute!"

Brandon began laughing. Matt got the joke and he laughed too.

"Don't worry. I'll keep an eye on you, but you can fly for a while. Keep control and get used to the feel of it."

For the next half hour Matt flew the plane. He watched the scenery change below him, and the clouds skitter by above him. He checked each gauge and made sure everything was as it should be. He understood, now, why Brandon, Mark, and their dads loved flying so much. And he really understood that poem, *High Flight*. As he thought of the line that said, "*Put out my hand and touched the face of God*," it made him think of Mark, and he knew right then that his big brother was there with them in spirit.

Chapter 9

Matt was feeling pretty good about flying now. He kept the plane on the correct heading and he kept it level. Every once in a while Brandon would have him make a turn, and then turn back again. He was getting good at it.

"You're a natural," Brandon said.

"You really think so?"

"Yeah, it looks like you feel easy about it already." Matt had settled back in his seat, relaxed. His tension had disappeared, and now it seemed more fun handling the plane.

Brandon looked over his shoulder. Kirby was watching the scenery go past. "Kirby sure likes flying, doesn't he?"

"He always has. Wonder if he knows how far it is to the ground?"

When he heard his name, Kirby leaned forward and gave Matt a big wet lick on his left ear. Matt chuckled and wiped his ear with the shoulder of his tee shirt.

"He sure looks better than the day Mark and I found him," Brandon said. "You know how Mark was: always looking out for some critter that was hurt or lost. I think he'd have had a whole menagerie if he'd had his way about it. He just couldn't look the other way from a lost animal – always had to take 'em home."

"I remember he was pretty skinny when you guys brought him home," Matt said.

"Skinny? Cripes! You could see every rib and every vertebra in his back. We found him scratching at a road kill rabbit that was frozen to the highway. He was all dirty and covered with burrs – a real mess. Of course, Mark had to stop and when he saw how skinny he was, there was no question. The dog was goin' home with him. We took him to your house and your parents were gone, so we gave him a bath in your bathtub. He was *really* skinny when he was wet. Then we cut all the burrs out of his coat and Mark made him a big bowl of food. Your mom had a big pot of leftover stew in the refrigerator and Kirby's eyes just about popped out of his head when he smelled real food. He gulped it down, and then he laid down on the living room floor and went right to sleep."

"I remember when I came home he was there. Mark and I began plotting how we could get mom and dad to let us keep him," Matt said. "Obviously, we did it, 'cause here he is." He reached back with his left hand and scratched Kirby's head.

"He's a lucky dog to get rescued like that. I don't think he'd have made it much longer on his own. It was about twenty below zero that night. He'd have probably laid down somewhere and froze to death. And now look at him, all filled out, and handsome as heck." Kirby's tail hammered against the side of the plane.

"Where do you s'pose he came from?"

"I don't know, Matt. Someone must have abandoned him. He must have been on his own for a long time, 'cause he wouldn't get that thin overnight. I can't believe anyone that heartless – who would just throw out a nice dog like him. He's such a sweet guy."

"You s'pose he was a hunting dog?"

"I think one of his parents was. He looks like he's half golden retriever and half collie. But who cares? He's a good friend. That's why Mark bought that stuffed duck for him, since we thought he was part retriever. I doubt that Kirby ever had a toy before, and when Mark gave it to him, he carried it around for a couple of days before he finally put it down. He loves that old thing."

"What happened to its other leg?"

"Mark and Kirby were playing fetch and things got a little rough and poor Donald lost a leg. I suppose he'd swim in a circle now – if he could swim."

Matt laughed and reached over his shoulder to scratch Kirby's ears. "How's Donald doing, Kirby?" he asked. The dog picked up the duck and held it in his mouth, as if to let Matt see for himself. "He looks good. Thanks, Kirby."

"See that city down there?" Brandon asked.

"Yeah."

"That's International Falls. When we cross that river, we're in Canada. I'll take over now – unless you think you want to try to land this thing."

"No way! Take it back," Matt said hastily.

"Okay. I have it," Brandon said, and Matt took his hands and feet off the controls. "That was great, Brand. Thanks for letting me do that."

"I knew you'd like it. We'll let you fly some more later. Right now we have to land and get inspected."

Brandon called to the tower. They gave him landing instructions and a few minutes later they were hurtling down the runway after a perfect touchdown. Brandon taxied the craft to the hanger that the traffic controller had told him to go to, and the Customs Inspector came out to check the plane.

The two boys got out and showed the man their passports and Kirby's papers. He looked over the plane as they walked into the terminal and used the bathroom. They stopped at the snack bar and picked up a couple of sub sandwiches and sodas. By the time they were back to the plane, they were cleared to proceed to Nestor Falls. "Have a nice trip, eh?" the Customs Inspector said as he waved them off.

Brandon taxied to the far end of the runway, lined up the plane, and then called in for take off clearance. He was told to go ahead, and as he throttled up the engine to start down the runway, he said to Matt: "Take hold of the yoke so you can see what take off feels like."

Matt put his hands on the yoke and as the speed increased, he felt the yoke come back toward him. "Pull back gently," Brandon said, and the plane began to lift off the tarmac. They climbed for a short while and Brandon said, "Push it forward just a little and level out."

Astounded to see that Brandon's hands weren't on the yoke but poised just above it Matt blurted out: "Brand! Did I just take off?"

A big smile spread across Brandon's face. "Like I said. You're a natural."

Matt's heart was pounding, but he wore a smile as wide as the horizon.

Chapter 10

Brandon took control and lined the plane up on the heading for Nestor Falls. Then he told Matt to take over and to keep the plane on that heading. Happy to take control again, Matt soon relaxed. He felt comfortable about flying. Keeping his eyes on the gauges, just in case, Brandon sat back in his seat and relaxed.

They chatted about many things as they flew on northward. It seemed like very little time had passed when Nestor Falls came into sight. "The airport is next to the bay. See it?" Brandon asked.

"Yeah, I see it," Matt replied.

"Make a wide turn and go to it from the west." Brandon said, and then he called the airport and requested permission to land. The controller's voice came back with clearance, and to approach from the west, just as Brandon had already guessed by the direction of the waves on the bay.

Matt slowly turned the yoke and the plane responded. While he was making the turn, Brandon checked the gauges again. "Okay. Now swing toward the airport. I'm going to throttle back a little. Be ready for the plane to dip a little as it slows down. You'll feel the difference, but don't panic."

"Brand! I'm not going to land this thing!"

"I'll be right here all the while. Just do what I tell you. If I thought you'd crash, I wouldn't let you try it. I'm right here if anything goes wrong."

A sweaty sheen broke out on Matt's forehead as he thought of trying to land the plane. Just as Brandon had said, he felt the difference as their airspeed slowed and the plane began to drop. The yoke seemed to get heavier. "Now I'm going to give it a little flaps," Brandon continued. That will lower the stall speed, like an airbrake, and allow us to fly slower as we land."

Matt nodded that he understood. He felt the control come back as the flaps made the engine work against their drag.

Brandon lowered the airspeed a little more. The plane felt even heavier and more sluggish to Matt. "It's feeling heavy," he said.

"It's supposed to. Now push the yoke in a little and bring the nose down." Matt complied and they dropped slowly toward the earth.

"Now, see the end of the landing strip up ahead?"

Matt nodded yes.

"We want to be just a little ways up when we get over that," he said, noting the large sign that designated the number of the runway. "Push it in a bit after we pass that sign."

Matt pushed the yoke ahead a little more. Brandon applied more flaps and eased the throttle back a bit. The plane began to drop again. "Good. Now just a little farther and then start to drop forward, but slowly."

They were over the runway now and the ground was getting close. "Okay. Ease it forward but be sure to keep the nose up. Don't let it hit nose first." Brandon eased the throttle back and the plane slowed even more.

"Brand, maybe you should take it," Matt said with a trace of fear in his voice. "I'm not sure I can do this."

"You're doing fine. Just a few more feet. Ease it down."

A few seconds later there was the chirp of tires hitting the pavement with a slight bump. The airplane was on the ground. Then the front tire touched down and they were hurtling down the runway. "Okay! You're on the ground. Firmly but steadily, push on the brakes," Brandon said, his smile beaming.

Matt applied the brakes and the plane slowed. Brandon eased the throttle back to idle.

Matt exhaled. "I think I held my breath almost the whole way," he said grinning.

"There. You just made your first landing." Brandon put his hand out to shake with Matt. Matt took Brandon's hand and then threw his arms around his friend. He hugged him as hard as he could. Tears streamed down his cheeks when he let go. "Thanks, Brand. That was the coolest thing I ever did."

"By the time you're old enough to try for your pilot's license, you'll be a shoe-in," Brandon said.

Chapter 11

"Okay. Left rudder. Take us back to that cross runway and turn. Park it next to the hanger."

Matt grinned as he pressed his foot on the rudder pedal and the plane began turning. Brandon gave it a little more throttle and soon they were stopped in front of the main hanger.

"Well, you know what they say?" Brandon said smiling.

"What's that, Brand?"

"Any landing that you can walk away from is a good one."

They both laughed and Kirby barked as if he understood the joke too.

"I'll get a cart and unload the stuff while you take Kirby out for a walk. I'd bet he needs a potty break," Brandon said. "Then you can go to the terminal building and get us something to eat. I think our plane is that black one with the red wings and trim, but I'll find out for sure and load up the stuff. We need to get going pretty soon."

"What's the hurry?"

Brandon nodded to the northwest. "See that big bank of clouds? Looks like a big front is moving in. I don't want to waste a lot of time before we take off. We're flying right at that front and I want to be landed in Clearwater Bay before it gets there."

Matt nodded, climbed out, opened the side door and unhooked Kirby from his harness. Brandon handed him some money for the food. Then he walked off toward the hanger to make sure which plane was theirs and to find a cart to haul their gear down to the dock.

Kirby galloped back to Matt after quickly doing his business behind the hanger. "C'mon Kirb. Let's get some lunch."

The terminal building was not much more than a corrugated steel hut with an office and a lunch counter where pilots could get a sandwich and coffee. "You sit here and stay," Matt said to the dog as they approached. Inside, a lady in a waitress uniform got up from a stool where she had been watching TV and took a position behind the counter. "Hi, Hon. What can I get you?"

"Hello," Matt said. "Can I get some burgers and fries to go?"

"Sure. How many and what would you like on them?"

"Give me four with the works and one with just ketchup. He looked at Kirby, watching through the screen door, Donald in his mouth, his tail wagging furiously. "And two large orders of fries, and six of those big cookies over there," he said. "And a six pack of *Cokes* and six bottles of water."

"Your furry friend doesn't like mustard and pickles?" she chuckled. Matt smiled. "No. He's kind of fussy about his burgers."

The TV fastened to the wall was tuned to the weather channel. Matt studied the radar picture that showed a massive front over Manitoba, and right now, it looked to be about the same distance from Clearwater Bay as Nestor Falls.

"Are you the two who are taking that Beaver up to Clearwater Bay?" the waitress asked.

"Yes Ma'am. My friend, Brandon, and I and Kirby."

"Which one is Kirby? The furry one? Or the handsome one out on the dock?" she asked.

"He's the furry one."

"You guys should think twice about going out there today. That storm is coming pretty fast. Maybe you should wait till it passes, eh?" Matt had to grin, he loved the way Canadians always put that "eh" on the end of a sentence and the way she pronounced the word *out*, sounding more like *boot.*

"That's why we're taking the food to go, Ma'am, so we won't waste any time."

"Well, you keep an eye on those clouds and get out of the air if they get too close. You'll be in a peck of trouble if you get caught in that storm. If it gets bad, you come back here and we'll take care of you till it passes."

In a short while she had the hamburgers wrapped in aluminum foil and the fries dumped into little boxes. She put six cookies into a white paper bag and then transferred all of the food into a plastic bag with handles. The drinks went into another bag, and she set them on the counter. Matt pulled out the money Brandon had given him and paid the bill. "Thank you, Ma'am."

Matt stepped to the door and looked into the sky. The cloud bank was just about to block the sun and the sky had turned to a reddish orange ahead of the blackness that was coming behind it.

He walked through the door. The waitress called to him: "Don't forget about that storm, sweetie. God speed!"

Matt marched across the tarmac to one of the six docks that stuck out into the bay. Kirby was pacing him closely, sniffing the aroma of hamburgers. Five or six planes were tied up to each dock. Brandon was talking to a man who worked at the airport, or perhaps, who owned it. They were both looking northwest at the front moving in toward them.

"There's going to be some rough weather," the man said. "When that cold front hits this warm, humid air, there's going to be some dandy storms. You guys make sure you're off the lake before it hits."

Brandon assured the man that they weren't going to do any sightseeing. They were heading straight to Clearwater Bay. "Ah! Here's our lunch," Brandon said. "We're taking off right away so we'll get a jump on the storm." Kirby followed a little farther behind Matt as he walked along the dock. Now he seemed more interested in the smells of the dock and the water.

"Let's get him in one of the back seats," Brandon said to Matt as he climbed out onto one of the pontoons. "And then let's get going." Matt picked up Kirby and handed him over. Brandon coaxed him up on a seat and belted him in with his harness that he had removed from the Cessna.

"Brandon tells me it was you who made that landing," the man said smiling.

"Yes sir. My first one," Matt said with a grin.

"That was real pretty. Just as light as a feather."

Matt's smile was as wide as the wings of the Beaver. "Thank you sir," he replied. "Actually, today is the first day I've ever flown a plane, but I have a good teacher." He nodded to Brandon.

"You guys take care and mind that storm. We'll see you when your customers start showing up next weekend." He turned and walked down the dock toward the Cessna that he would service and then store in a hanger for the summer.

Chapter 12

When he stepped up into the co-pilot seat, Matt realized that compared to the Cessna, the Beaver was enormous. Once inside, he got a better look at the plane's large size. There were four seats for passengers behind the cockpit and a large cargo area.

Matt could see their duffle bags, fishing gear, and Kirby's dog food stacked among the cargo already loaded. A cargo net that was fastened down to hooks in the sides and floor of the plane held it all securely in place.

"Jeez Brand! This thing is huge."

Brandon looked up from checking the gauges and smiled. "Yeah. She's a big girl, isn't she?"

"How do you know she's a girl?" Matt said grinning.

"Look at that name below the numbers –*Edna*. I think that's a girl's name, isn't it?"

"I don't know about a girl, but maybe a grandma's name," Matt said laughing.

"Well, let's see if this big thing will get off the water," Brandon said. He flipped switches and pressed the start button. The 450 horsepower *Pratt and Whitney* engine sprang to life and the prop began turning faster until it was nothing more than a blur. "She sounds good. Nice and strong," Brandon said.

"Can you hop out and untie the ropes?" he asked. Matt opened the door, jumped down to the pontoon and untied the ropes that held the plane to the dock. When Brandon nodded okay, he climbed back up into the co-pilots seat and buckled in. Brandon had his headset on and motioned for Matt to put his on. "You read me?" he asked. Matt nodded yes. Brandon pushed in the left rudder, revved up the engine and they began to taxi out into the bay.

"Is this your first take off on water?" Matt asked.

Brandon winced. "You don't have to shout. Just talk normal." Matt giggled.

"Yeah, it's the first time, but it's not much different. Dad says just remember to keep the nose up so the pontoons don't dip in too much." They went to the southeast end of the bay and turned the plane into a moderate northwest breeze. There was a slight chop on the water. Brandon raised his eyebrows up and down and grinned. "Hang on! Here we go!"

He pushed the throttle forward all the way and they began riding the waves out toward the middle of the bay. There was a little vibration from the waves hitting the pontoons but otherwise the feeling wasn't much different than taking off on asphalt. Kirby slobbered all over the window as he looked out at the water. Matt watched Brandon's feet and hands as he moved the rudder and pulled on the yoke. The noise of the pontoons hitting the waves died away and he was looking down at the bay, dropping away. Little rivulets of water dripping off the pontoons sparkled as they fell toward the lake. Though large and cumbersome looking, the big plane was really quite a good flying machine. Weighing in at over 5,000 pounds, it left the water with such ease.

"She handles real nice," Brandon said. "She's not a speed demon – cruising speed is about 140 mph. But she's got a good feel to her." They gained altitude and swung east looking for the Canadian Pacific railway that ran along the eastern edge of the Lake of the Woods. The plan was to follow it and then swing west when they got to Kenora. From there it was a relatively short distance to Clearwater Bay. "Watch for the next big town," Brandon said in the headset.

"Crow Portage?" Matt asked, and Brandon nodded. "Ready for a burger, Brand?"

Brandon wiggled his eyebrows and smiled. "Yeah. I'm famished."

Matt dug into the bag, unwrapped a burger for Brandon, and set a box of fries on a little pull-out drawer that may have been put there for the purpose of holding food. He opened a bottle of ***Coke*** and set it on the pull-out, too.

Then he opened a burger that had an X penned on it with a magic marker. That one was Kirby's. He broke off about a third of it and held it back over the seat. Wet lips engulfed his fingers up to the first knuckles as Kirby gulped in the bite. "Jeez, Kirby! Take it easy. I don't need my hands washed with your spit." Kirby's tail wagged furiously.

Matt opened a burger and fries for himself, and by then, Brandon was ready for his second. He finished feeding Kirby his burger and then shared his fries with him. Soon they were eating cookies and Kirby was getting about half of each cookie from the two boys.

Matt gathered up the wrappers and packed them into the plastic bag just as Brandon said, "There's Crow Portage." Matt looked down at a small town and then gazed off to the northwest where the storm front was getting closer.

"Brand… do you see those clouds?"

Brandon nodded. He didn't look happy about how close they were getting. The front covered the entire horizon; the thunderheads were building up to thousands of feet high. Lightning flashed inside the big black clouds and they could imagine the horrific wind. "Looks like it's coming pretty fast," Matt said.

Brandon nodded and stared to the northwest again. He shook his head. "I don't like it. Maybe we should turn back."

"You think we'll get caught in the storm?"

"I don't know, Matty. We'll keep going for a while and see what happens."

They flew on. In a short time they could see Sioux Narrows ahead. Brandon looked to the northwest again and shook his head. "If we go all the way to Kenora, that storm will be on us before we get to Clearwater Bay."

"Are you sure?"

"It's moving fast Matty."

"What's our other choice?"

"Well… we can figure a course from here to Clearwater Bay and cut across the lake."

"I thought Dad said not to do that."

"He didn't know a storm would come up. If we plot a compass heading and stick to it, I don't see how it will hurt anything. It'll cut off a lot of miles. This old girl isn't real speedy, so a difference of a hundred miles will mean a lot of time. At our airspeed, it will get us to Clearwater Bay forty-five minutes sooner… if we bypass Kenora."

Matt wasn't sure it was a good idea, but he trusted Brandon.

"Well, if you think we can do it, let's give it a try."

"Okay. You take over flying for a few minutes while I get the map and plot a course."

"You want me to fly this big thing?" Matt asked skeptically.

"Sure. It's no different than the Cessna… just bigger."

Matt gulped. He put his feet on the rudder pedals and took hold of the yoke. "Okay?" Brandon asked. Matt nodded. "You have control," Brandon said as he released the yoke.

Matt held on tightly and tested the plane a bit by turning the yoke just a hair. The plane turned just like it was supposed to, and then he turned it back to the former heading. He looked over at Brandon who was watching him. "No problem," he said grinning. Dang! He was flying a Beaver – nearly three tons of airplane with pontoons. "If somebody would have told me this morning when I woke up that I'd be flying two different planes today, I'd have told them they were nuts," he said to Brandon. Brandon just smiled and winked.

Brandon poured over the map and put a ruler across the intended heading. Taking a reading on the compass, he figured in his head the correct bearing.

Matt flew on, enjoying the feeling of power, having the time of his life flying the big plane. But he couldn't keep his eyes off the huge bank of clouds that were getting closer by the minute.

Chapter 13

Brandon checked his calculations. Then he re-checked the map and stored it away. "I'll take it back now," he said.

Matt nodded. "You have control," he said as he released the yoke and took his feet off the pedals. Brandon banked the plane to the left and headed toward the storm front that was quickly getting larger and closer.

As they left the eastern shoreline of the Lake, they could see larger expanses of water dotted with islands of every shape and size. The sunlight sparkled off the water, like someone had thrown a handful of diamonds on a green carpet. "Boy there's tons of islands," Matt said.

"Yeah. Over 14,000 of 'em," Brandon said. "That's why they called it Lake of the Woods. The guy who discovered it was French and he named it *Lac aux Iles,* or Lake of the Woods in English."

"How do you know all this stuff, Brand?"

"I don't know. I guess I just like to read about discoveries. You know this guy who discovered it – his name was Jacques de Noyon – was only about 20 years old when he found it way back in 1688." Just think. A guy just a little older than I am right now was the first white man to see this place.

"What was he looking for? A fishing hole?" Matt asked grinning.

"He was looking for the same thing every explorer was looking for in those days – a passage to the Pacific Ocean. Of course, there was no such thing, but a lot of explorers were out there looking for it. They all thought there was a water route that they could sail to the Pacific. It's the same thing that Lewis and Clark were looking for on their expedition."

Matt looked out ahead at the endless dots of land spread out over the surface of the huge lake. "Boy. If a guy came down on one of those, it'd take 'em a year to find him."

"Well, we'll just have to be sure not to end up down there," Brandon said.

They flew on toward the ever growing bank of clouds. It was beginning to look like the storm was about to reach them. "How much farther to Clearwater Bay, Brand?"

Brandon looked at the clock on the dash. "If my calculations are correct, I'd guess that we have about a half hour of flying yet. I'm not sure we're going to get there ahead of the storm, Matty."

Matt could see the worry in Brandon's face, and he could hear the concern in his voice. Just then a bolt of lightning shot across the sky. The storm would be upon them sooner than they had thought. "Better check Kirby," Brandon said. "Make sure he's strapped in tight, and then tighten your belt, too." Matt slid between the seats and tightened Kirby's belt and then walked to the baggage area and checked the tie downs holding the cargo net.

"Everything's tight and secure back there, Brand."

"Good. Strap in, Matty. It's going to get rough."

The cloud bank was several thousand feet high, much higher than they wanted to fly. If they tried to fly above it, the clouds would block their view of where to land, so the next best option was to fly through it, and hope they would see Clearwater Bay. Sudden wind gusts rocked and swayed the plane. Brandon handled it expertly, but he had to work hard on the rudder pedals to stay on course. Then the rain hit, making a loud racket as it pounded on the metal skin of the plane.

Brandon turned on the windshield wipers. They tick-tocked back and forth, barely keeping the water off as the rain increased and the wind rocked the plane.

The clouds closed in as they flew deeper into the storm, cutting off any visibility of the water and islands below, like being enveloped in the middle of a dense fog. Brandon reached up to the dash and tapped his finger on the altimeter.

"What's wrong, Brand?"

He tapped the gauge again. Then he tapped the airspeed gauge and the rate of climb gauge. "All three of these gauges are run by a thing called a Pitot tube. It's a small opening on the front of the wing that makes these gauges work. It measures air pressure and calculates airspeed and altitude. Sometimes that tube gets plugged, and then the gauges don't work. It must be plugged now. All of them have just gone dead."

"Do we need them to stay flying?" Matt asked. His voice quivered with little fear..

"No. We can fly without them, but without the altimeter we don't know how high we are. In fog like this you tend to lose altitude just because you can't see where you're going, so I've got to keep the nose up and keep us level."

"So… we're okay, then?"

"We have to watch, Matty. Keep your eyes peeled, in case we get too low. We don't want to crash into one of these islands." Brandon was tense, but he tried not to let it show. He didn't want to frighten Matt. "Just watch close, and if you see water or trees, yell."

"I'm all eyes, captain."

The wind increased and the rain came down in torrents as they flew deeper into the storm. Brandon considered his options. He didn't like them. Either they would come to the back side of the storm and be in the clear, or he would have to set the plane down on the lake and take shelter behind one of the islands until the storm passed. Neither plan sounded very good right then.

Wind gusts were hitting hard from the right, and Brandon desperately attempted to keep the plane lined up on the proper heading. The plane shifted to the left each time the wind gusted. He wasn't sure, anymore, of how far he had been blown off course, or how far he had to go to get back on the right course. They were in trouble and he hoped he could get them out of it without wrecking the plane, or worse yet, injuring or killing himself, Matt, and Kirby.

Chapter 14

The wind steadily roared, rocking the Beaver to one side and then the other. Rain poured down in sheets; the wipers hardly kept it off the windscreen. The clouds had become so dense it was impossible to see anything.

"Brand! I can't see anything!" Matt said with a measure of fright in his voice.

"Just keep looking, Matty. As long as we can't see trees or water, we're still high enough." He reached up and banged the altimeter gauge again as if hitting it might make it work again. "Damn thing! Shit!"

They were still flying at cruising speed, so Brandon cut the throttle back a little to slow them in case he had to take some sudden, drastic action. Of course, it was impossible to stop a float plane quickly, unlike a wheeled plane with brakes. A float plane just slides to a stop, like a boat.

"We're gonna have to set her down on the water," Brandon said grimly. "We can't keep flying blind like this. We'll crash into an island and that'll be it." Brandon switched on the landing lights, hoping to give him more visibility. But all they illuminated was thick fog closing them in.

Matt nodded that he understood. He unconsciously reached down and tugged on his seatbelt to tighten it even more. The plane bucked and rolled as the storm raged. The Beaver began to drop slowly toward the lake. The swirling clouds and rain were so dense that they could see nothing beyond the front of the plane, making it impossible to know what might be in their flight path.

Matt strained his eyes staring into the clouds and rain; his head started to ache. He massaged his forehead, and just then he had the first glimpse of a tree. "Brand! Trees on the right!"

Brandon quickly turned his head and saw the tops of pine trees flashing by in the fog. He turned the plane to the left. The trees disappeared. "Keep watching," he said to Matt. "We're getting close now!"

The plane dropped a few feet lower and Brandon applied a little flaps to slow them down some more. Matt got a glimpse of water below. “Brand! We’re over water right now!”

Brandon cut the throttle back, gave the plane more flaps to keep it from stalling, and eased the yoke slightly forward. They dropped lower and the water surface became fully visible, just ten feet below. But they were moving much too fast to attempt touching down – visibility was nearly zero.

Then Matt saw the first boulder sticking up out of the water. “Brand! There’s big rocks down there! Go to the left!” Brandon turned the yoke and they moved away from the rocks and the shallow water. A large island was just barely visible on their right.

They kept moving over open water and suddenly they heard a slapping noise from the left side of the plane. Brandon saw the wing tip just barely clipping tree branches at the waterline of an island. He turned the yoke sharply to the right and moved them away.

They settled a little lower. They could see water again, and it appeared to be free of rocks. “Just a little lower now,” Brandon said quietly. The pontoons just started skimming the water when Matt yelled. “Brand! Brand! Ahead! An island!”

Brandon had seen it, but it was too late. They were too close and coming in much to fast. Nothing would prevent the Beaver from colliding with the island. He pulled the lever that dropped the water rudder into the lake, hoping it would slow them a little more, and allow him to steer the plane like a boat.

Fifty yards ahead the island was lined with large boulders right down to the water’s edge. To the left Matt saw a sandbar covered with small willows sticking out from the island, gradually tapering into the lake. “Brand! To the left! The bank is lower and no rocks!”

Brandon spotted the sandbar. He pushed the rudder as hard as he could with his left foot to turn them toward a pebble covered beach. The aluminum pontoons screeched as they slid across the small rocks and sand, and then up a gradual slope onto the island.

The head high willows were about as thick as a pool cue. The landing lights beamed through the darkness. Leaves and branches flew like they were being shot from a salad shooter as the plane cut though the willow grove. Brandon cut the throttle but there was little else he could do without brakes. Forty feet of wings miraculously missed rocks and trees as they chewed through the willows.

"Hang on, Matty!"

The prop was beginning to slow down and the drag from the sand and pebbles on the pontoons was slowing the forward movement of the plane. They cleared the willows and came to an open area just before dense woods. Just when they thought they were going to make it without any damage to the plane, Brandon saw a huge boulder right in their path, about the size of a back yard tool shed. He stomped as hard as he could with his left foot on the rudder control, but there was nothing for the rudder to work against and it did no good. Matt ducked his head as the prop, still spinning at many thousand revolutions, hit the boulder and disintegrated. The nose of the plane crashed into the huge rock and the plane slammed to a stop. Matt leaned forward and held his hands over his head, and when he finally sat upright again, the plane was not moving. The nose was against the boulder.

A little grin of relief spread across Matt's face when he realized they had not been killed. "Whew! That was exciting." He turned to Brandon and then his mouth dropped open. Only the small bit of light from the instruments revealed Brandon slumped over his yoke, blood streaming from a cut above his left eye. He appeared unconscious. "Brand! Oh no! Brand! Are you okay?"

Realizing that the engine was still running, he reached to the dash and began flipping switches until it shut down. Once the engine stopped, the lights went out on the instrument panel and the plane's interior plunged into total darkness. The sky lit up with a bolt of lightning and he looked over the seat to see if Kirby was still there. The dog was sitting still strapped in, looking ahead, and wagging his tail. "You okay, Kirb?" The dog leaned forward and licked him on the face.

Matt unbuckled his seatbelt and moved over toward Brandon. He carefully turned his head to see the three inch long cut just below the hairline above his left eye. "Brand! Are you okay? Come on, Brand! Wake up!" He put his head on Brandon's chest and listened. He could feel and hear a strong heartbeat. Matt looked around in the dark cockpit and tried to stay calm, but the raging storm, the crash, and Brandon's injury were too much for him to handle all at once. Tears filled his eyes and he put his arms around Brandon. After several minutes, Kirby licked the side of his head and that brought him back from despair. "You're right, Kirby. I gotta keep it together and take care of Brand. I gotta get something to stop the bleeding." The dog wagged his tail in approval. He got up and moved to the back of the plane where the cargo was still snugly held in place by the cargo net. He had to feel his way through the dark. The only light came from the flashes of lightning that lit up the sky every few seconds. He went back to the cockpit but nothing happened when he flipped the switch for the interior lights. "No lights," he said to himself. Brandon had talked about where emergency equipment was on the plane earlier, so he felt his way along the fuselage again until his hands touched a small locker on the side of the plane. There he found a flashlight and turned it on. On the wall above the door was a metal first aid kit. He unclipped the bracket and took the case back up to the cockpit.

The kit contained all sorts of bandages, a bottle of alcohol, a bottle of Iodine, cloth tape and Band Aids. He found a gauze pad and pressed it to Brandon's forehead. It quickly soaked with blood. Several pads applied with a little pressure took longer to become blood soaked. After four bunches of gauze pads had been completely saturated, the bleeding slowed down. With three pads folded over, Matt taped them to Brandon's head. They turned a little red from blood, but they seemed to suffice for the time being. "Well," he thought to himself. "It's up to me to take care of Brand and Kirby now." He looked around the plane and started figuring out what his next move should be.

Chapter 15

The trees above them bent over in the wind, their branches screeching against the metal skin of the plane. The rain, still coming down in torrents rattled against the windows. Matt sat there listening to the ticking of the engine as it cooled. Maybe he should just sit still and wait for Brandon to wake up. Brandon would know what to do. He felt his eyes filling with tears again, but he wiped them clear and took a deep breath. He checked Brandon's head again with the flashlight and the bleeding was much slower now. He sat back down on the edge of his seat and looked around, not certain what to do next.

But he knew it was now up to him to take charge. Brandon was unconscious, and might be for a long time. "Kirby, we're in a fix here," he said. The dog happily wagged his tail, obviously not concerned with their situation. Matt had to smile at Kirby's innocence of the predicament.

"Well, old pal. I think I should get Brand out of that seat and make a place for him to lie down. I don't know how long he'll be knocked out, so I think I should try to make him comfortable. What do you think?" Kirby thumped his tail as if he approved.

Matt moved back between the seats to the cargo area and surveyed the mound of baggage. "If I move this stuff up to the seats," he thought to himself, "...there's room for him to lie down... if I can get him back here... " He unhooked the netting, removed it from the pile of food and gear, and stashed it under the back seat. He walked back to the front of the plane to check on Brandon. The bleeding seemed to have stopped, so he carefully took the bloody bandage off and taped another on. He listened to his friend's heartbeat again. It seemed steady and strong. "Well, he's okay for now," he said to Kirby.

He walked back to the pile of cargo and slid their duffle bags under the other back seat where they would be easy to reach. The bulk of the cargo was food, so, at least they weren't going to be hungry.

Matt started looking over the boxes, trying to determine if there was anything he could use right away. The first thing he found was a large box with six brand new sleeping bags. They were for the so-called cabins at the outpost camps. Matt opened the box and piled the sleeping bags behind the last seat on the left. They would be useful now.

He carried boxes and bags of food and kitchen supplies, stacking them on the floor between the passenger seats. When the space was full, he filled the seat. He even had to coax Kirby to his seat in the cockpit and then filled Kirby's seat with boxes, too.

After a couple of hours, it seemed much darker. There was less lightning and his flashlight was getting quite dim. So when he found the case of oil lamps and several gallons of lamp oil at the bottom of the stack, he was rather pleased. He filled one of the lamps with oil, and then stored the rest along with the oil in Kirby's former seat. With the lamp lit, it was much easier to work in the plane, and it felt a lot safer.

The seats and the spaces between them were completely full, but there was still more boxes of supplies to be moved out of the way. Some things he knew he didn't need – a case of outboard oil, several boxes of extra shear pins, three new propellers for the outboards, and a five hundred foot roll of rope that was going to be used to tie up boats to the docks, life jackets, boat cushions and several anchors. He opened the cargo door and tossed the boxes out onto the ground. Now he had a good space cleared out in back of the plane. He spread out two of the open sleeping bags on top of each other to make a place for them to lie down. He'd saved a couple of boat cushions, too, for pillows.

"Now, I've gotta get Brand out of that seat and back here," he thought to himself. Brandon outweighed him by fifty pounds and he was doubtful that he could move him. But he couldn't just leave him there, slumped over the yoke. He moved up between the pilot and co-pilot seats and unclamped Brandon's seat belt. "Well here goes," he said to Kirby. The dog watched with great interest.

From behind, Matt wrapped his arms around Brandon's chest under his armpits and lifted. He was able to move him a little, and he took a step back. Brandon slid onto the floor and Matt sagged down with him. He got behind him again and managed to pull him a couple of feet. Bracing his feet against the legs of the passenger seats, he could move Brandon a few inches at a time. He did the maneuver a couple of times and Brandon's feet were finally clear from under the yoke, resting on the pilot's seat. That was when he noticed that Brandon's left ankle was swelled to twice the size of his other foot.

"Oh no, Brand. Your ankle is broken!"

Matt tried to put that out of his mind temporarily and moved Brandon a few feet closer to the cargo area. Three more pulls and he had the unconscious pilot slid onto the sleeping bags. The bags were all messed up from dragging Brandon across them, but with a little lifting and pulling he managed to get them straightened out again. The exertion had him sweating and panting. Kirby came to him and licked his face as he sat on the floor catching his breath. He hugged the dog and tried to keep the tears from coming. But he couldn't hold them back. He buried his face in Kirby's coat and sobbed, scared to death that Brandon wouldn't wake up. Just the thought of being left here alone terrified him.

Chapter 16

Matt felt like the weight of the world had fallen on him and he just couldn't hold it back. The tears kept flowing. Kirby sat next to him on the floor and put Donald in his lap. Matt stroked the dog's head. He wiped his eyes and tried to gather his wits. He took the duck in his hand and smiled at Kirby. "I've got to keep it together and take care of Brand. We've got plenty of food and we're in here out of the weather, so we'll be okay. I just gotta keep my head." He handed the duck back to Kirby. "Thanks for letting me hold Donald," he said. He took a deep breath and felt a little better.

Matt stared at Brandon's left ankle. It was a nasty sight, badly swollen, and his foot appeared swollen in his shoe, as well. He untied the shoe, but it came of with much difficulty. Then he carefully pealed off Brandon's sock. He didn't know anything about broken bones, but he guessed that Brandon had been pushing hard on the left rudder when the plane struck the rock. That had probably caused the injury.

"Mom always put cold on my ankle sprains and kept them elevated," he thought. He looked out the window. Rain was still pouring down. He looked around for something to put water in. The only things he could find were Kirby's stainless steel food and water pans. "I'm gonna borrow your pans, Kirb," he said to the dog. "We're going out for water, and I suppose you better get to pee before we bed down. Sorry, Boy. But I guess we got to go out in the rain."

Kirby seemed to be in favor of getting outside. Matt opened the fuselage door, and he though it was too far to the ground for Kirby to jump. He climbed down the ladder to the pontoon and called Kirby to the door. "Leave Donald here… so you don't lose him," he said. Kirby put the duck down on the duffle bags. Matt lifted him out of the plane and onto the pontoon. "Go potty Kirby," he said, and the dog trotted off into the dark. With both dog pans and the flashlight, he followed the path that the plane had cut through the willows. They had come quite far from the edge of the lake. "Holy crap! We must have gone thirty yards into the woods," he said to nobody in particular. The rain was still falling steadily, making a hissing sound as it hit the lake water. Matt studied the darkness all around, hoping to see a light from a cabin or a lodge, but there was nothing but black. He rinsed out the pans, then scooped up water in each, and started back up the path to the plane.

He went to the bathroom out in the woods, too, after he set the pans of water up in the cargo area. "Kirby," he called. "Let's go in." He waited a minute and then called again. Kirby came trotting up the path from the lake. "Come on. Let's get out of the rain," he said to the dog. He climbed up on the pontoon and Kirby hopped up, too. He hoisted the dog up into the doorway, climbed up himself, and pulled the door shut when he was safely inside.

His clothes were soaked by the rain, and he was shaking because he was cold. He pulled his duffle bag from under the seat, dug out some dry clothes, and shed the wet ones he was wearing. Now he was glad he had packed a couple of large beach towels for swimming. He dried himself off and changed into the fresh clothes. Then he dried off Kirby with a sweatshirt from the duffle. A tee shirt soaked in the cold lake water worked well for wrapping around Brandon's swollen ankle. He made a sling with the cargo net between one of the hooks on the side of the plane and the back of the last seat. Carefully he hoisted Brandon's injured ankle up into the makeshift sling.

"I guess we're gonna have a cold supper, Kirb. Is that okay with you?" Kirby knew the word supper. His tail began thumping. Matt found a can of peaches in one of the cases of food, and a can opener in a box of kitchen utensils. He put some of the peaches in an aluminum pie pan – he'd found a whole case of them – for Kirby. Then he tore open the sack of dog food and poured out a pile on the floor. The dog loved "people food" and quickly lapped up his share of the peaches before he ate the dog food. Matt ate the rest of the peaches from the can and drank the juice. It wasn't one of the best meals he'd ever eaten, but he was grateful for it, just the same.

He took the tee shirt from Brandon's foot, soaked it in the cold water again, and re-wrapped the foot. Then he dipped a clean sock in the water, wiped the dried blood off Brandon's face, and changed the bandage on his head. In an attempt to make Brandon more comfortable, he took off his other shoe.

Matt still felt chilly from being wet. He unzipped another sleeping bag, laid down next to Brandon, and spread it over both of them. Kirby snuggled in, too, with Donald held gently in his mouth. Matt's effort to stay awake in order to keep an eye on Brandon was soon overcome by exhaustion, and he fell into an uneasy sleep.

Chapter 17

Restlessness woke Matt several hours later. The oil lamp dimly lit the interior of the plane, but it was still very dark outside. He dipped the tee shirt in the cold water again and re-wrapped Brandon's foot. The swelling didn't look any worse than it had earlier, but the ankle was turning purple. It looked pretty ugly. He leaned over close to Brandon's face. "Well, you're still breathing, so that's a good thing," he said. He laid back down, pulled the sleeping bag over him, and listened to the raging storm. Once again, he could not resist sleep.

Matt felt a breeze blowing across his face. He opened his eyes to see Kirby furiously wagging his tail. Some light came in through the window, so Matt knew it was morning. Rain still splattered against the glass and he could see the trees still whipping back and forth as the storm continued. "What's up Kirb?" Matt said to the dog. "Gotta go out?" The dog went wild jumping up and down. He looked at Brandon, still unconscious, but his chest was still rising and falling. He seemed to be breathing very strongly. "Ok, Kirby. Let's go," he said.

He lifted Kirby out onto the pontoon and the dog disappeared into the woods. Matt jumped down off the pontoon and walked into the willows to take care of his morning call to nature, too. Kirby returned to the pontoon quickly, waiting to get inside. "You don't like this weather, either, Kirb, do you?"

He dried Kirby off with the same sweatshirt, dried himself off with a towel, and put on a dry shirt. He had gone out in just his underwear. Teeth chattering and shivering, he dried off his legs and feet and then put on his jeans again.

The bleeding on Brandon's forehead had stopped completely, so he just cleaned it off again and left it alone.

Matt went to the cockpit and peered at the instruments and radio controls. "I wonder how you use this radio," he said to himself. While he was trying to determine what to do to make it work, he heard Kirby jumping and fussing in the back. He turned and saw Brandon's right eye open, and he was partially sitting up. He stared questioningly at Donald resting on chest, where Kirby had put it. Obviously, he had difficulty in comprehending where he was and why there was a duck on his chest.

"Brand! You're awake!" He jumped to his feet, quickly moved back to the cargo area, and knelt next to him.

"Hey, Matty," Brandon said with a weak smile.

"Oh man! I'm so glad you're awake. I was so scared."

"What happened? How did I get back here?"

"We crashed. Don't you remember that?"

"I remember sliding through a bunch of willows, but nothing after that."

"We smacked into a big rock, and you hit your head and got knocked out. Dang, Brand! I'm so glad you're awake." He leaned over his friend and hugged him as hard as he dared. Brandon wrapped his arms around the boy and returned the hug.

Matt's eyes were shining with tears as he let go of Brandon. "How's your head feel?"

"Like someone hit me with a rock," Brandon said.

"How 'bout your foot?"

Brandon looked down at his elevated foot. He tried to move it a bit and winced with the pain. "Wow. That's pretty ugly. Do you think it's broken?"

Matt shrugged. "Do I look like a doctor? I think it could be broken… or a really bad sprain. Take two Aspirin and call me in the morning."

Brandon giggled a bit despite the pain in his head and foot. He put his arm around Matt's neck and pulled him closer. "You took good care of me Matty, even though you're a little smart butt."

They stayed close other for several minutes, and then Matt said, "Are you hungry?"

Brandon shrugged his shoulders. "Not so much, but I gotta pee real bad."

"Well, I'm not going to help you with that," Matt said, his eyebrows arched.

"Got one of those empty soda bottles handy?"

Matt searched the front of the plane, found an empty water bottle and took it back to Brandon. He removed his foot carefully from the sling and sat up. When he had finished taking care of business, he screwed the cap back on the bottle and set it near the door. "Empty that next time you go out," he said. "Have you tried calling on the radio?"

"I was just looking at it trying to figure out how it works when you woke up," Matt replied. "Last night, I just got busy moving all of this stuff so I could make a place for you to lay down. There was a lot of stuff back here."

Brandon pondered a bit. "I wonder how far Clearwater Bay is from here." He thought a moment, and went on. "We could be just an island or two away, or we might be at the other end of the lake."

"I was down by the water last night and I didn't see any lights," Matt answered. And I haven't heard any boats or planes, either."

Brandon gazed out the window at the storm. "Jeez that's a big storm. How long has it been raining like that?"

"It hasn't stopped once since we landed," Matt said.

"Maybe we should try the radio again," Brandon suggested.

"Can you tell me what to do?"

"Yeah. Go up there and I'll walk you through it."

Matt sat in the pilot's seat while Brandon instructed him on switches and dials, but nothing happened. "It's not coming on," Matt said.

"Maybe the fuses are blown, or the battery is damaged," Brandon said. "Do the interior lights work?"

"No, I tried them last night. They quit working when I shut off the engine."

"Well, we might as well get comfortable and wait till the weather breaks," Brandon said. "No one will be looking for us in this storm. We probably couldn't get a radio signal because of the storm anyway. When my foot gets a little better, I'll take a look at it. Maybe it's just something easy to fix. And we sure won't starve."

"There's lots of stuff, but no meat," Matt said.

"I think our dads took all the meat and food that needed refrigeration last week," Brandon said. "They left all this stuff for us to bring in. At least we'll have something to eat until they find us, and it's better than berries and twigs. Let's sort through it and see what we've got."

The empty box for the sleeping bags was still there, so Matt moved it next to the seats and began opening boxes. He held up a box of wooden stick matches. "Won't have to rub sticks together for fire," he said grinning. Next he removed a two-gallon can of cooking oil and put it in their grocery box.

There were two fifty pound bags of potatoes. Matt slid one out of the way but where it was easy to get to, and left the other one under the seats. He found onions, pepper, salt and bags of white and brown sugar. He put them in the empty box.

With his foot still wrapped with the wet tee shirt and suspended in the cargo net, Brandon just watched. "Looks like we've got enough stuff to stay alive for a while," he said.

"Yeah," Matt said. "I'll get all this stuff sorted, and next thing our dads will be knocking on the door to take us to the lodge."

"Well, just in case it takes a little longer than that, we might as well be ready," Brandon replied.

Matt sorted through the cases and found canned peaches, pears, cherries, and apples – all the ingredients that would be made into pies for the fishermen at the lodge. "And we won't have to wash dishes," he said as he held up the case of aluminum pie pans to show Brandon.

He found canned beans, corn, peas, green beans and bags of flour. He moved the box of kitchen utensils to the back and sorted through the last few boxes, finding spices and a case of aluminum foil.

"I sure hope we don't need all this stuff," Brandon said. "But it's good to know we can survive."

Five hours later, the clouds and wind were still making things ugly outside but at least the rain had stopped. "I'm going to take Kirby out," Matt said. "Then I'll get some more water."

"Fill those two empty pop bottles, too," Brandon said.

Matt and Kirby climbed out of the plane. Matt headed down the path of flattened willows to the lake. As he filled the two dog pans and the bottles with lake water, he gazed out across the water and saw just how close they had come to large rocks in the shallow water just offshore. Had they hit them, they might have destroyed the plane and sunk, so they were quite lucky to be high and dry on the island. He looked closely in every direction, hoping to see a boat dock or a cabin, but he saw nothing but water and trees.

Putting the water in through the open cargo door, Matt noticed Brandon was sitting up against the bulkhead. He looked a little better. "How you feeling, Brand?"

"My head doesn't ache so much, now, but my foot hurts like hell."

"Soak that tee shirt in this cold water and wrap it up again... and get it elevated," Matt ordered.

"Yes, Mom," Brandon said grinning.

Kirby came bounding up from the path. Matt lifted him into the plane. Then he found four rocks all about the same size and put them on the ground by the pontoon. "Brand?" he called out. "Is there a tool kit somewhere on this plane?"

"Under the co-pilot seat," Brandon responded. "What are you building?"

Matt grinned. "A barbeque grill."

Chapter 18

Sure enough, Matt found the metal box strapped down under the seat. When he pulled it out and opened it, he was happy to see a good variety of tools. He carried the box back to the cargo area and set it on the floor. "Do you think our dads would care if I take off that metal door?" he said pointing to a steel mesh door in the rear of the plane.

"I doubt it. That's where they usually put the cargo when they haul in fishermen or hunters. What are you going to do?"

Matt unlatched the door to the cargo hold and swung it open. It was heavy steel mesh welded to a two feet square angle iron frame. "I'm gonna put this door over those four rocks down there." He pointed to the rocks he had gathered. "And then I'm gonna put a couple of those oil lamps without the glass chimneys under it and we can cook over it." He was grinning like a Cheshire Cat. "All of the wood out there is soaked with rain, so this is the only way we're gonna have a fire."

A smile crept onto Brandon's face. "I think I'm pretty lucky to be lost with such a clever guy, Matty."

Matt dug out a large screwdriver and the correct size wrench and began taking the nuts off the back side of the door frame. In a few minutes, he had the door off and set it next to the cargo door. Then he retrieved four lamps, minus the chimneys, and filled them with oil.

Clouds still hugged the ground. The wind had settled a little, but there were still occasional hard gusts. Matt emptied the rest of the lamps out of the box, and cut the bottom out of the box with his knife. Then he carefully wrapped aluminum foil around the sides of the box. "Well, we'll see if this will work," he said as he stepped down onto the strut ladder.

After he had gotten the grate, lamps and box to the ground, he positioned the large box on the ground, marked around it, and scooped the sand out of the area, so the box could be set down in the depression. He positioned the four rocks at the four corners and set the door grate on top of them. He had to adjust a couple of the rocks for height to get the grate fairly level. He lifted it back off, set the lamps in the center of the pit, and lit the wick on each of them. When the lamps were all burning, he replaced the grate on the rocks over the flames. He stood back and admired his handiwork. It seemed like a good plan. He turned to Brandon and grinned. "How would you like your potatoes?"

"Jeez, Matty," Brandon laughed. "You sure are clever. I don't know if I'd have thought of that."

"We'll see if it works," Matt said. "I don't know if it will get hot enough, but I'd think it would be better than eating raw potatoes."

Matt climbed back up the ladder, found one of Kirby's stainless steel pans and the can of cooking oil. He filled the pan with potatoes and an onion and returned to the grill. With the empty pan on the grill, he poured a little oil into it, and then headed to the lake with the potatoes. He knelt on a piece of driftwood that looked like it had been part of somebody's dock or a stair step and washed the potatoes in the lake. Deciding that the piece of driftwood would make an excellent cutting board, he washed it off, too, and carried everything back to the plane. In short order, several potatoes were sliced and ready to fry.

He scooped up a handful of potatoes and dropped them into the oil, watching expectantly for the potatoes to sizzle, but not a single sizzle came from the pan. He waited for several minutes and then saw Brandon viewing the spectacle from the plane. "I think I need more lamps. The oil isn't hot enough."

Matt climbed back up into the plane and filled two more lamps with oil. He used a tee shirt for a pot holder to lift the pan from the grill, and the mesh grill from the rocks. After adding the extra lamps and replacing the grill and the pan, he said, "Now let's see if this works any better." Slowly, the potatoes started to sizzle, cooking like they were on a real stove.

"Way to go, Matty!" Brandon cheered from the plane.

Matt cut up the rest of the potatoes and the onion and filled the pan. The aroma of fried potatoes with onion wafted into the plane. "Holy smokes, that smells good," Brandon said. Matt climbed back up into the plane, found a box of salt and pepper, a spatula, and three pie plates. He returned to the grill and seasoned the potatoes. Brandon watched him with a sparkle in his eyes. He was impressed with how his little buddy had taken over so well.

Matt stirred the potatoes with the spatula, and while they cooked, he went to the willows to cut a couple of forked sticks, about the size of a regular table fork. He whittled each of them to sharp points and then speared a nice brown slice of hot potato from the pan on the grill. Climbing back up the ladder, he handed it to Brandon. "Try this," he said grinning.

Brandon carefully bit the slice of potato. He closed his eyes, smiled, and then chewed lovingly. "That's the best potato I've ever eaten, Matty."

Matt stirred the pan again. The entire pan of potatoes looked done, so he clamped onto it with a pair of pliers, and set it in the doorway of the plane. He took the grate off the fire and snuffed out the lamps.

Up in the plane again, he scooped out a pile of potatoes onto one of the pie plates and handed it to Brandon. He put some more on another plate for himself, and left a portion for Kirby. He hadn't realized how hungry he was until he began eating. Brandon ate ravenously, and managed to grin between bites. "Best meal I've had in a long time, Matty."

"Glad you like it, Brand," Matt said as he squirted some ketchup on his potatoes. "…'cause I think it's what we're gonna be eating for a while." After they had consumed the potatoes, Matt opened a can of apples and shared them with Brandon and Kirby. "Well," he said, "we might get hungry for meat, but at least we're not gonna starve."

Chapter 19

"How much water and soda do we have left?" Brandon asked.

Matt checked the stash of beverages. "Two waters and three sodas," he said.

"Two things we need to do right away," Brandon said. "First, we have to find a way to boil water. I don't know if the lake water is safe to drink, and I don't want us to get sick. There are Beaver in this lake and they have a parasite that can be harmful to people, so to be safe, we need to find a way to boil the water we drink. And second, we need to see if the radio will work, so we can try to call for help."

Matt nodded in agreement and began searching through the cargo that he had stored in and under the seats. The only thing he could think of for boiling water were Kirby's stainless steel pans. He found a bunch of zip lock bags that purified water could be stored in; he showed them to Brandon.

"We need something bigger to boil it in," Brandon said. "…or that's all we'll get done from now on."

"Yeah, but there's nothing else to use."

Suddenly, one of those "light bulb" looks came to Brandon. "How about one of those two gallon oil cans? We can pour the oil into some of those bags, wash out the can, and use it to boil the water. We can store the water in it, too. Two gallons will last a lot longer. We can put the oil in the empty pop and water bottles, and the rest in the bags."

"One can of oil is already partly gone. Maybe we can empty two cans, and we'll have twice as much at one time. When one is empty, we'll still have water to drink while we boil another one. We won't ever run out."

"Good idea," Brandon said.

Matt set the two cans of oil by Brandon and tossed him a box of large zip lock bags. After they had filled the empty bottles, Matt held one of the bags open while Brandon poured it nearly full of cooking oil. Carefully zipping it shut, Matt set it in an empty box. They filled six more bags. Now they had two cans for water.

"Have we got any soap?" Brandon asked.

"I've got shampoo in my duffle bag," Matt said. He rummaged around until he found the bottle. "I'll take them down to the lake and see how clean I can get them," he said, and out the door he went.

Matt filled each can about half full of lake water and then poured in some shampoo. He screwed the lids on tight and shook the cans until they were full of soapy suds. He poured the soapy water out and rinsed them several times until the water ran out clear of suds. Then he moved to a spot on the beach where the water was not full of soap and filled the cans nearly full. With the bottle of soap in his back pocket, he carried the cans back to the plane.

"They're as clean as I can get them," he said to Brandon. "If we burp soap bubbles, we'll know I didn't get them rinsed enough," he said laughing. He filled four more lamps with oil and added them to the pit with the others. After he lit all the lamps, he replaced the grill and set the cans on top. "Now, we'll see if it gets hot enough," he said, quite proud of his accomplishment.

"It was hot enough to cook the potatoes," Brandon commented. "So it should get hot enough to boil the water."

Over an hour later Matt noticed steam coming from the top of the cans. He jumped to his feet. "Brand! It's starting to boil!" Sure enough, the steam indicated that the water was just a few degrees below boiling point. In a few minutes, they would have four gallons of safe drinking water.

"Let it come to a full boil," Brandon said. "It will cool off during the night and tomorrow we'll be in business. We already have plenty for tonight."

Half an hour later, Matt capped the cans, set them aside, and snuffed out the lamps. Then he took Kirby for a short walk while Brandon used the pop bottle again. He climbed up into the plane and shut the door.

"How's your foot feeling, Brand?"

"Better. It looks pretty ugly, but it doesn't hurt as bad."

Matt unwrapped the wet shirt from Brandon's foot. It did look better than it had. The swelling had gone down and Brandon moved his toes a bit – something he couldn't do earlier without great pain. "It's all purple and black, but it doesn't look so fat," he said.

"I think I'll sleep with it out of that sling," Brandon said. "Can you pull off my other shoe and sock?" Matt took off Brandon's other shoe and sock and then took off his own. He arranged their sleeping bags and lay next to his friend. He pulled the other sleeping bag over them. Brandon turned his head toward Matt. "Thanks for taking such good care of me, Matty," he said quietly.

"No problem, Brand."

Chapter 20

Matt felt Brandon stirring and saw that light was coming in through the windows. Kirby sat beside him, his tail whisking back and forth across the deck. He turned over to see if Brandon was awake.

"Hey Brand. Your eye is open!" he said as he sat up. The swelling had gone down around Brandon's left eye, enough to let him open it partially.

"Yeah, I think I'm gonna be able to open it all the way soon," Brandon said. "How about you take a look at that cut on my head... see if it needs anything before I get infection and croak?"

Matt carefully lifted the bandage from Brandon's forehead. The gash appeared to be healing well. "It's not all red and nasty looking now," he said. It's got a good scab, and it looks like it's healing." Matt found a bottle of water, poured some onto the corner of a clean tee shirt, added a bit of shampoo, and then carefully washed the cut on Brandon's forehead. He rinsed it off, dried it, and applied a new bandage from the first aid kit.

Then he said to Kirby, "Got to go OUT?" Kirby jumped up and down at the magic word. Matt opened the door, climbed down the ladder to the pontoon, and lifted Kirby down onto the ground. The dog took off for the woods like a shot.

"I'm gonna have to get out of this plane and do that too, Matty," Brandon said.

"You gotta go *out*?"

"Yeah," Brandon laughed. "I gotta go... and soon."

"I'll find you a crutch," Matt said, and trotted off into the woods. He saw Kirby up ahead in a clearing in some fairly tall grass. Kirby was stopped still and was staring ahead into the grass. Matt watched as Kirby took a careful step forward, and then another. The dog stood perfectly still, one foot suspended, his body as tense as a coiled spring. "He's probably sneaking up on a grasshopper or a frog," Matt thought to himself. He was just about to say something to the dog when a bird about the size of a small chicken sprang up out of the grass and flew off. Kirby lunged and just missed it as it flew across the meadow, disappearing into the woods. "That looked like a grouse," Matt said to the dog. "Let's see if there are any more."

Matt picked up a heavy branch to use as a club. He and Kirby began walking slowly through the grass. Kirby's nose was working overtime trying to pick up the scent of another bird, but there were no more. "Well, we tried," Matt said. "Let's go back and tell Brand about that bird."

When they returned to the plane, Brandon was sitting in the doorway of the cargo hold. "We almost caught a bird," Matt said excitedly as he approached. "It looked kinda like the grouse we hunt at home, and when it flew up it made the same sound. Kirby almost caught it."

"Probably a Spruce grouse," Brandon said. "Dad told me about those birds. They're almost tame and real trusting. The explorers who discovered this land caught lots of them for food. They used a stick with a noose and just slipped it over their heads or hit them with a club. They called them Fool Hens. They're about the same size as the grouse in Wisconsin, but the Spruce grouse has more black with tan markings instead of the brown and tan like our Ruffed grouse."

"Are they good to eat?"

"Oh, yeah. They're similar to the Ruffed Grouse. They should be real good."

"I found this branch that we can fix up as a crutch for you, so you can keep off that bad foot," Matt said. "Go take care of your business, and I'll open some cans for breakfast."

With a heavy knife, Matt chopped off the branch on either side of the V, leaving a five inch stub on each side. He then tied some socks and a tee shirt in the crotch for padding. It was rather crude, but it was a crutch.

Brandon made his way down the ladder with Matt's help. He eyed the crutch with appreciation, and then hobbled off to a secluded spot for his morning duties.

Matt looked through their groceries, chose to open a couple of cans of sliced apples, and then climbed back down to the pontoon.

Brandon returned and they sat on the pontoon eating apple

slices right from the cans, sharing with Kirby. “Well, this isn’t as good as a couple of eggs and toast,” Brandon said.

“Yeah, but just think,” Matt replied. “We’re lucky to have all that stuff. Let’s just hope that our dads will find us soon so we don’t have to eat canned peaches and apples all summer.”

“I’m sure they’re out looking for us right now,” Brandon said. “It’s a big lake, but they won’t give up until they find us.”

Chapter 21

After Matt cleaned up the cooking area, Brandon decided to see about the radio. He climbed carefully back up into the plane and used the seat backs to steady himself as he hopped on his good foot to the cockpit. "Wow!" he said as he looked out the windshield. "It's a good thing we weren't going any faster when we hit that huge rock or we'd have been killed."

"We were going fast enough," Matt said.

Brandon flipped some switches and watched for the radio dials to come to life, but nothing happened. He switched some other gadgets on and off and then looked at Matt. "The battery is dead… or it's been damaged. We don't have any power."

"I'll go see what it looks like," Matt said. He opened the door on his side of the plane, climbed down the steps onto the pontoon. He made his way up to the nose of the plane and saw right away that they were not going to get the radio to work. When the propeller shattered against the rock, large pieces of it had ricocheted back into the engine cowling. The radiator was punctured, and a hole smashed in the side of the battery. All of the battery acid leaked out; the battery was useless. He walked back to the door and looked up at Brandon. "No good. The prop flew into the battery… it's toast."

"No fixing it?"

"Not without a gallon of glue and a couple of gallons of battery acid… and maybe a magician to help."

Brandon sighed. "Well, I guess we'll just have to wait for someone to find us, then."

Matt looked at the sky. "I don't think it's ever going to be clear again. It's been cloudy and foggy like this since we crashed."

"Sometimes these big fronts take a long time to go through," Brandon said. "There's no way they'll see us in this fog. We can make a signal fire by the lake when things eventually dry out, but until then I think we're stuck here."

"Well, we've got food and a place to sleep," Matt said. "Guess it could be worse."

"Yeah, it could be worse. But with 14,000 islands for them to search, we might be here for quite a while, especially since we weren't on our planned flight path." Brandon looked miserable. "I'm sorry I got you into this, Matty. I really screwed up."

"It wasn't your fault, Brand. This just happened. We just had bad luck."

Brandon smiled, but he shook his head sadly. "I'm kind of bad luck for your family. First, I'm driving when Mark is killed, and now I almost killed you, too."

"Horseshit, Brandon!" Matt exclaimed loudly. "Don't you ever, ever think you were at fault for Mark or for this. It just happened! Brandon, I love you as much as I ever loved Mark, and I won't listen to you saying stuff like that. This was just bad luck and we'll be okay. It was just as much my fault for not trying to make you go back. So quit blaming yourself. Understand?"

Brandon's face showed a little astonishment with the younger boy's outburst. But knew it was because of the way they felt about each other, like brothers. "Okay, Matty, okay. No more talk like that. We're good here. We'll be okay."

Matt climbed up into the cockpit and threw his arms around Brandon's neck. "I'm going fishing now," he said, and hurried to the back to find his fishing gear. He didn't want Brandon to see the tears in his eyes.

Matt rummaged around in the cargo hold, found his fishing pole and a couple of baits, climbed down from the plane and walked toward the lake. "He's grown up a bit, hasn't he, Kirby?" Brandon said to the dog. "Go with Matt, boy, while I tidy up the place." The dog jumped from the plane and trotted down the path to the lake.

Chapter 22

Matt was still a little angry with Brandon as he walked toward the lake, stomping on any bush or stick that was in his way. But in a short while, he cooled off and slowed his pace. He stopped by the shore where they had slid the plane onto the island, climbed up on a rock, and gazed at the lake. Just then Kirby joined him, wagging his tail furiously.

"Did Brandon send you to watch over me?" he said to the dog. "Let's see if we can catch a fish for supper." Hearing the word supper excited Kirby. Matt could see the bottom for a long way out into the lake. "This doesn't look like a very good spot, Kirby. I think we'll walk along the shore and find a place where the water's a little deeper."

Much of the shoreline was covered with small rocks, easy to walk over. Only occasionally they had to climb over a larger boulder as they moved down the island. They walked out on a point that protruded from the shore. The water was much deeper there. "This looks like a good spot," Matt said. The dog wagged his tail with approval. Matt tied spinner to his line. He reeled up the extra line and cast out into the deeper water. When the lure had dropped to the bottom and the line went slack, he began reeling the spinner back up toward him. He felt a couple of bumps when the lure hit a rock or some weeds, but he knew it wasn't a fish striking so he kept reeling.

He reeled up the lure and cast again, a little to the left. Again, he felt a bump or two as he reeled in. He kept working the point and cast all across it. Kirby lost interest, lay down in the gravel and went to sleep. Matt was beginning to think they would eat potatoes again for supper. But then his lure suddenly felt very heavy. He gave a sharp snap with his rod to set the hook. "I've got one!" he yelled. Kirby jumped to his feet.

Matt soon had doubts that the heavy weight on the line was a fish; it wasn't moving or fighting back. It was then that he saw a large branch hooked onto his lure coming up through the clear water. "Dang. Just a stick," he said. Kirby watched as Matt slid the stick to shore and unhooked his lure. "Well, at least that got us excited for a while," he said to the dog. Kirby sniffed the stick, lay back down, sighed and closed his eyes. More than an hour passed. Matt was beginning to lose his confidence when he felt a hard thump on the line. He pulled back hard to set the hook, and this time his reel began singing as the fish took out line. "Whoa! Kirby, I've got one! It's for real this time!" he yelled. Kirby sat up and barked as Matt worked the fish. It was not giving up easily and he had all he could do to keep it from taking out all of his line. He didn't dare tighten the drag on the reel any tighter for fear the fish would break the line. He'd gain some line and then the fish would make a run and take it all back.

Then he saw a flash of silver in the water as he manipulated the fish close to shore. "I wish you had hands and a landing net," he said to Kirby. Now he could see it. "Holy smokes! It's a big northern pike," he said. Kirby wagged his tail. There was no way he could lift the fish from the water so he kicked off his shoes, and holding the pole with one hand he quickly took off his socks. He waded into the water up to his knees and then reeled up his line so there was about a pole's length of line between the tip of the rod and the fish. The big northern was tired out and lying on its side, gills working slowly, trying to replenish the oxygen it had used up in the fight. Matt led the tired fish up close, and when he had it between him and the bank, he tossed the pole up onto the grass, put both hands under the fish and tossed it up on the shore. It almost landed on top of Kirby. He took off into the woods with his tail between his legs. Matt quickly scrambled up onto the shore, tackled the thrashing fish, and tossed it again farther on the shore so it wouldn't flop back into the water.

The fish flopped and thrashed some more, but it wasn't getting back into the lake. "Kirby! Come on back. It won't hurt you," he said laughing at the dog. Kirby poked his nose out of the brush and stared at the fish, but he wouldn't come any closer. "You big chicken," Matt said.

He grabbed the fish behind the head and took out his spinner, reeled up the line. Then he wiped off his feet in the grass and put on his socks and shoes. "Come on, Kirby. There'll be fresh northern fillets for supper tonight."

Matt carried the fish by its gill flap back along the shoreline. By the time he reached the willow path it had quit flopping around and was a little easier to carry. He found Brandon sitting on the pontoon studying a map of the lake. "Hey, Brand. How about some fresh fish for supper?" he said holding up the fish.

"Jeez, Matty! That's a dandy," Brandon beamed.

Matt puffed out his chest. "Oh, it's nothing so great… for a world famous fisherman like me."

Brandon laughed. "You're really something, Matty."

After they had admired the big fish, Matt brought the driftwood plank and a fillet knife to Brandon. When Brandon was finished filleting the fish, Matt washed the pieces of meat in the lake, and tossed the head and guts out as far as he could, where scavengers would get them. Then they put the meat into zip lock bags and stored it in the shade until supper time. "That was some pretty good fishing, Matt," Brandon said. "We'll eat good tonight." Then after a little contemplation he said, "I think we need to build a signal fire pretty soon, so we can be ready if a plane comes over."

"Do you think they're looking for us?" Matt asked.

"I don't know. It's still so overcast and rainy looking, and they probably don't know that we're lost yet. I bet our dads think we waited out the storm… just what we should have done."

"Well, we didn't and what's done is done," Matt said. "Once it clears off, they'll start looking."

"Yeah, I'm sure they will. But there's a heck of a bunch of islands for them to search, and we don't know how far off course we are. They'll probably start looking for us near Kenora, and I have no idea how far from there we are. So we might just have to get comfortable here and wait for a while."

"Well, it could be worse. We could have crashed in the water, or the plane could have burned… and we'd be dead. So, I think we're in pretty good shape."

Brandon patted the pontoon beside him and Matt sat down. Brandon put his arm over Matt's shoulders. "With your food gathering skills, we're going to be just fine, pal."

Chapter 23

That evening Brandon cut and deboned the fish fillets, rolled the pieces in flour and salt and pepper, while Matt prepared another pan of his delicious fried potatoes. The wonderful aroma wafting from the pit had Kirby sitting as close as he could get to the fire. "Kirby," Matt said. "Get back! You're gonna drool in the food." He pushed the dog farther away.

They ate until all of the food was gone except for one big piece of fish. Matt offered it to Brandon.

"No way. I'm stuffed. You eat it."

"I can't. I'm gonna explode," Matt groaned. He offered the fish to Kirby. Kirby was full, too. That didn't happen very often. He sniffed it and then took it, almost grudgingly.

"That was a great dinner, Matt," Brandon said. "Thanks to your good ideas and fishing skill, we're eating pretty darn good."

Matt just grinned.

They cleaned up the cooking site and put things away for the night. It was still rather dreary, but they sat watching the lake and the clouds, hoping to perhaps hear the hum of a search plane. By the time dusk settled in, the only sounds they had heard were the quacks and cries of ducks and loons. Everyone took a potty break and climbed into the plane. Brandon was getting along much better on his bad foot, and although the left side of his face was still black and blue, the swelling had gone down considerably, and he could see quite well with his left eye.

They slipped off their shoes and socks, spread out the sleeping bags and lay down. "You know," Brandon said. "Tomorrow we should think about taking a bath."

"Yeah," Matt said grinning. "I've noticed you smell a little like Kirby."

"You don't smell so sweet yourself."

Matt smiled. "Okay. Tomorrow a bath. G'night, Brand."

"Night, Matty."

For the first time in several days they woke to find sunlight streaming in through the window. "Brand! Look! The clouds are finally gone."

They arose and opened the door to a glorious morning of sunshine. A nice breeze blew in off the water. Matt climbed down, gave Kirby his freedom, and then helped Brandon down the ladder.

"I'll clean the pans down at the shore so we can have some breakfast," Matt said.

While he cleaned the cooking pans, he looked out over the massive lake. Islands dotted the surface of water for as far as he could see. "Lotsa water," he said to nobody in particular.

Brandon had opened cans of apples and peaches when he returned. They dumped them together into one of the pans and heated them up. "I sure could go for some bacon and eggs," Matt said.

"Or some pancakes," Brandon added.

But instead, they ate apples and peaches, and they were glad to have that.

They brushed their teeth after breakfast, and then decided to take a bath in the lake. Matt carried the soap and fresh clothes while Brandon slowly hobbled along with his crutch. When they finally got to the edge of the lake, they each sat on a boulder and took off their shoes and socks. Then they both stripped off their clothes and stepped into the water. "Yeeeeeoww!" Matt said when his legs hit the cold water. "Are you sure we can't just stink?"

"It won't be so bad once you're used to it," Brandon said. He moved into deeper water, hobbling on one good foot and one crutch. Matt followed and they both stopped when the water was at mid-thigh. "That's deep enough," Brandon said. With his hands he dipped water over his head and body and began lathering his hair with shampoo and his body with soap. Matt did the same and soon they were both covered with soap suds. "Only one way to get rinsed," Brandon said. He let himself fall backwards into the water, went under, rubbed off the soap and quickly got to his feet. "Nothing to it," he said through chattering teeth.

The last thing Matt wanted to do was to duplicate Brandon's rinsing method. But he had little choice, so he dropped into the water. It felt like a thousand needles had stuck into his body. He rubbed furiously to get the soap rinsed off and then scrambled to his feet. "Holy cow!" he yelled as he waded at a rapid pace for shore. Brandon turned to watch Matt just as he stepped out of the water. "That wasn't so bad, now, was it?" he said grinning.

"Jeez," Matt whined. "It's a good thing I don't have to pee. I think it would come out icicles."

Brandon laughed, even though he, too, was rather cold. But the sunshine warmed them up as they dried off with Matt's big beach towels. When they had dressed and were carrying their dirty clothes back to the plane Brandon said: "You smell a lot better now."

"I'm glad I don't offend you any more," Matt said grinning. "What's next?"

"I think we should find wood for a signal fire... in case a plane flies over," Brandon said.

"It's still wet. Do you think it'll burn?"

"If we pour lamp oil on it, we'll get a lot of smoke, and that's really what we need. And if we get it out in the sun it'll get dried out."

"Okay," Matt agreed. "Let's gather up some wood, then."

Chapter 24

The boys explored the shoreline near their campsite and found a large boulder, about three feet high, out in the open and nearly flat on top. "This'll make a good place for a signal fire," Brandon said. With that decided they started gathering up wood and piling it on the boulder. Brandon wasn't much help with one bad foot – his broken ankle was beginning to hurt and it was swelling again from being used too much. So Matt gathered and carried the wood and Brandon pulled himself up on the rock. First he laid the heavier branches that Matt carried to him in a square, piling them like a log cabin. Once the pile was nearly three feet tall, Matt brought smaller brush and branches and Brandon filled the inside of the square with the smaller pieces.

After working steadily for several hours they had an enormous stack of broken branches, driftwood and small logs, ready to light if a plane came over. "We'll leave a couple bottles of that lamp oil down here, and a box of matches in a zip lock," Brandon said. "Then if we see or hear a plane, one of us… well, you most likely, will have to run down here and light the fire."

"I'll get all that stuff, and some paper and cardboard, too," Matt said. He started toward the plane. Brandon climbed down off the rock and began hobbling back toward their campsite.

They met about mid-way and Brandon said, "You notice how a lot of these willows have sprung back up? Our path is getting harder to find and harder to walk in."

"Yeah, I noticed that. The only place that's still clear is where the prop chopped them off like a weed whacker."

By the time Brandon reached the plane, Matt had dropped off the kindling and oil and had caught up with him again. "Brand? I wonder how big this island is."

"No idea, Matty. From the shore where we took our bath it looks like it goes a long way in both directions. Hard to say how wide it is. Why?"

"I thought maybe we should see how big it is. And maybe we can find something that might be useful."

"That's a good idea, Matt. But I won't be very useful hobbling around in the brush with this broken ankle. I'd just slow you down."

"Do you think there's any Grizzl Bears on this island?"

Brandon laughed. "No, I doubt that there are any Grizzl Bears. Maybe a Black Bear. Grizzl Bears are a lot farther north."

"You think there's Black Bears?"

"I doubt it, Matty. But they could live on the island if it's big enough and there are enough small animals and berries and stuff for them to eat... but I really doubt it. Most likely there are some raccoons, and beaver, and maybe a few otter... and those spruce grouse. There could be a few squirrels and maybe a moose, but probably nothing too dangerous."

"Well, if there's no Grizzl Bears, I'm not too worried," Matt said with a wide grin.

After a lunch of vegetables and potatoes, Matt called Kirby and announced, "We're gonna take a little hike and see what's here."

"Okay, but just remember we're on an island, so if you get lost, find the water and start walking until you find our path."

"I'll remember that. You gonna be okay?"

"Sure. I think I'll hobble down by the water and see if I can catch a fish for supper."

"I'll carry your fishing pole and tackle box down for you," Matt said. "When you get to the lake, go to the left and there's a point that has deep water all around it. That's where I caught the northern."

"Sounds good, and thanks for carrying my stuff. It's kind of hard to carry much with this stupid crutch in my hand."

Matt left the tackle box and pole sitting on a big rock near the end of the path. He met Brandon as he started back. "Well, catch us some supper, and maybe Kirby and I will get lucky and find a McDonald's or Pizza Hut on the other side of the island."

Brandon laughed. "I'll have a double quarter pounder if you do," he said.

Matt and Kirby set off on their journey into the woods to explore the island.

Chapter 25

The brush was thick in some places; countless rocks and boulders strewn over the island, and downed trees that littered the forest made walking in a straight line very difficult. Matt and Kirby took quite a while to cover any distance, but they worked their way toward the middle of the island. Matt marveled at how the huge pine trees seemed to spring up out of nearly solid rock, with hardly any topsoil, or even sand. Somehow, their roots seemed to find a way down between the rocks to make a living. "Look at these trees, Kirby. They send their roots down into a little bit of dirt and hang on for dear life."

There were no signs of anyone ever being there before them. No trees had been cut; no trails had been made. But there were signs of habitation other than humans. In the clear areas where grass grew over the limited ground, Matt saw tracks of birds and small animals. Had he paid more attention in Cub Scouts he probably could have identified the creatures by the tracks they made, or by the poop they left behind. Kirby's nose made grunting sounds as he sniffed at all the new strange scents. Matt knew some tracks were made by raccoons, and others that looked as if they had been made by some type of squirrel. As they crossed one of the grassy meadows, a spruce hen flew up just ahead of them. Kirby took off chasing it through the trees. "Kirby! Come back here!" Matt called out, and Kirby returned panting.

"We'll watch in this grass from now on. Maybe we can catch one of those and have some KFC tonight for supper." Kirby wagged his tail furiously as if he understood what that meant.

After walking aimlessly for over an hour, Matt could see the sparkle of water between the trees up ahead. "There's the other side," he said to the dog. They were just a few yards away from the shoreline when they heard the startling sound of a rifle shot. Matt instinctively ducked and grabbed onto Kirby. Then there was another shot and the sound of an outboard motor. "Kirby. There's people here. They can help us!"

He hurried toward the water and as he stepped up to the edge of the woods Matt saw something swimming across from the next island. He had to look closely but finally figured out that it was a cow moose. All he could see was its head sticking up out of the water. He was just about to step out onto the rocks when another shot sounded and the water near the moose turned red with blood. The moose swam a couple more strokes, and her hooves thrashed on top of the water. Then she sank out of site. Matt looked to the right and saw a boat with three people in it flying down the lake as fast as it could go.

Instead of waving to them, he stepped back into the woods and crouched down, holding Kirby's collar. He wanted to see what these strangers were up to before he showed himself. The motor stopped and the boat drifted to the spot where the moose went under. "Get in there and get her," the man sitting in front holding the rifle said to the man in the middle.

Matt watched as the middle man, much smaller than the other two, leaned over taking off his shoes. Then he stood, took off his shirt and pants, picked up a rope and dove over the side of the boat. After what seemed like a long time, he came back to the surface, gasping for air. "It's tied on," he said. Matt realized the voice was that of a boy, not a small man. He had tied the rope to the moose. "Swim over there and get out," the front man said pointing to the island where Matt was crouching. "We'll drag her over to the shallow and pull her in."

The boy swam toward the island. The two men in the boat appeared to be Indians with their dark features and long black hair. They were both large and mean looking in their flannel shirts, jeans, and tattered cowboy hats. Meanwhile, the boy had reached the bank a short way from Matt and stood there in his underwear, shivering. He looked to be about thirteen or fourteen, thin, and also an Indian. His long black hair hung to his shoulders, but his skin was not as dark as the other two. Trying to get dry, he brushed the water off himself with his hands. Matt knew from experience – that water was cold.

The men started the motor again, drove the boat up near the shore a short way down the lake and got out. Both were wearing hip boots. They pulled the boat up on the shore and then started pulling on the rope. The carcass of the moose was soon visible, gliding through the water.

Kirby was excited to see other people, trying to break free from Matt's hold to go and greet them. "Kirby," Matt whispered. "Ssshhh. Lay down!"

The boy standing on the shore turned to look when Matt tried to quiet Kirby. Matt froze. The boy stared into the woods a few moments, and then turned and walked back to the boat. He climbed in, stripped off his wet underwear, and put on his dry clothes. "Bring the knives here," one of the men said. The boy did what he was told. They had drug the moose up onto the shore and began to field dress it. "I've got to go. I'm gonna go in the bushes," the boy said. The men nodded and paid no more attention to him.

Matt crouched lower in the brush and tried to keep Kirby's wagging tail from making noise. The boy walked into the woods just a few feet away and looked right at Matt. "Who are you?" he whispered.

"My name is Matt, and my friend, Brandon is on the other side of the island. We crashed our plane on the island a few days ago during the storm."

"Are you hurt?"

"My friend has a broken ankle, but otherwise, we're okay."

The boy looked over his shoulder. "Those guys are my uncles and they're poachers. If they know you're on the island they'll come and steal everything you've got. You gotta keep that dog quiet until we leave."

Matt nodded that he understood.

"How far are we from Clearwater Bay?" Matt asked.

"Never heard of it," the boy answered. "I gotta get back or they'll come looking for me. I'll try to come and see you guys in a day or two. Will you still be there that long?"

Matt nodded again.

"Be quiet, now." The boy put his finger up to his lips. "And wait for me to come back." He turned and slipped off through the trees.

"You took long enough, you lazy little snot," one of the men said.

"I'm sorry I had to go. That cold water made me," the boy apologized.

"Yeah," the man snarled. "You just wanted us to do all the work. You're lazy just like your Ma was. Now git your ass in the boat 'n shut up. You're lucky we take such good care of you."

The boy climbed into the boat while the men loaded up the four quarters of moose meat. One of them got in and started the motor while the other pushed them into deeper water. Then they sped off down the lake. As they began to turn around an island, Matt saw the boy look back at him.

"Come on, Kirby. We've gotta tell Brandon about this."

Chapter 26

On the way back to the plane, Matt and Kirby stayed on the lookout for another spruce hen. Each time they came upon a grassy meadow, they snuck forward slowly, Kirby just ahead sniffing the air, but they didn't run across any of the birds.

They came to another shoreline. Matt studied the surroundings a few minutes trying to determine which way would get them back to the plane. One of the islands looked familiar, so he decided to go to the left. He hadn't walked far when he found the path to the plane and just beyond, Brandon sat on a rock near the shore fishing. "Hey, Matty. Look here," Brandon called out. He lifted a stringer with three nice walleyes.

"Wow! Brand! Walleyes! Those look great."

"How did your exploration go?"

"I saw some people."

"What? Did you talk to them? Can they help us?"

"They were poachers. Did you hear them shooting?"

"Shooting? What shooting? It's been pretty windy on this side of the island. I didn't hear anything."

"They shot a moose in the water."

"At this time of year? Well, then they're poachers. There's no moose season open now."

"They had a kid about my age with them, and he dove in and tied a rope on the dead moose. He swam to shore right next to me and Kirby, and he saw us."

"Then what?"

"He didn't tell the others, but he came back and talked to me, so the others didn't hear him. I think he was forced to go with them. They treated him real bad like he was their slave. He said they were his uncles and they were poachers and that I should be real quiet 'cause if they found out we were here they'd come and take all our stuff. They were real mean looking guys, so I don't think the kid was exaggerating."

"There were two adults?"

"Yeah… real nasty looking, like they'd just as soon shoot you as look at you."

"Which way did they go?"

Matt pointed to the west. "The kid said he'd try to come back and see us in a couple of days."

"No kidding? Do you think he will?"

"I don't know. Maybe. If he was a bad guy like the others, he'd have yelled at them when he found me."

"That makes sense. Wow. You really had an adventure."

Matt nodded. "I wonder if we should try to cover up our path from the shore to the plane. I'd hate to have those two poachers find us and steal all our stuff. And they've got guns."

"Good idea, Matt. Maybe we should hide our signal fire, too," Brandon said as he stepped carefully from the rock. He picked up his crutch and then the stringer. "Let's have supper and then we can figure out what to do about those guys."

When they got to the plane Brandon filleted the fish and Matt got some potatoes ready. "I'd like to make a wood fire for cooking and save the oil," Brandon said. "But I don't want those poachers to see the smoke."

"We've got lots of oil. I hope we're not here long enough to run out."

"Okay. So tell me everything you saw," Brandon said as they ate the fish and potatoes. "Don't leave out a thing."

Matt started with missing the grouse and finished with finding Brandon sitting on the rock. "That's it. That's everything."

"Hmm," Brandon pondered. "Makes me wonder just where we are on this lake. If those guys came by boat, they must have a way to a town near here. They wouldn't be living way out in the middle of the lake on an island. I wonder how far we strayed off course in that storm. We might be closer to Minnesota than we are to Canada."

"You think we're that far south?"

"We could be. We flew for quite a while in that storm before we crashed. Our dads are probably looking for us way up in the opposite corner of the lake."

Darkness was closing in as they finished their supper. When Matt had cleaned the pans, they climbed into the plane and pulled the doors shut. "Better lock them tonight," Brandon suggested.

"Yeah. Good idea. I'll feel safer knowing they can't just walk in on us."

They settled down on the sleeping bags.

"Brand?"

"Yeah, Matty."

"You think those guys would hurt us?"

"I don't know, Matt, but I'd rather not find out. If they're poaching, that's one thing. But they may be more than just poachers, and up here, there's not much for law. So we should hope they stay far away from this island."

"I wonder if that kid will come back."

Chapter 27

Adam Whitehorse Happalti sat on a small wooden stool in the corner of the cabin, reading from a copy of *The Call of the Wild.* It was the only book he had managed to bring with him to this desolate place. He had read it so many times he nearly knew the entire book by heart. Although his uncles went to town each month for supplies, he had never found the courage to ask them to buy him another book or two. He was trying to stay out of their way as they cut up the moose they had killed earlier in the day. When they had some meat ready, Adam hung the pieces in the smokehouse just a short way from the front door. He did what he was told to do, but otherwise, he tried to keep his distance from his uncles and their hot tempers.

"How did it ever come to this?" he thought to himself.

Just a little over a year earlier he had been living in Rochester, Minnesota, going to school, playing soccer and acting like any other normal fourteen year old kid. His parents were great and they were providing him a good life. Then on a night that he would never forget, his parents were on their way to pick him up from school so they could go to dinner and a movie. It was snowing, which was nothing unusual in Rochester. They had stopped for a red light when a car rammed them from behind. Their car slid on the slippery pavement and was hit by a snowplow crossing the intersection. They were both killed instantly. Adam's world was turned upside down.

His dad had emigrated with his parents from Finland when he was a child. His grandparents on his father's side of the family had died when he was a small boy. No other family could be found.

His mother had two brothers who lived somewhere in Canada or northern Minnesota. They were his only legal relatives. But he didn't know where they lived, and he'd never met them.

Adam was put in foster care for several weeks. When the authorities located the uncles, they agreed to take the boy in, and were awarded the estate of his parents, with the stipulation that after funeral expenses were paid, the remaining money from the sale of the Rochester home and other property was to be put in a trust fund for Adam, so he would be ensured of a college education. But after his uncles had taken him away, the welfare department seemed to put Adam's file away and forget about it. There was never any follow up to see that he was in good hands.

Adam's uncles turned out to be less than stellar people. Instead of putting the money that was rightly Adam's into a trust fund, they bought for themselves a new boat and motor, a four wheeler, and a snowmobile. They bought a small bed and put it in the loft of their cabin, and for all practical purposes, Adam became a servant who did the cleaning, cooking and most of the work around the cabin while the uncles fished, hunted and drank.

Adam's mother was a full blooded Ojibwa Indian and Adam inherited her dark skin, noble features and black hair. The Finnish ancestry from his father softened the high cheekbones, large nose, and skin tone of the Indian blood, making him appear just darkly tanned all the time. The unique combination of genes made him quite handsome. But unlike most fourteen year old boys, he seldom smiled and rarely laughed. His life had become nothing but work, if only to avoid a beating.

His uncles could not be called "pillars of society". They were hard, crude men who lived by poaching both fish and game, and stealing whatever they could get their hands on. They owned a small parcel of land on the southwest shore of Lake of the Woods and spent most of their time scouring the land for whatever they could find to bring in a few dollars.

Their old Ford pickup was beat up and rusted, but it ran well, and it got them to and from town. Baudette was almost 50 miles away by way of a rutted and rock strewn path they called a road. Their only reason for going to town was to pick up gas and groceries, and occasional parts for their outboard motor. They also met monthly with a man who bought the stolen goods they had acquired.

A generator providing electricity was about the only modern convenience in the log cabin consisting of one large room that served as kitchen and living room with stone fireplace at one end. Off the main room were bedrooms for each of the uncles. In the loft above the two bedrooms, Adam's bed and a couple of wooden boxes to hold his clothes were the only furnishings. The rest of the room was bare. He had nothing of his own – nothing that even suggested that a boy lived there at all.

"Get your lazy butt over here and haul this venison to the smoke house," his uncle Carl growled. Carl was the older of the two and gave all of the orders.

Adam got up from his stool in the corner. He carried a large pan filled with chunks of fresh moose out the door to the smoke house situated on the bank of a small creek that ran across the property. Sweet smoke billowed out as he opened the door. He skewered the pieces of meat onto stainless steel hooks, hung them on a rack inside, closed the door and walked back to the cabin.

"Clean some potatoes and get them boiling," his uncle Ed barked. Adam did as he was told. While he cleaned the potatoes, his uncles finished boning the meat and hung the rest in the smoke house. They reserved the loins for supper.

"Get this meat cooked up," Uncle Ed said as they walked out the door. We're gonna wash up."

Adam dredged several slices of venison in flour and dropped them into a pan on the stove. The hot oil sizzled and the frying fresh meat and sliced onions filled the cabin with a delicious, tantalizing aroma. His uncles came back from washing up at the creek and poured themselves drinks from a bottle of rye whiskey. "Hurry up with that food, boy, and don't burn them steaks. I want mine a little rare."

Adam shoveled the food onto platters and set it on the table. Then he sat next to the window and looked out over the lake as the men ate and drank. When they were full Uncle Carl shoved the platter toward Adam. "There's some left. Take it."

Adam took the leftovers and sat down away from his uncles as they began to drink in earnest. "Please don't let them get drunk tonight," he prayed silently. But his prayer wasn't to be answered.

A couple of hours later, both uncles were roaring drunk, stumbling around, laughing and singing. Adam just sat near the corner and looked out the window, trying to make himself small and invisible. "Clean this place up you lazy little shit!" his Uncle

Ed slurred.

"Yes, Uncle," Adam responded obediently.

He heated a kettle of water, poured it into a sink and began washing the dishes. Just as he finished Uncle Carl tipped his chair over and passed out on the floor. "Lightweight!" Uncle Ed yelled, laughing. "Look at this dipshit," he slurred to Adam. Adam nodded and continued putting the dishes away. "You ignorin' me, boy?"

"No, Uncle. I was just busy trying to clean up the mess," Adam said.

Ed stared at him for a few moments and then seemed to forget him. "Goin' to bed," he said and staggered off into his bedroom. Adam shut off the lights, climbed up the ladder to his loft, took off his clothes and slipped into his hard bed. He could hear Uncle Carl snoring below him on the living room floor. His eyes filled with tears as he lay thinking about what a hell his life had become.

"I've got to get out of here," he said to himself. "Or I'm gonna end up dead some night when they get drunk."

Just then he heard Uncle Carl floundering around, trying to get up. "Wha the hell? Who pushed me down on the floor?" Adam peaked over the side of the loft and saw his uncle on all fours, crawling toward his bedroom. There, lying on the floor where Carl had fallen over, Adam saw a key on a small key ring. A plan quickly took shape in his mind, and it didn't take long for him to decide to put it into action.

Carl usually locked the front door when they went to bed – to be safe from a burglar who might try to get into the cabin, but mostly he did it to be sure that Adam didn't try to run away. But tonight the door was unlocked and the key was there on the floor. In his drunken stupor, Carl had forgotten to lock the door. This was Adam's perfect opportunity. And now there was someone to run to.

Chapter 28

Adam waited until he could hear snoring from both of the bedrooms below him so he knew both uncles were passed out cold. He got up from his bed, dressed in jeans, a tee shirt, a hooded sweatshirt, socks and tennis shoes. He took the pillow case off his pillow and filled it with other clothes. He didn't have much, some extra underwear, tee shirts, jeans, shorts and a few pairs of socks. He carefully climbed down the ladder, making sure not to make any noise, and picked up the key from the floor. He grabbed his heavy jacket from a hook near the door as he snuck out, locked the front door from the outside and tossed the key into the bushes.

The moon was up and nearly full so it was easy to find his way to the smoke house. He opened the door and put several chunks of the fresh meat that had hardly begun to smoke in a clean stainless steel pail with a clean towel over it. He figured that some of the meat should rightly be his, since he had to dive into the cold water to retrieve the dead moose. But he didn't want to steal anything else from his uncles that didn't belong to him.

He was going to steal one thing, though, and if his uncles ever caught him after this, they'd probably kill him for doing it. He was going to take their boat and motor – their lifeblood – their only possession that they really relied on. Of course, the boat was actually his, since it had been bought with his money, but he knew that wouldn't matter to Carl and Ed. There was a canoe beached on the shore next to the boat, too, but he was sure they'd catch up to him if he took that. But he was confident that he could get away far enough and fast enough with the motor boat so they wouldn't find him. All he could do was hope for the best.

He put his clothes and the meat into the boat, untied it from the small dock and pushed it off into the lake. He quietly put the oars into the oarlocks and began rowing away from the shore. The right oar had a loud squeak. He stopped, found an empty outboard oil bottle, and let the few remaining drops of oil drip into the oarlock. The squeak was gone. He smiled to himself and began pulling hard on the oars. He wanted to get as far from the cabin as possible before dawn.

After rowing for over an hour, Adam felt it was safe to start the outboard. He squeezed the primer bulb, set the throttle to midway, and the motor started on the first pull. He flipped the shift lever into forward and off he went down the lake. The moon and stars gave him enough light, but after several miles, he decided to put to shore and wait for dawn.

He tipped up the motor, pushed the nose of the boat up onto a gravel bank, and settled down in the bottom to rest. With the light of dawn he could find the right island. His heart beat fast as he thought of his decision to leave his uncles. He had to make this getaway a good one. They'd be so angry that he'd be in for the beating of his life if they ever caught him.

"If that kid and his friend have people coming for them, and if I can get there before they do," he thought as he gazed up at the stars, "…I can get back to civilization and have a life again." He tightened his heavy jacket around his neck, settled back and closed his eyes. Just as he began to doze off, he heard a loud splash in the water near him. He froze, thinking that Carl and Ed had followed him in the canoe. He slowly sat up and looked into the dark only to see a beaver swimming across the water. He smiled, pulled his hood up over his head and settled back in the bottom of the boat.

Adam wasn't sure how long he had slept but the sun was quite high in the sky when he opened his eyes. He felt confused at first, unaware of why he was in the boat. Then he remembered his flight from his uncles. He sat up and looked around.

The journey through the darkness, though, did have him confused about just where he was. He looked up and down the lake until he thought he had it figured out. "I've got to go around those islands, and then I think that next one on the left is where that boy and his friend are," he thought to himself.

He pushed the boat off the shore, stepped to the back, lowered the motor and gave the starter cord a pull. The motor sprung to life and he backed it into deeper water. As he passed the next two islands, he saw the island that they had chased the moose from, and he recognized the island where he had seen the kid and the dog.

"That's the one right there," he said to himself. He turned toward the island and cut the motor just as he came to the shore at the same spot where they had quartered the moose. He put his clothes and the meat on the beach, and then removed his pants, shirt, shoes and socks. He found a stick that would suit his purpose and then he pushed the boat out away from shore.

He got into the boat as it drifted into deep water and pulled the starter cord. The motor came to life. He revved the throttle to about midway and wedged the stick between the throttle handle and the back seat. He slid over the side into the water, maneuvered the boat so it was pointing up the lake towards his uncles' cabin, reached over the side and pushed the shift lever forward. Adam dropped off the side and watched as the boat began moving up the lake. His plan had worked. The stick kept it from turning to either side. He watched it for a little while, then swam until he could touch bottom, and waded the rest of the way back to shore. By then the boat was far away and still going.

"It'll go until it hits an island or the shore, and then I hope those two drunks find it," he said to himself. "And if I'm lucky they'll think I fell in and drowned… and that will be the last I ever see of them."

He wiped himself dry with an extra tee shirt, took off his wet underwear, and put on dry clothes. "Well, now. Let's see if I can find these guys." He picked up the bundles and started walking.

Adam found the trail left by the kid and his dog quite easily where they had trampled weeds and broken branches. He wasn't sure how large the island was, but the trail was clear, and it would surely lead him to the kid, his friend, and the crashed plane. His only fear was that their rescuers had already come, and that he might be stranded on the island alone.

Chapter 29

"You want eggs or pancakes for breakfast?" Matt asked as he sorted through the cans of fruit and vegetables.

"Hmm. Let's have pancakes. We had eggs yesterday, didn't we?"

"Okay. Pancakes it is," Matt said, picking up cans of beans and peaches. He unlocked the cargo door and opened it. "Looks like a nice day," he said as he climbed down, and then lifted Kirby down. Kirby took off for the woods, and Matt did the same. When he returned, Brandon was just coming down the ladder.

"How's the foot feeling, Brand?"

"Not too bad. It's tender, but if I'm careful, I can make it work pretty well."

"Your face is looking better, too," Matt said.

"That's good. I'm glad I'm not so ugly anymore."

"No, I didn't say you were ugly," Matt laughed. "I just meant that the cut on your forehead is healed up, and the black eyes are only purple now. Much less ugly."

They both laughed. Brandon walked carefully to the woods while Matt lit the lamps under one of the food pans and dumped in the cans of beans. He was stirring the beans when Kirby and Brandon came back. "Won't be long now," he said. The beans started to steam. "You know, I'm getting kinda tired of peaches and beans, but I guess we should feel pretty lucky… we could be eating bugs and worms."

"Yeah, you're right, Matt," Brandon replied. "But I sure could go for a good juicy hamburger about now."

They ate the hot beans and then had the peaches for desert. Matt cleaned the pan and utensils in the lake. He was just finishing when Brandon and Kirby came down the trail. "Let's get the signal firewood piled down behind that rock so those poachers don't see it," Brandon said. "We can throw some of it up on top of the rock again and light it if we hear a plane."

Matt agreed. He climbed up on the rock and tossed the wood and kindling down. Brandon stacked it behind the rock where it couldn't be seen. Then they pulled a few more of the willows along the shoreline upright so their path was hidden. "That'll keep them from seeing us," Matt said.

"Yeah. But from now on, we have to be listening for an outboard or shooting."

They walked back to the plane. Matt decided to take Kirby hunting for another spruce hen. "We saw one yesterday but we weren't expecting it, so it got away. We'll be more careful, just in case it's back there today."

"Good luck," Brandon said. "I hope you get one. They'll be as good as chicken."

"Just like KFC?"

"KFC?"

"Yeah. Kentucky Fried Chicken," Matt laughed.

"Wouldn't that taste good? Especially if we had mashed potatoes to go with it?"

"Well, we might have to settle for just the chicken. I'll see what I can scare up," Matt said. He selected a good strong stick to crack the bird over the head if they found one. "I'll be back in a couple of hours."

"I'll be down by the lake trying to catch some more fish... not that I don't have faith in your hunting ability... but just in case," Brandon said grinning.

"Okay, Brand. Don't fall in." Matt and Kirby started off into the familiar woods in search of something to go with their vegetables for dinner that night. He was getting used to being out in the forest; each time he went there, he liked it even more. "I could live on an island like this if there was a place to get a burger now and then," he thought. "Come on, Killer. Find me a grouse," he said to Kirby. The dog dashed back and forth, investigating each and every smell he came across.

Chapter 30

Uncle Ed woke with a terrible hangover. Still in his clothes and lying on top of the covers, he lay for a while trying to let his head clear. "Adam!" he shouted. "Get some coffee going."

In the next room, Uncle Carl woke when he heard his brother yelling at Adam. He, too, was terribly hung over and had a throbbing headache. He rolled to his side, sat up and swung his legs off the bed. "Get some breakfast cooked, you lazy snot!" he shouted through the door.

Both were slow getting on the move and both came out into the kitchen at almost the same time. "Where the hell is that kid?" Carl grumbled. "Adam! Get up, you lazy brat!"

Carl peered up at the loft, expecting Adam's face to appear over the railing. No one was there. A startled expression came to his face when he climbed the ladder far enough to see that Adam and his clothes were gone. "Ed! Adam's run off!" he shouted, nearly falling down the ladder.

The two men scrambled into their boots and scurried to the door. Ed grabbed the doorknob and pulled. He was surprised to find it locked. "Give me the key," he said.

Carl felt inside his pocket. Then he checked the other pocket, and his shirt pockets as well. "I don't have the damn thing," he mumbled.

"Well, where the hell is it?"

"How the hell should I know? I don't remember locking the door. You s'pose that kid stole the key and locked it from the outside?"

"Damn kid!" Ed said. "We gotta take the hinges off."

"Well, hurry it up. I gotta pee real bad," Carl said dancing from one foot to the other.

Ed dug a screwdriver from a drawer and started taking the hinges off the back side of the door. All the while, he cussed Adam. "There. That'll do it," Carl said as the last screw fell to the floor. He stuck the screwdriver into the slot between the door and the jamb and pried. The door slid out of the opening and fell toward them. Ed grabbed it and stood it against the wall.

As they stepped from the cabin, the first thing they looked for was the old pickup. It was right where it was suppose to be. Carl ran to the edge of the woods to pee. When he looked toward the lake, he let out a groan. "He's stole the boat," he hollered.

"That brat! I'll kill him!" Ed yelled.

They ran to the shore and looked up and down the lake, expecting to see Adam in the boat. "That stupid kid. I knew we shoulda left him in that foster home in Minnesota."

"Let's not get into that again. I still say it was worth it to get the money from Naomi's estate."

"Well, we're gonna have to take the canoe and see if we can find the little brat," Ed said.

"Let's get some coffee and grub first. Then we'll go find him and skin him alive."

The men hurried back to the cabin and after they ate a quick breakfast, they carried the canoe down to the lake. "Which way?" Ed asked.

"He was acting kind of strange the other day when we shot that moose. I wonder if he went that way. Maybe he saw something on that island that he thought would help him get away from us?"

"What do you suppose he saw?"

"Maybe somebody was there. He seemed to take a long time when he said he was shittin.'"

"Why didn't he just run then?"

"How the hell do I know? I don't even know if that's the way he went, but we gotta go one way or the other, don't we?"

"Yeah, you're right. Let's go that way first. He's got a good head start on us, so we're gonna have to paddle as fast as we can if we want to catch him."

"There ain't no way to get to town that way. So if he's out there we'll find him. The boat can't go forever with the gas that was in it. We're gonna keep lookin' till we find him, and then he'll be one sorry brat."

The canoe moved quickly through the water with the force of the two large, strong men paddling. Not only were they skilled in canoeing; their anger motivated them even more.

They had gone a little over a mile when Ed stopped paddling

and held up his hand. "Wait. Listen!"

Carl stopped paddling, but the canoe glided silently onward. "I hear it," he said quietly.

Ed pointed to the right. "Over there… around that island!"

They paddled feverishly and in a few minutes they reached the island where they could hear an outboard running. They turned and skirted the island, and the sound got louder. Ed pointed and nodded. "Right around that point," he whispered.

Again they paddled briskly, with every intention to surprise whoever was in the boat. As they rounded the point they saw their boat, up against a fallen tree in the water, motor running, and the prop churning the water. They paddled to it, but they found no sign of Adam. Ed boarded the boat and shut down the motor.

"What the hell?" he said. He pulled the branch that Adam had wedged into the motor to keep it headed straight. "What do you suppose that kid did?"

"Maybe he's up on this island hiding from us," Carl said. He got to the front of the canoe, stepped out onto the shore and began looking up and down the edge of the water for tracks. Then he walked into the edge of the woods, checking for some disturbance made by a person walking through. "He ain't been here. There's no tracks."

Carl returned and stared at the branch and the empty boat. "The life jackets are still here. S'pose he fell overboard?"

"Maybe so. But what's this stick in here for?"

"I hope the little snot is drowned," Carl said. "We're lucky to be rid of him."

"Yeah, maybe so. But I think something's not right here." Ed gazed down the lake.

"What do you mean?"

"I think that kid is pulling a fast one on us. Maybe he did fall in and drown, but I got my suspicions."

Chapter 31

Adam stepped into the woods and found the spot where the boy and the dog had been hiding. He hid his clothes and the pail under a pile of brush. Then he began tracking them through the woods, looking for mashed grass, disturbed leaves and broken branches. "This kid wasn't trying to hide his path," he thought to himself as he walked along.

He thought he would just try to follow the trail, and if that didn't work, he'd follow the shoreline until he saw them. "He said they crashed a plane here, so there must be some damaged trees or something," Adam thought to himself.

He had walked for nearly half an hour taking his time, following the signs, when he saw something white moving through the tall grass ahead. He was puzzled for a moment, and then he realized it was the tail of that dog he saw the previous day with the boy. Just beyond the edge of the woods behind the dog he saw the boy, stalking quietly through the tall grass, wielding a long stick.

"Well, now I'll see if I've made the right decision," he thought. He stepped from the brush into the grassy meadow. "What are you hunting?" he asked.

He saw the boy stop dead in his tracks, staring at him. The dog heard him and came galloping toward him. He didn't know if the dog was mean, but he decided to hold his ground. The dog rubbed against him and licked his outstretched hand. "Hi, fella," he said, squatted and ruffled the dog's ears. The dog stretched up and licked his face with a big wet tongue.

"He'll lick you to death if you let him," the boy said as he approached.

Adam smiled. "I love dogs. I used to have one, but… well, that's in another time." He offered his hand. "I'm Adam."

"I'm Matt." He accepted the handshake, looking over Adam's shoulder toward the woods. "Are those other guys with you?" he asked quietly.

Adam shook his head. "No. I ran away."

"What do you mean? Ran away?"

"It's a long story, but don't worry. I'm not a poacher. I had to help them or they would've beaten me."

"How'd you get here?" Matt asked.

"I stole their boat."

Matt's eyes widened. "You've got a boat?"

"No. I sent the boat out into the lake, and I hope they'll think I fell overboard and drown. Then maybe they won't come looking for me. I was really hoping to get off this lake with you and your friend."

"We don't have a way off the lake. Our plane is busted."

"Don't you have a radio?"

"It's busted, too. We were flying in that storm a few days ago and our altimeter thing broke. We couldn't tell how high we were and suddenly we were almost on the water. Then there was this island in front of us and luckily we hit it where it was low and just covered with willows. We were going fast enough to slide up on the island until we smacked into a big rock. That rock busted our prop, and a piece of it busted the battery. So we've got no battery… and no radio."

"Dang. I thought I was escaping. All I did was find someone else stranded on the lake."

"Well, at least you won't be getting beat up."

Adam smiled. "Who's with you? Your dad?"

"No. My friend, Brandon. He's eighteen."

"Who was flying the plane?"

"Brand was. I flew it, too, but not when we were crashing."

"You know how to fly?"

"Well, Brandon was teaching me earlier when it was clear. He's a good pilot. He's been flying for two years."

Adam laughed. "Apparently not such a good pilot. He crashed into an island."

Matt joined him with a laugh. "Well, it *was* nasty weather, but I guess it wasn't the best thing to do."

"How old are you, Matt?"

"I'll be thirteen next fall, if I live that long," Matt said. "How old are you?"

"I'm fourteen… almost fifteen."

"Well, let's go back to our camp so you can meet Brandon, and we'll see what we can do about getting all of us off this island," Matt said, taking the lead. Adam fell in behind him, and Kirby trotted along beside Adam, close enough that Adam could scratch his ears, and overjoyed that he had a new kid to play with. "Your dog sure is friendly," Adam said.

"Yeah, he was a stray that Brandon and my brother rescued. He's about the friendliest dog I've ever seen," Matt said. Kirby wagged his tail. He knew they were talking about him.

Chapter 32

Adam was wide eyed as they walked up to the huge plane sitting in the midst of the willow grove. "Jeez! You guys are lucky you didn't get killed!" he said as he studied the splinters of propeller and the smashed engine cowling. He climbed up on the rock and peered into the open engine cover. "It looks like everything else is okay. Only the battery and the radiator got smashed. That was pretty bad luck. How fast were you going when you hit this rock?"

"We were almost stopped by the time we got here," Matt said. "The willows slowed us down a lot." As he neared the cargo door he called out: "Hey, Brand! Are you in there?" There was no answer so he stepped up and looked in to see if Brandon might be sleeping. Then he turned to Adam and said, "He's probably down at the lake fishing."

Adam looked inside the plane and saw all the cargo. "Wow! You've got enough food for a year in there."

"It's all vegetables... no meat, but yeah, we've got a lot of stuff. We were hauling it to the lodge that our parents bought. They went up last week. Brandon and I had to finish school first, and then we were coming up for the summer. They took the other plane – an Otter – and left this one for us to fly up there. Come on." He urged Adam to follow. "Let's find Brandon."

The two boys hiked down the path to the lake. They found Brandon fishing from a boulder at water's edge. "Hey, Brand! Look what I found," Matt said.

Brandon turned and smiled as he eyed the stranger. "Our savior?"

"Well, not quite," Matt said. He motioned for Adam to follow. Adam noticed Brandon's black and blue foot soaking in the cold water.

"Brandon, this is Adam. Adam, Brandon."

Brandon turned, stepped off the boulder and carefully waded onto the shore. The two boys shook hands. "Nasty looking foot," Adam commented.

"Actually, it's a lot better than it was. Nurse Matty, here, fixed me all up."

"See those black eyes?" Matt said. "I gave him those when he smarted off to me."

Brandon laughed and so did Adam. "Yeah," Brandon said. "Be careful of Matt. He's a killer."

"Actually," Matt went on. "Brandon got that cut on his head and those black eyes when he kissed the windshield while parking the plane against that rock."

They all chuckled.

"So have you come to rescue us?" Brandon asked. "Where's your boat?"

"Well, that's not exactly what I had in mind," Adam said. "Actually, I was hoping you guys would rescue me."

Brandon looked questioningly at Matt. Matt shrugged. "It's a long story, Brand. We can talk about it while we eat. I'm hungry. Did you catch any fish?"

"Sorry, Matt. Not even a bite. I guess it'll be potatoes again."

Adam spoke up. "I've got about five pounds of fresh moose tenderloin with me."

Matt's and Brandon's eyes lit up. "Meat? *Real* meat?"

"Yeah. Fresh yesterday, just waiting for us to cook it."

"Then, what are we waiting for?" Matt said.

Brandon dried off his feet, put on his socks and shoes, and the three walked the path to the plane. "Wait here," Adam said. "I'll run back to get my stuff. I left it just in case you guys were like my uncles." Adam left to retrieve his clothes and the pail of meat, and returned in about a half hour. He removed the towel to show them the meat.

"Oh, man! Does that ever look good," Brandon exclaimed.

"I'll light the fire," Matt said as he removed the grate and lit the oil lamps.

"We've got all kinds of stuff for cooking in the plane," Matt said to Adam. While they climbed into the plane to find what they needed, Brandon prepared the potatoes. Adam looked through the box of spices and other things, and selected a few items that he took outside. Matt watched as Adam sliced the steaks from the loin, and then coated them with a mixture of flour, salt, pepper, and other seasoning in a zip lock bag. When the pan was full of sizzling steaks, he said: "They won't all fit in the pan. We'll cook them in two batches. They won't take long unless you like them well done."

"I like mine a little pink," Brandon said, and Matt nodded that he agreed.

The aroma of frying potatoes and onions and moose steaks made all of them drool, especially Kirby. He was nearly standing in the fire pit. "Get back, Kirbo, or you'll get burned." Kirby just wagged his tail and panted, waiting for his share.

When the steaks were nearly done, Adam sliced some onion into the pan and just as they turned golden brown he proclaimed that the steaks were ready. They each speared a steak with one of the home made forks and scooped some potatoes onto an aluminum pie pan. They sat on the pontoon to eat.

Brandon cut off a piece of steak and popped it into his mouth. "Oh, man," he moaned as he closed his eyes and chewed. "That's about as good as anything I've ever tasted."

Matt chewed and nodded his approval. Adam smiled at his new friends and their enjoyment of the meat. "I'm glad you like it," he said. "I'll cut some more and put them in the pan." He fried three more steaks; they disappeared quite rapidly.

Kirby had gobbled up his share and most likely never even tasted it. When they were finished, they all leaned back against the pontoon and sighed. "Adam? That was fantastic," Brandon said. "Now, tell us about how you got here, and why you're with those poachers."

Adam frowned. "Well, it's kind of long story...."

Chapter 33

"I lived in Rochester, Minnesota until about a year ago when my parents were killed in a car crash. My mom was a full blooded Ojibwa Indian from this area. Her parents raised her and her two brothers near here. They were the two guys Matt saw me with yesterday. Mom was real smart and got a scholarship to go to college in Rochester to be a nurse. She graduated from nursing school at the Mayo Clinic, and then she was a surgical nurse there.

"My Dad moved here from Finland with his parents when he was a boy. He was an anesthesiologist and they met in an operating room during an operation. One thing led to another, and they got married a year later… and then I was born.

"They both had good jobs and worked hard. We had a nice house and nice neighbors, and everything was great. I was in 8th grade and I played soccer, and I did pretty well in school. I had a lot of friends, and everything was really good.

"Then last year they were on their way to pick me up after school, and they got rear-ended at a stop light and their car slid on the ice into the path of a snowplow… and they were killed.

"The next few weeks were a nightmare for me. Several of our neighbors and friends offered to take me in, but the welfare people wanted me to be with a relative. But I ended up in a foster home because they couldn't find any relatives that would take me. My mom's parents had died when I was a baby, and I never knew anything about my Finnish relatives, so I had no one.

"Then about ten months ago the welfare people located my two uncles. They showed up all nice and proper and took custody of me, and took over my parents' estate. We weren't rich, but we had a nice house and some savings. Uncle Carl and Ed promised to put the money from the sale of the house into a trust fund for me for college, and enroll me in school and see to it that I was taken care of.

"When we got back to their shack on the lake shore, I knew I wasn't going to school… or college… and it wasn't long until I was nothing more than their housekeeper and cook. They took all of my money and spent it on a four wheeler, a snowmobile, and a new boat and motor, and they've drank up most of the rest of it. I really don't care about the money, but they drink a lot and then they get really mean, and I'm scared that someday they'll get drunk and beat me up real bad... or even kill me. I try to keep out of their way, but they still slap me around a lot for no good reason.

"So yesterday when I found Matt hiding in the woods, I decided that I'd sneak away and find you guys. I figured that you had a radio and you were just waiting for help. I thought maybe I could get out of here with you and find some way to make it on my own... back in Minnesota, or anywhere away from those two old drunks."

Brandon was visibly moved by Adam's story. "I'm so sorry to hear about your parents, Adam."

Matt had tears in his eyes, too. "Brand and I know all about people you love getting killed in a car wreck. My older brother, Mark, was killed a while ago in one, too."

"Sorry to hear that," Adam said.

"Mark and I were best friends," Brandon said. "And I..." He hesitated a moment. "... was driving when it happened."

"But it wasn't your fault, Brand. Don't forget that," Matt added hastily.

"I sure understand why you don't want to live with a couple of drunks," Brandon said. "Unfortunately, we wrecked our battery when we crashed and the radio doesn't work. But we're hoping that a search plane will come by soon. Now that the weather has cleared they should be out searching for us."

"I've been up here for quite a while," Adam said, "and I've only seen a couple of planes in all that time. You know that there's over two thousand square miles of lake here, don't you?"

"Yeah, but there must be planes flying back and forth all the time to the resorts."

"We're way on the western part of the lake, real close to the big open part where there're no islands for a long way. It's forty miles across up here, no places for resorts. I hate to say this, but I don't think we're gonna get rescued by any planes just flying by on their way someplace. If someone in a plane is going to find us, they'll have to be out here looking for us."

"You say we're way out in the western part of the lake?" Brandon asked.

"Yeah. Just a few miles west of here, the lake gets real huge, with very few islands. It's like an ocean."

"We must have been blown a lot farther off course than we figured," Brandon told Matt. "We were up near Kenora when the storm hit us. They'll be up there looking first, and it's hard to tell how long it'll be before they come down this far, if they ever do. They probably figure we're on the bottom of the lake someplace... and they're looking for bodies."

"Well," Matt said. "If they're looking in the wrong place, then we're gonna have to figure out how to rescue ourselves."

Adam turned and stared at the pontoon they were leaning against. "Could we get these pontoons off the plane?"

"I s'pose so," Brandon answered. "They're just bolted on."

Adam stood and walked to the end of the pontoon, looking it over. "Suppose we got them off. They're just like two big canoes without a hole in them to sit in. Do you think we could lash them together and make a big raft? I'm sure we could figure out a way to keep them together and a way to sit on them. We could even rig a way to steer it."

I big smile spread over Brandon's face. "We could sail out of here."

Adam grinned. "And I know right where there's a pickup truck with the keys on the visor... waiting for us."

Chapter 34

The boys talked about their rescue for the next several hours until darkness started to fall upon them. Just as they were about to climb into the plane, Matt looked up and saw strange lights in the north. "It looks like a search plane," he said excitedly, pointing to the illumination on the horizon.

"That's the Aurora," Adam said. "The Northern Lights."

"I've seen them a couple of times," Brandon said, "but at home we don't see them too much. There are too many other lights and we're too far south. It's been so cloudy and foggy that we haven't seen them here until now."

"My mother used to tell me the story of the Aurora," Adam said. He stared at the lights with a far off gaze in his eyes.

"Tell us, Adam," Matt said.

Adam smiled. He remembered his mom telling him the story:

"Long ago in the days of darkness the world was covered with water and the great God caused the water to recede leaving dry land for man. And there was a race of God fearing people called the Mongols who called the God, the Great Manitou. This God told the Mongols to take all they could carry and he would lead them to the fertile plains of the Continent and they would prosper. But the world was dark and the people became lost and many died. So the Great Manitou caused the Northern cap of the world to become covered in ice crystals that would capture the rays of the hidden sun and reflect them up into the sky so his people could see where they were going. These people became the forerunners of all the Indian Tribes. The great ice prisms split the sun's rays into all the beautiful colors of the spectrum and because of this, people for thousands of years have witnessed the wonderful miracle of the Northern Lights."

"Wow! Cool story, Adam," Matt said.

Adam was glad to be here with his new friends that he could talk to, and who wouldn't yell at him for no reason. "My mom used to tell me lots of nice stories about their people and the old days," he said. "I can remember most of them because I asked her to tell them to me so many times."

"Well, let's get some sleep now," Brandon said. "Big day tomorrow."

Matt lifted Kirby into the plane, and the rest followed. Brandon found a couple more sleeping bags, laid one on the floor with the first two, and then zipped the remaining two together to make one big blanket for them all to sleep under. They all undressed and piled the clothes on the deck behind the seats. "You get in the middle, Adam," Brandon said. Kirby crawled up next to Adam, put his duck next to Adam's chest, and then snuggled at his feet. "Kirby must like you," Matt said. "He's entrusted you with Donald."

Adam stared at the duck. "Oh, now I get it. Donald Duck," he said laughing.

They pulled the top sleeping bags over them and Matt snuffed out the lamp. They remained silent for a few minutes, and then Adam said, "I'm sure glad I met you guys."

"Me, too," Brandon said.

"Me, three," Matt said. They all giggled.

In a short while they were all asleep, Adam with a slight smile on his face for the first time in many months.

Matt's stomach was growling. He tossed and turned and then it dawned on him that it was daylight. He turned toward Brandon and was surprised to see that Adam wasn't between them. Alarmed, he sat up and saw that Kirby was missing, too. Then he smelled something wonderful and looked toward the door that was partly open. He crawled over to it and slid it fully open to see Adam and Kirby sitting next to the fire pit, Adam stirring something in the metal pail that had held the venison the previous day. "Jeez! You're up early," he said yawning.

"Kirby woke me up. I think he had to pee," Adam said. "So I decided to get up and make breakfast."

"That smells great. What is it?" Brandon said sitting up amidst the sleeping bags.

"It's moose stew, or as close as I could get to moose stew with what I found in the plane."

Matt and Brandon dressed, climbed out of the plane, and both hustled off to the woods. When they came back Adam was scooping portions of thick stew out onto pie plates. There were large chunks of moose steak, carrots, peas, corn, and potatoes, all swimming in thick gravy with slices of onion in it. Matt scooped a spoonful into his mouth and began fanning. "Whoa! Hot! Hot!"

Brandon was a bit more careful. He took a smaller bite and chewed lovingly. "Dang, Adam. That's amazing!"

Adam beamed as the boys voiced their approval of his culinary skills. "I've done all the cooking for the last ten months, so I guess I've learned a few things about making stuff taste reasonably good. I don't know how Uncle Carl and Uncle Ed survived before I came there. They can't make toast without ruining it."

"Well, this is much more than good! This is delicious." Matt shoveled more stew into his face. "I don't care if we ever get rescued, if we can eat like this all the time."

They put a good portion of the stew in an aluminum pan for Kirby. He attacked it as if he hadn't eaten for a week.

The entire pot of stew was gone. Matt scraped all the last remnants from the pail and savored every drop. He lay back against the pontoon and let out a loud burp. "Oops. Where are my manners," he laughed.

They all rested after their huge breakfast, chatting about their upcoming rescue plans. After a while Adam gathered up the pans and headed to the lake. "Here," Matt said as he wrestled the dirty stuff from his new friend. "I'll do that. Cripes. You got up early and cooked. You don't have to do all the chores here, Adam,"

"But I'm used to doing all the work," Adam responded.

"Well, not any more, pal. Now you're one of us, not a slave."

"While Matt's cleaning the dishes, let's see about taking these pontoons off," Brandon said. He used his crutch to get up, and then he moved to where the strut was fastened to the pontoon.

Adam found the tool kit in the cockpit after Brandon told him where to look. Then he surveyed the nearest pontoon to determine what they had to do to remove them. He wondered if it could be done by three boys with limited tools. With certain determination, he and Brandon sat straddling the pontoon and began removing bolts.

Chapter 35

By the time Uncle Carl had finished making scrambled eggs and bacon, the entire cabin was full of smoke. He and Uncle Ed were trying to eat the miserable breakfast. "Your cookin' ain't much to speak about," Ed said chewing on the burnt eggs with bits of charred bacon mixed in.

"Then, you do it next time," Carl grumbled.

"We need to find that damn kid. I still think he tried to pull a fast one on us."

"What do you mean? You don't think he's drowned?" Carl asked.

"Why would he have a stick jammed in the steering of the motor? Why wasn't he holding onto the steering arm? If he fell overboard, the motor would have turned and kept goin' in circles. Unless it hit him when he was in the water, he should've been able to swim to shore. He's a good swimmer."

"But, why would he leave?"

"Why? Cripes, man. Why wouldn't he? It's not like we treated him real nice. I really wouldn't blame him if he left."

"But where would he go? He can't walk to town, and there's no way he'd find his way to anyplace that would help him."

"I still keep thinking about the other day when he went into the woods. He was acting kinda funny."

"You suppose he saw someone there?"

"Yup. That's exactly what I think. And I think he went back there yesterday and met up with 'em."

"Well, we'd better find out. He knows too much about us. If he goes to the law and they find all that stuff we've swiped in the shed, we'll be in a heap o' trouble."

"I know. We'd better head out and find that brat."

"Well, we can't go today. We've got to meet Tiny outside of Baudette. He's ready for another load of stuff."

"Yeah, I know. But tomorrow or the next day, we're gonna find that kid and whoever he's with."

The men put their dirty dishes in the sink and sauntered out to the storage shed behind the cabin. Inside were TVs, stereos, fishing gear, guns, and everything else that they had stolen from cabins and resorts that had been closed up during the winter months. Before they had their newfound wealth that they took from the sale of their dead sister's house, they had trapped in the winter time, but burglary proved to be much more profitable.

Tiny was a dealer in stolen merchandise; they took a load to him every few weeks. Then they used the money he paid them to buy gas, food, and a few bottles of whiskey.

They loaded the pickup with an assortment, locked the shed, tied an old canvass tarp over the load, and headed down the rutted road toward Baudette. There they would meet their fence and sell the items to him.

A couple of hours later Tiny pulled into a wayside outside of Baudette in a large van. He shut off the motor and waited for his partners. Tiny was a huge man, six feet six inches tall, tipping the scales at nearly three hundred and fifty pounds. The three of them were old friends and had been doing business for years. "Where's that kid of yours?" Tiny asked as Carl and Ed pulled into the wayside. They got out their truck and walked over to Tiny's van.

"He done run off, but we're gonna find him and kick his worthless ass," Ed said.

"Run off? Where'd he run off to?"

"If we knew where he run off to, he'd be with us, dumb ass," Carl growled.

"You better find him. He knows too much about our little enterprise, here. We sure don't want him talkin' to the cops."

"Don't you worry. We'll take care of him… that's if he ain't already at the bottom of the lake."

They unloaded the stolen merchandise into Tiny's van as he made a list of each piece. When they were finished, he did his figuring with a portable calculator. "Looks like about five hundred and fifty bucks today," he offered.

"Five fifty! No way! Seven hundred if it's a dime," Ed argued.

"Oh, no. Some of that electronic shit is obsolete as soon as it comes out of the stores. Best I can do is six even."

"Six fifty."

"Six and a quarter," Tiny said. He knew the bargaining was over.

"Done," Ed said.

Tiny counted out six hundred and twenty five dollars from a thick wallet and handed it to them. "There you are, and it's been a pleasure."

"See you in a month," Carl said as he and Ed got into their truck.

"A month it is. And don't forget to take care of that kid, or we'll all be in jail." Tiny drove away.

Ed and Carl drove into Baudette to fill the large gas tank in the back of the truck. Then they stopped at the hardware store. They needed a few things for the cabin, including a new lock, since theirs was now worthless without a key. Then it was on to the liquor store where they bought a few bottles of whiskey. They tied the tarp over their supplies, and then decided to have one for the road at the saloon. Six hours later they staggered down the street trying to find the truck, drunk as skunks.

"Where the hell did we park that damn truck?" Ed slurred.

"Beats me. You were drivin.' Didn't you watch?"

"Wasn't me drivin.' It was you, wasn't it?"

"Don't make no difference who it was, dumb ass. Where the hell did we put it?"

Just then the local sheriff pulled up alongside them as they staggered along. He recognized the two brothers, and he knew they were in no shape to drive. He pulled ahead of them, stopped, and stepped out of his car. "You fellas aren't going to drive anywhere tonight, are you?"

"Huh? Hey, Sheriff. What's up?" Carl said as he finally figured out who was talking to him.

"Carl. Ed. You two been drinking a bit?"

"Just a couple, Sheriff. We lost our truck."

"Why don't you guys come with me? We'll give you a nice bed to sleep in for the night. Tomorrow you can find your truck and head back to the lake."

"Tha sounds good, Sheriff. Don't it Carl," Ed said.

"What you arrestin' us for, Sheriff?"

"I'm not arresting you. But if you drive in that condition I *will* arrest you. I'm just giving you a bed for the night. You're free to leave in the morning when you're in better shape to drive. I'd hate to see two such upstanding citizens as you smack that truck into a tree on the way home."

"Wal, as long as were not arrested, I guess that's okay," Carl said swaying back and forth.

The sheriff opened the door and the two drunks stumbled into the back seat. When they arrived at the Sheriff's Office, he helped them out of the car, and then locked them in a cell for the night. Technically, they hadn't done anything wrong and they weren't under arrest, but he was glad he had prevented them from being in their condition. They'd surely kill themselves and maybe some poor, innocent bystander, too.

Chapter 36

By the time Matt had scrubbed the pot and cleaned up the homemade utensils, Brandon and Adam had the tool box out and were working on removing the right pontoon. "How's it going?" he asked.

"This should be pretty simple," Brandon said. "They're held on with twelve bolts and we've got a socket wrench that fits. When we get the bolts out, we need to figure a way to tip the plane so we can slide the pontoon out from under it."

Matt walked around to the other side, backed away until he was at the tip of the opposite wing, and studied the task. "If I remember my geometry right, I think the plane should tip pretty easy if we can push down on this wing tip," he said loud enough for the other two to hear him. "It's something to do about leverage."

"Yeah, you're right, Matty," Brandon replied.

"Who was that guy who said: 'Give me a lever and a place to stand and I will move the earth?'" Matt asked to no one in particular.

"Can't say as I remember, Matty," Brandon said. "But you've to the right idea about tipping the plane."

"I think it was Archimedes," Adam said.

"Yeah! That's the guy," Matt said grinning.

Matt crawled under the fuselage and found the spool of nylon rope that he had tossed out the first day. "I'm gonna tie this around the wing tip and find someplace to anchor it on the ground. Maybe we can pull the wing down." Adam and Brandon nodded and kept working.

Matt realized he couldn't reach the wing from the ground. He climbed up the pontoon brace which was like a ladder and managed to get up onto the wing. Then he crawled slowly out to the tip of the wing with the spool of rope under his arm, looped it over the tip of the wing with a slip knot, and then dropped the spool of rope down to the ground. Then he tightened the knot so the rope was snug on the wing and slid down to the ground on the rope.

"I'm ready here whenever you guys get that pontoon loose."

"Just a couple more bolts," Brandon answered.

A few minutes later Brandon and Adam climbed over the pontoons and made their way to Matt through the brush. "I think we can pull the rope around that big boulder," Matt explained. "Once the wing is pulled down, we can tie it off and the pontoon will be free."

Brandon and Adam agreed. They looped the rope around a large boulder and began pulling. The wing tip began to come down toward them. As they pulled they cinched the rope around the rock, and soon they had the wing tip lowered more than two feet.

"Tie it off and we'll see it that's enough," Brandon said.

Adam tied a knot around the rock and they carefully released the rope. The wing tip raised a little as the knot tightened, but it stayed put. They all crawled back across the left pontoon. The right side support structure easily cleared the pontoon by a foot. "You guys grab that end," Brandon said nodding to the front of the pontoon. Adam and Matt got hold of their end, Brandon grabbed the back end, and they slid the pontoon out from under the plane.

"Wow! That wasn't so bad," Matt said as they surveyed the loose pontoon. "It doesn't weigh as much as I thought it would."

"It's like a real big canoe, with a top on it," Adam laughed.

"Well, that's one down. Now we can let this side down and work on the other one," Brandon said.

"We should put something under the wing strut that will keep it up at about the same height as the pontoon," Matt suggested. That'll make it easier to tip this way."

"Good thinking, Matty," Brandon said. Adam and Matt gathered a few rocks and a log and put them down so they would support the metal strut.

They loosened the rope and let the plane settle down on the log. Adam and Brandon began taking the bolts out of the left pontoon. Matt rigged the rope on the tip of the right wing and found that there weren't any large enough rocks to anchor it, so he cleared the brush out from around the base of a pine tree and wrapped the rope around it. Once again, they pulled the wing tip down, anchored it, and then slid the pontoon out from under the support structure. More rocks under that side kept the plane level when they let it back down.

"It's not such a high climb back inside now," Matt said looking at the plane resting more than a foot closer to the ground.

"Well," Brandon said. Now we have to figure out a way to connect the pontoons together, and a way to steer and propel our little raft."

"I've got a couple of ideas," Adam said. But I'm getting hungry. S'pose we could find something to eat first?"

"I wish we could catch one of those grouse," Matt said.

"What grouse?" Adam asked.

"Kirby almost caught one a few days ago. It was like what we hunt for at home, but It was more black than brown like our grouse are."

"Fool hens!" Adam said.

"What?"

"That's what the Indians call them. They're real trusting; they don't fly often, and if they do, it's just a short way. You can catch them with a snare, or sometimes just hit them in the head," Adam said.

"S'pose we can get some?" Matt said excitedly.

"Got any string or twine?"

Chapter 37

The steel door clanged loudly as the deputy opened the cell that Carl and Ed were sleeping in. "Time to wake up gentlemen," the young deputy said.

Ed opened his eyes and then shut them tightly against the light pouring in from the hallway. He opened them a slight bit and saw the uniformed deputy standing in the doorway looking at him. "Are we in the slammer?" he asked.

"Just as guests. You're not arrested," the young man said.

"How'd we get in here?" Carl asked as he sat up on his bunk.

"You boys had a few too many and lost your truck. The sheriff saw you wandering around the street looking for it. He invited you to sleep it off here. I've got coffee if you want some."

"Mighty nice of you. We'll be right out," Carl said. He stood up and immediately leaned against the cell wall to keep from falling over.

Ed swung his legs over the side of his bunk and sat with his face in his hands. "We gotta quit drinkin' that cheap whiskey. It makes me feel awful the next day."

"As much as you drunk, it's no wonder you feel ugly," Carl said.

They staggered out of the cell and walked down the hallway to the office where the sheriff was sitting behind a desk. The deputy was standing at the front counter talking to a local citizen about a barking dog. "Mornin' boys. Feeling a little peeked today?"

"Just a tad, Sheriff. Mighty obliged that you gave us a place to sleep."

"I didn't think you were in any shape to drive anywhere... and besides... you couldn't find your truck," the sheriff said grinning. "Coffee?"

The two poured themselves a steaming cup of coffee and sipped at it. The sheriff walked to a safe, opened it and took out an envelope. "This is yours. We always search anyone who is put into a cell, just in case. You had this wad of money in your pocket, Carl. I locked it up for safe keeping."

"Uh, thanks, Sheriff," Carl said. He grabbed the envelope and stuffed it in his pocket.

"That's a lot of money to be carrying around – almost five hundred dollars. What are you boys doing with that much cash?"

"We been savin' up and thought we might need some supplies," Ed said. "So we came to town. But, of course, we went to the tavern first… and we seem to have forgot our supplies."

"Well, I'd suggest you get them and head home before you get into trouble. Shouldn't be waving that much money around and then get all drunk. Somebody's apt to knock you in the head and take it from you."

"You're right, Sheriff. Mighty obliged for your hospitality."

The two lumbered out of the office and walked down the street. "We were lucky he didn't arrest us, but I don't like it that he saw all that money," Carl said.

"Let's find our truck and get out of town."

They walked down the street until they found the truck. They checked the supplies in the back and retied the tarp over it. "Let's get some breakfast before we leave," Carl said. "I don't think I can eat that shit you cook."

"Ain't never said I was a cook," Ed grumbled.

They walked to a café, ordered breakfast, and downed several more cups of coffee. The breakfast made them feel a little better, so they got the truck and headed out of town. The road to their cabin was not much more than a trail that had been cleared of trees, so they bumped and bounced along. Their hangovers felt even worse.

By the time they got back to their cabin, the previous night's booze had both feeling quite poorly. They unloaded the groceries and decided to call it a day, as they felt too ugly to do much more. They would look for Adam tomorrow.

Chapter 38

Matt found a spool of heavy butcher's twine in one of the boxes on the plane. He climbed down the support ladder just as Adam returned from the edge of the woods with a long branch. He cut all the side branches off with a knife, and trimmed each side of the fork at the tip to about three inches.

Then he made a loop about the size of a coffee can with a slip knot, hung it from the fork, and tied it on loosely with another short piece of string. Then he measured enough string to reach the back end of the stick and cut it off.

"Now, all we have to do is find a fool hen, walk up carefully, and lower this noose around her neck. Then when she flies, the noose tightens and when she hits the end of the string, the sudden stop breaks her neck."

"No foolin'? You think that'll work?" Matt asked.

"My people have been doing it that way for generations. When the first white men came to this land, they would have starved to death had it not been for the fool hens. They found that they could catch them real easy, and there are lots of them, so taking a few to eat won't hurt the population any."

"You guys go and hunt for them," Brandon said. "My foot is hurting from all the walking. I'm gonna stay here and get some potatoes ready to boil. If you bring back a grouse, we'll have grouse and potatoes for supper. If not, we'll have potatoes."

"Does Kirby hunt?" Adam asked.

"He's half Golden Retriever and half Collie, I think. He seems to have a pretty good nose," Matt said. "He almost caught that first grouse when it flew."

"Will he stay with us if we take him along?" Adam asked.

"He'll stay with us as long as I tell him to," Matt said. "Come on Kirby. Let's go find some KFC," he told the dog.

Adam just laughed as they started toward the woods to find some grassy meadows and, perhaps, some grouse.

They came to the first meadow and Adam stopped Matt at the edge. "See what he does," he said.

"Kirby," Matt addressed the dog. "Hunt them up!" Kirby started slowly through the grass, his nose testing the air. The boys could hear him snuffling, checking out all the scents. Suddenly he stopped and stared ahead of him. "He smells one, I think," Matt said quietly.

"Can you make him wait for us?"

"Kirby, stay. Wait for me," Matt commanded. Kirby looked over his shoulder at them and stood his ground, not moving. The boys slowly walked up behind him. Adam looked ahead into the grass and saw the bird's head move. "It's right there," he whispered. He extended the pole in front of him and began to lower it. Matt could see the loop getting closer to the bird's head. Just as it settled over its neck, the bird ducked down and scuttled away. "Missed him!" Adam whispered.

They moved forward a little farther and saw the bird again crouched down in the grass. Adam lowered the noose just over the bird's head again and then he said: "Go get him Kirby."

Kirby leaped forward and the bird sprang up from the grass. The loop was around its neck and it slid off the end of the stick as the bird rose up. The bird was about five feet into the air when it hit the end of the line and its neck jerked back. The grouse dropped to the ground. Kirby ran up to it and picked it up, its wings still flapping. He turned and brought it back to the boys, looking quite proud. By then the bird had quit flapping and was limp in Kirby's mouth. Adam took it from the dog, patted him and told him what a good boy he was. Kirby's tail wagged at supersonic speed. Adam turned and showed the dead bird to Matt.

"Wow! That was cool," Matt said.

"Nothing to it when you know how, and if you have a dog that minds like Kirby, it's even easier."

Matt carried the bird as they set off again, but the next grassy meadow they found was not holding any birds. A short way farther through the woods, they came to a small patch of grass that excited Kirby as soon as they were near. "He smells one," Matt said.

They told Kirby to hunt, and when he stopped, looking intently at the tall grass, Adam stepped slowly up to the dog and saw the grass moving ahead of him. "I see it," he whispered. He lowered the noose and began to move forward so he could see the bird's head. But he stopped dead in his tracks. "Call Kirby back!" he said urgently.

"Call him back?"

"Hurry! Do it now!"

"Kirby. Come!" Matt commanded. The dog looked but hesitated. "Kirby! Come! Now!"

Kirby turned and trotted back to Matt. Then Adam carefully and quietly stepped back a couple of steps, and then took off running away from the grass. "What the heck?" Matt said.

"Wrong kind of game," Adam said pointing to the edge of the grass where a skunk was ambling along. Matt's eyes got big. The skunk waddled off into the brush unconcerned.

"Whew. I don't think that would've made very good stew," he laughed.

They worked their way across the meadow in the opposite direction the skunk had taken. They came to another patch of grass and Kirby seemed to have found something. "Want to give it a try?" Adam asked.

"You scared it's another skunk?"

Adam grinned and shrugged. "I doubt it is. I'll do it."

They moved forward and Matt saw the bird crouched in the grass. "Give me the stick," he whispered. Adam handed over noose. Matt leaned forward and slipped it over the bird's head. "Get him Kirby!" he whispered urgently. The dog bounded forward, the bird flew up, and in an instant they had their second bird for supper.

"Dang! That's the coolest thing I've ever seen," Matt said as he took the string from the dead bird's neck.

"I think two's enough, don't you?" Adam said.

"Yeah. No need in taking more than we need."

The two new friends and their trusty hunting dog started back toward the plane with the makings of a fine feast.

Chapter 39

Brandon was sitting on one of the pontoons as Matt and Adam came into the clearing. Kirby ran ahead and alerted Brandon that the boys were on their way back. "How did you do?" he asked as they came through the brush.

"We got two," Matt said excitedly. "You shoulda seen it Brand. It's really cool. You just slip that string over their head and they fly up and break their necks."

"What are you making?" Adam asked when he saw the three branches at Brandon's feet."

"I'm trying to make paddles for our raft," Brandon said holding one up. He had cut three fairly stout sticks with a fork in one end and tied short pieces of rope close together between the forks, resulting in a thick rope net stretched across the two sides of the forks. "I think this will work okay. Don't you?" he said handing the paddle to Adam.

Adam looked it over and smiled. "That's really good work Brandon. That should work great."

Brandon seemed pleased with his effort. "I'm going to finish the other two if you guys will start making supper."

"I'll take the birds down to the lake and clean them," Adam said. "Matt, would you fill that pail about half full with oil and get it heating?"

"Sure. What are we having?"

"How about deep fried chicken and French fries?"

"Oh boy! That sounds good. I'll start slicing these potatoes that Brand peeled," Matt said. Adam took the birds down to the lake, skinned them, cut them up, and carefully washed the pieces.

Matt had the oil heating over the fire by the time he returned. Adam climbed up into the plane, found flour and spices, and prepared a breading mix in which he rolled the pieces of grouse. He let a drop of water fall into the oil. It spun across the surface and sizzled. "Oil's hot," he said, and then he carefully dropped in the first piece of grouse. The oil bubbled and popped the way it should, so he put in the other large pieces of both birds.

"What you gonna do with those other parts?" Matt asked looking in the pan.

"I'm going to boil the backs and gizzards and hearts when we're done and make soup for tomorrow."

Brandon gave Adam an admiring stare. "You sure are clever, Adam. I'm glad we met you."

"Not as glad as I am," Adam said smiling widely.

In just a short while, Adam fished the grouse pieces from the oil with a slotted spoon. They were golden brown with a crunchy outside crust. He laid them in a pie pan lined with cardboard to soak up the oil that drained off, and covered it with foil to keep it hot. He dropped a couple of handfuls of the cut potatoes into the oil, and in a few minutes those potatoes were brown and floating on top of the oil, ready to be taken out. Adam fished them out, put them in another pan next to the grouse, and put the last of the potatoes in the oil. "Let's eat this while the other potatoes are frying," he said. Matt and Brandon had been teased for the last few minutes with the wonderful aroma. He didn't have to say it twice.

Matt bit into a piece of grouse. "Oh, my gosh! Adam, you're a genius. This is delicious."

"You've outdone yourself, Adam," Brandon said smiling as he chewed his grouse.

Adam beamed, happy for the praise but also happy that he had made such good new friends. "It's my blend of twenty one spices and herbs," he said with a southern drawl.

Brandon and Matt roared with laughter.

They all took turns giving Kirby bites as they ate for the next half hour until everything was gone. "That would have made *The Colonel* proud," Brandon said.

"Whew. No kidding," Matt said as he licked the grease from his fingers. "KFC don't hold nothing to that."

"I'm glad you guys liked it," Adam said. "It's quite a change to cook for someone who appreciates it."

Adam poured the oil into an empty can, cleaned out the pail, added water and the left over parts of the grouse, and set it on the fire. Then he peeled and cut up an onion and tossed it into the pan. "I'm gonna cook this tonight, cover it with aluminum foil and set it in the edge of the water overnight. Then tomorrow I'll make us some good stew so we will have lots of energy to paddle our raft out of here."

"I've been thinking about that," Brandon said. "Take a look at that screen frame that separates the cargo hold from the main fuselage. I think we can take it out and put this door that we've been cooking on back in it. Then if we line up the pontoons, we can bolt it to them. It'll hold the pontoons together and make a place for us to sit to paddle the raft."

"That's a great idea, Brand," Matt said.

"The wind's been steady from the north east the last two days," Adam said. "So if that keeps up, we'll be heading at just the right direction to get to my uncles' cabin. If they come looking for me like I think they will, we can slip around them and get back to the cabin before they do. Unless they've gotten more careful than they have been, we should be able to steal their pickup and make it to town and find some help. They'll think I'm out here hiding and won't take any precautions to be quiet. They'll think they can just find me and I'll go back peacefully. I doubt that they know about you guys, so they'll never expect us to be going toward the cabin while they're here looking for us."

Later in the evening, as they settled down, visions of their dangerous adventure excited the boys. But their excitement was mixed with a little fear, too.

They took off their shoes and socks and outer clothes and crawled under the sleeping bag. Kirby snuggled next to Matt. "You got any more of those Indian stories?" he asked Adam.

"Yeah, my mom used to tell me lots of them when I was a little kid. You want to hear another?"

"Yeah, tell us one," Brandon said.

Adam thought a few seconds and smiled. "This was one of my mom's favorites:

"The Legend of the Snowbirds... Many years ago there lived in the Ojibwa encampment at the mouth of the Kaminisiqua River, a beautiful young Indian maiden, beloved by all. Her name was White Dove and she was very talented, making beautiful jewelry and gifts of silver. Two days before the feast of Thanksgiving, White

Dove and her lover, Nanokarisi, left to take gifts to her grandmother who lived in the mountains. They stopped to eat a light lunch on the way. As they finished they felt a cold wind bearing down on them. Nanokarisi climbed to the top of a high hill and saw ominous black clouds bringing a snow storm toward them. Fearful, Nanokarisi urged White Dove to hurry back to the camp. They ran as fast as their legs could carry them. The storm burst forth in all its fury after they had gone but a short distance.

"The wind howled around them, whipping heavy snow on them and blinding their vision. They wandered aimlessly until nightfall, and then cold, exhausted and hungry, they lay down in the shelter of a large rock and embraced, sharing their body warmth.

"The Thanksgiving Feast was at its height when the Chief announced that he feared the two young people had been lost in the storm. All of the braves volunteered to search for them. After four days they found the young couple sleeping the Great Sleep from which there was no awakening.

"The braves and the Chief pleaded with the Great Spirit to do something, but the Great Spirit told them he could not bring them back, and that they were now living in the realm of the Great Manitou. He told them that he could not control the coming snows, but he could give them a sign in the future to warn them that the snows were coming.

"As the braves watched they were amazed to see the bodies of White Dove and Nanokarisi disappear into the snow, and in their place appeared two little, soft, gray birds with striped heads. They flew into the air and darted from left to right showing off their snowy plumage.

"Where these birds come from or where they go, no one knows. But when you see them swirling around in large flocks, take heed, for as surely as night follows day, Snow is not very far away."

Brandon and Matt were smiling in the light of the lamp. "Matt," Brandon said. "We sure got our money's worth when we got this guy on our team."

"No foolin," Matt said smiling at Adam. "Cool story. G'night guys."

Chapter 40

Adam was the first to wake up the next morning. He was thinking over the plan they had made the previous evening, sure that Carl and Ed would come looking for him. Unless their boat had kept going out into the big part of the lake where there were no islands, they would surely have found it. And, even though they weren't real smart, they would wonder why the stick was jammed into the steering arm. They would eventually figure it out – that he had tried to fool them into thinking he was drowned. And they would be just angry enough that they'd spend weeks looking for him.

He remembered that they had an appointment with Tiny, and he was sure that they probably had gotten drunk and spent the night in town, or in a ditch somewhere on the way back to the cabin. They didn't trust him in town, and they didn't trust him alone, so they made certain he wasn't going to run off by locking him up at the cabin when they went to sell their stolen goods.

He had laid out his plan to Brandon and Matt and they thought it was a good idea. They would push the pontoons down to the lake and then bolt on the heavy screen partition from the plane. Then they'd store a few cans of food and water bottles on the raft, just in case things didn't work as planned. All they could do, then, was wait until they were sure Carl and Ed were looking for Adam, build the signal fire on top of the rock, and when they heard Ed and Carl's outboard, they'd light the fire with hope that the uncles would see the smoke and come to investigate. Whichever way they came around the island, the boys would paddle the raft the other way, keeping the island between them and the uncles.

Adam figured that when Carl and Ed found the fire, they'd surely check out what else was there. For sure, they wouldn't be able to keep their hands off all the cargo in the plane. It would take them a quite a while to load their boat full, and while they were doing that, the boys would paddle back to the cabin and take the truck. It all had to work just right or they would find themselves in open water with two nasty, angry men who wouldn't think twice about shooting them and sinking their bodies in the lake.

"Maybe this is crazy," Adam thought. "I might just get us all killed with this idea."

He laid there mulling it over, watching the light grow as the sun rose higher across the water. Matt rolled over and there came a muffled noise from under the sleeping bag. Adam giggled; Matt opened his eyes and grinned. "Did you hear that one?" he asked.

"Who could miss it?" Adam laughed. "I'd bet Carl and Ed did too."

"You guys are pigs," Brandon said. He pulled the sleeping bag over his head. Suddenly he shot out from under the covers. "Whew! Matty! That's nasty under there."

They all laughed and poked at each other. Kirby jumped in, too, licking and barking. "Well, I guess it's time to get up anyway," Matt said. They all got up, dressed, and stepped out of the plane into a glorious sunrise. "Looks like a good day for raft building," Brandon said.

Adam started rummaging for some breakfast items. "What are we having?" Matt asked, grinning expectantly at Brandon.

"If I can find everything I need, I'm going to make pancakes ... or something close."

Brandon and Matt exchanged glances. "Is there anything we can do to help?"

"Get the fire going... and make sure the pans are clean. I'll do the rest."

He found what he needed, climbed down from the plane and began working on the breakfast. He made a thin batter with flour, baking powder, a little oil and water. Then he coated the bottom of the dog dishes with oil and set them over the fire. While the pans heated, he removed all of the slices from a can of peaches and put them in an aluminum pie pan. Then he put brown sugar into the peach juice left in the can and set it to the side of the flames to heat. He poured some batter into the hot pans, and in no time the thin batter was bubbling on top. He slid a spatula under the pancake and flipped it over. "Oh my God!" Matt exclaimed when he saw the first golden brown pancake.

Adam flipped the other pancake. "Just a minute more." A few seconds later, he took the pancakes out of the pans and put them in an empty pie pan. He speared a couple of the peach slices, laid them on top of each of the pancakes, poured warm syrup over them, and handed them to Matt. "Try this pal."

Matt stared at it open mouthed.

Matt rolled up one of the pancakes like a tortilla with a slice of peach inside and took a bite. His smile blossomed as he chewed. "Adam, will you marry me?" he said. They all laughed.

Adam made pancakes for Brandon and himself, and of course, Kirby got his share, too. When the batter was all gone, all three boys and Kirby were quite full and satisfied. "Adam, you absolutely amaze me," Brandon said. "How did you learn all of that?"

"I liked to cook with Mom, and when Carl and Ed took me to their cabin, all we ate was fried moose, deer, potatoes, and fish. I got tired of always the same thing, so I started cooking some other stuff. From then on, Ed and Carl saw to it that I did all the cooking. I made do with what they had. Sometimes you can cheat on a recipe a little to make it work. These pancakes were a little heavy. If I had some eggs and some butter they would have been better."

"They were fantastic," Matt said. I like 'em heavy."

After breakfast they cleaned up the pans, and then they pushed the twenty-foot long pontoons down the path and put them side by side near the water. Then Brandon and Adam climbed up in the plane and removed the cargo hold partition frame. They carried it down to the lake and laid the partition on top of the pontoons. With a little adjusting they managed to get about a dozen of the bolt holes in the pontoons lined up with openings in the steel mesh, and bolted it down. They screwed the rest of the bolts into the other holes so there wouldn't be a chance of water leaking into the pontoons.

"When we're ready to leave," Brandon said, "all we have to do is get the mesh door from our cooking grill back on… and our raft will be finished."

Matt brought down a couple of the sleeping bags and some rope. When the platform was finished, they would tie the bags down to make a more comfortable place to sit. He carried the paddles down, too, and set them close by.

"Now, we'd better get the wood for the fire ready, and load up some water and a little food. Then we'll just wait for Carl and Ed to show up."

Chapter 41

Carl and Ed rolled out of bed and did their best at making breakfast, filling the cabin with smoke just as they had the previous day. "We're gonna have to find that kid or we're gonna get real skinny… the way you cook," Ed said.

"If you think it's so easy, you give it a try," Carl grumbled.

After they finished the cremated eggs and bacon, they unloaded the other groceries from the truck into the storage shed. Then they pumped gas from the tank in the back of the truck to fill up the generator, the outboard tank, and the four-wheeler. Then they went back to the cabin.

"Do you really think that kid is alive?"

"I think he's smart enough to stick that branch in the steering and hope that we thought he had fallen in and drowned," Carl said. "And I think he's down on that island where we shot that moose the other day. I reckon he found something there that made him think he could get away from us."

"Well, then… we better find him. If he gets back to civilization, he might tell about our little enterprise with Tiny, and about our poaching, and we'll end up in the crowbar hotel."

They were both still feeling quite hung over, so they decided to wait until the next day to start looking for Adam. Both had bad headaches, and the thought of bouncing around for hours in the hot sun out on the lake wasn't too pleasant. Instead, they decided to fix the cabin door. They removed the old lock, threw it away, installed the new one, and attached the hinges back on the door.

They attempted to fry some moose steak that evening, and again they filled the cabin with smoke and could barely chew the overdone meat. "If nothin' else," Ed said, "that kid sure could cook."

"His ma was a good cook. I s'pose that's where he got it," Carl said.

"If we find him, what you plannin' to do to him?"

"We'll see when we find him. But he's gonna get a beatin' for sure, one way or the other."

They turned in with intentions of getting a good night's sleep, ready to search for Adam in the morning.

After another dismal attempt at cooking breakfast, they loaded their rifles and lumbered down to the boat, tied up to the rickety dock. Carl got in the back and started the motor. Ed untied the boat, pushed it off and jumped in. Carl turned the boat to the east and motored along slowly, looking for any sign of Adam. "Watch for a body," he told Ed. "But I don't think we're gonna find one. If he drowned he should be floatin' by now, but I reckon he's still alive, and I think we're gonna find him down on that island."

They motored along, circling each island they came to, watching for a body washed up on shore, or entangled in tree branches that hung over the water. It took a while to move down the lake, and to make sure they covered the entire area.

Chapter 42

Everything was loaded on the raft and the boys had pushed it into the water so just the tip of the pontoons were on shore, keeping it from floating away. Matt and Adam had built up a good stack of wood for the signal fire. They poured a bottle of lamp oil onto the wood and left a box of matches near it so they would be ready to quickly light the fire when it was time.

It was late afternoon by the time they had everything ready except the door they were using for the grill. "You think they'll show up today?" Matt asked Adam.

"I think they'll be lazy and lay around the cabin today. It usually takes them a couple of days to recover from a trip to town. I think tomorrow will be the day we should start watching for them."

They brought out their fishing poles and spent the afternoon casting spoons and spinners, trying to catch some fish for supper. It was a beautiful, sunny day with hardly any clouds so they took off their shirts, enjoying the warm sun on their backs. Matt noticed several dark bruises on Adam's back. "What happened to your back, Adam?" he asked.

"Uncle Carl," Adam responded sullenly. "I don't remember what I did to get those new ones, but it probably was something like not having the breakfast ready on time. It doesn't take much for him to hit me."

Brandon stepped closer to look at Adam's back. "Holy shit! He did that for no reason?"

"Now you see why I had to get away from those guys. Carl is the worst. He hits for no reason at all sometimes. Ed isn't so bad, but he's scared of Carl, too. Nice life, huh?"

"I can't believe you didn't kill them in their sleep," Matt said.

"Believe me. I thought of it," Adam said with a scowl.

"Fish don't seem to be biting," Brandon commented. "Anyone getting hungry besides me?"

"Yeah, me!" Matt said. "I keep thinking about that grouse stew Adam told us about last night."

"Well, then, let's go back to the plane and see what's on the supper menu." Brandon threw a questioning glance toward Adam.

Adam smiled and picked up the pot sitting in the cool water. He lifted the foil and smelled it. "How does chicken pot pie sound?"

Brandon and Matt could hardly get back to the plane fast enough. Brandon peeled potatoes and Matt started the fire. Adam found his ingredients, mixed up a broth concoction with spices, added the grouse meat, liver, gizzard and heart cut into fine pieces, potatoes cut into chunks the size of dice, a can of corn, and a can of peas. When it started to boil, Adam said: "Ok, now the top." He began making something very similar to the pancake batter, but much thicker like dough. Then he stirred up a little flour and water in an empty vegetable can.

"What's that for?" Brandon asked.

"It'll thicken the juice and make it like gravy," Adam said as he poured the mixture slowly into the pot. He stirred, and when the broth was thick and delicious looking, he removed the pot from the fire. Then he sprinkled some flour on a piece of foil covering the cutting board and spread his dough out, pressing it until it looked like a pie crust. He carefully placed it over the top of the stew, tucked the edges in against the side of the pot, and cut some small holes in it with a knife. "That will let the steam out, so it doesn't blow up," he said. Matt and Brandon just watched with fascination.

He made a balloon looking contraption with aluminum foil, crimped it tightly over the top of the pail, and set it over the fire again. Then he went to a big rock and sat down. "It needs about twenty minutes," he said.

"I'm amazed," Brandon said. "You should be a chef when we get home."

"I'd like to do that. I like cooking," Adam said. "It's a way to make people happy."

"I'm about the happiest guy in the world right now... if that stuff tastes half as good at it looks," Matt said rubbing his empty belly.

They guessed at the time. Adam lifted a corner of the foil to reveal the finished pot pie. "It's ready." He removed the rest of the foil.

Brandon and Matt looked down into the pot. The dough had

formed a golden brown crust on top of the stew. "Oh, dang! Adam, that looks great," Matt said reaching for a pie pan. Adam scooped out a portion of the stew for each of them, and then one for Kirby. He blew on Kirby's to cool it off. "Be patient, Kirby. It'll be too hot for you. Just wait a second." Kirby jumped up and down. He was ready to eat.

With a huge cooking spoon Matt shoveled in a big bite of the stew. "Oh, jeez," he said fanning his mouth. "That is fantastic."

Adam gave Kirby his pan and then attacked his own. They ate in silence and in a short time the entire stew was gone. Brandon just shook his head and looked at Matt. "He did that with the stuff we'd have thrown in the lake."

Adam shrugged and grinned. "Waste not; want not," he said.

They cleaned up the cooking mess and soon it was getting dark. They climbed in the plane, undressed and got into their bed, tired from the work on the raft. It didn't take long for them to drop off to sleep.

"Peaches or apples with your pancakes this morning?" Adam asked as Matt opened his eyes.

"Jeez, Adam. You're up early. I don't care."

"Apples," Brandon said rolling over toward them. "Couldn't sleep?"

"Yeah, I slept well. But I'm thinking today is the day we're gonna see if we get away with this little plan… or not."

"We'll make it work," Brandon said. "Don't worry."

Adam made breakfast pancakes again, but with apple slices, sugar and a little cinnamon. Matt and Brandon couldn't decide which they liked better – peaches or apples. "Maybe we should stay another day and try cherries?" Matt said.

"I don't think Carl and Ed will give us another day," Adam said. "They'll come today for sure. We should put the door in the frame on the raft. If they don't come, we can take it back out and use it to cook. You guys get ready. I'll go to the other side of the island and watch for them."

"What?" Matt asked. "What happens if they see you and shoot you or something?"

"They won't see me, I guarantee. I'll get up in a tree, and I'll see them as soon as they're in the channel on the other side of the island. When I see them, I'll give this a blast." He held up a compressed air horn that he had found in the survival pack in the plane. "You'll hear this easy, and when you do, light the fire and get ready to push off." He pulled the trigger on the small canister. A loud, high pitched horn sounded. Kirby scurried off into the brush. "Come on, Kirby. I'm sorry. I didn't mean to scare you," he said. The dog came carefully back, with his tail between his legs. Adam knelt down and patted Kirby's head.

"I'll wait until I see which way they're coming around the island and then I'll hightail it back here… and we'll go the other way."

"Can you get back here fast enough?" Brandon asked.

"It's a long way for them to go around the island either way. I can cut across the middle in lots less time – I'll be running. We've got some good trails, now, with all the exploring we've done, so I can make it pretty fast. They'll just be looking for the source of the smoke, and not in much of a hurry. They don't know we're expecting them, so they'll try to sneak up on us."

"What about that air horn? They'll hear that."

"They're not the brightest guys in the world. With the boat motor running, they'll hear it but they won't know what it is."

They all agreed that it was a good plan. Adam started down the path toward the other side of the island. "Adam, you run fast… and don't get caught," Matt called out.

"Don't worry about me. I'm quick," Adam said. He grinned, turned, and disappeared into the woods.

Matt watched his new friend leave. His stomach churned with an uneasy, sick feeling that something was sure to go wrong. "Kirby. Get Donald. Let's go down by the lake." The dog grabbed his toy and galloped toward the water. Matt and Brandon sat on the end of the pontoons after they tied Kirby with a short piece of rope so he wouldn't wander off. And then they waited.

Adam trotted through the brush and woods to the west end of the island. Carl and Ed would surely come from that way. He found a tall pine tree and climbed up into it nearly three fourths of the way and sat on a large branch. "Come on, guys. Show yourselves," he said to himself.

The minutes became an hour, and then two. Adam was getting sore from sitting on the branch when he heard what he thought was the far off whine of an outboard. He was fully alert and scanned the water watching for his uncles.

Then he saw the unmistakable bulk of the two big men coming around an island a few hundred yards up the lake. He turned back toward Matt and Brandon and squeezed out a short blast from the air horn.

The boat slowed and came to a stop. They had heard the air horn but they didn't know what it was because of the motor noise. They stopped the motor and listened, talked and pointed. Adam climbed down from the tree and snuck near the edge of the island to see which way they would choose.

Then he saw Ed pointing excitedly toward the island. Adam turned and he could see smoke above the trees. Matt and Brandon had lit the fire. Carl pulled on the starter cord. Adam watched from the brush until he saw they were turning to the east. He turned and ran as fast as he could, back toward his friends.

It took him less than ten minutes to get to the raft. Brandon and Matt were visibly relieved to see him. They had bolted the grill door back into the frame and had everything ready to go. "They're coming around from the east end!" Adam gasped as he ran up to them. "Push off and we'll head the other way."

Brandon climbed up on the raft and Matt lifted Kirby up to him. Then he and Adam pushed the raft out until the water was up to their knees and then they jumped on. They all picked up paddles and turned the raft to the west, paddling as fast as they could, Brandon on the right, Adam on the left, and Matt switching side to side as needed. At first they zigzagged back and forth until they got a rhythm down, and then the raft moved through the water at a good rate. In a short while they were around the end of the island, heading into the channel where Carl and Ed had appeared. "Just keep going straight down this channel for three more islands," Adam said, excitedly. "Then we have to veer to the left and around a couple more. Then we should be at the cabin."

"You're sure you know where you're going?" Brandon asked.

"Yeah, I'm sure. I've been back and forth here a dozen times over the last few months," Adam said pulling on his paddle.

Kirby was running back and forth from back to front and enjoying the ride immensely. "What do you think of this Kirby?" Adam said. The dog stopped and licked his face.

"He thinks this is great fun," Matt said.

"Let's hope it stays fun, and that we don't end up in the gun sights of those two," Brandon said looking over his shoulder back down the lake.

The pontoons floated high in the water, making very little drag, easy to paddle and steer, despite the raft's large size. They covered a lot of water in a short time "How far is it all together?" Matt asked.

"Probably about four or five miles. Hard to tell with all the zigzagging we have to do around these islands," Adam answered.

"Well, they have to zigzag too," Matt said. "We'll have plenty of places to hide if we hear them coming."

"Yeah. Keep your ears open! If we hear them coming we can't outrun them, so we'll have to try to hide."

Chapter 43

Carl and Ed took it slow and easy, trying to make as little noise as possible as they rounded the tip of the island and started back down the other side. "The smoke is just up ahead," Carl said. Ed nodded. They ran the outboard slowly, just barely above an idle. They didn't want to alert Adam, or whoever was on the island.

They came to the willow grove and saw the remains of the signal fire, still smoldering on top of the rock. Carl cut the motor, lifted it up and let the boat glide up onto the shore. Ed jumped out and pulled it up farther so it wouldn't float away.

"Somebody's been here a while," Carl said quietly. "Look at all the tracks."

"No kiddin.' Looks like they had some kind of boat or canoe. See these marks in the sand?"

They followed the marks in the sand that the pontoons had made when the boys slid them to the water's edge. "Tracks of three people," Ed said observing the three different sets of footprints. "And a dog, too."

They walked slowly and quietly, until they came to the plane, not knowing if there was someone still there. Ed stopped and stared at the plane. Carl ran into the back of him, still looking at the tracks on the ground. "Watch where you're goin'!" Ed snarled.

"Well… git out of the way, then."

"Look at that!" Ed said pointing at the huge plane.

"Well, I'll be," Carl said. "There ***was*** other people here. They must've crashed that plane."

The two men walked to the front of the plane and saw the smashed motor cowling and the remains of the prop. "They busted their battery. That's why they didn't radio for help. Must be why they made the signal fire."

"You s'pose somebody saw the fire and came and got them?"

"If'n it was a plane we'd o' saw it," Carl said. "Must've been somebody in a boat."

"So, let's see if they left anything that we might want," Ed said turning back toward the cargo door.

They walked back to the cargo door, opened it, and climbed

inside. "Holy shit! Look at all the grub and stuff!"

They dug through the cargo like a couple of pigs rooting through a trough of slop. "Man! We've got us a treasure here," Carl said.

"Let's load it up and get out of here before somebody comes back. Somebody surely is comin' back to get all this stuff… and to fix the plane. We better take all we can get right now."

They carried armfuls of cargo back to the boat, but quickly realized there was more than the boat could haul in one trip. "We'll take one load back and come back to get the rest, and hope the owners don't get back here first."

They filled the boat until it was dangerously overloaded. Carl waded to the back and climbed in. Ed pushed them off, climbed over the bow and sat on what little was left of the front seat. Carl lowered the motor and backed them away from the shore. "We're gonna have to go real slow or we'll take water over the side," he told Ed.

"Go as fast as you can without sinking us," Ed shouted back over his shoulder. "Good thing it's not windy or we'd have to leave some of this stuff."

They started down the lake slowly. A confused look suddenly came to Carl's face. "Did that plane look funny to you, Ed?"

"Funny? What do you mean? A plane sitting in the middle of the woods looks funny, sure."

"That was a float plane, right?"

"Yeah, I didn't see any wheels."

"Did you see pontoons?"

Ed looked dumbfounded. "Wasn't pontoons, either, was there?"

Carl looked worried. "There was three people there for sure, and the pontoons were gone, so what do you suppose they did with them?"

"Holy shit! They made a raft… sure as hell!"

"And Adam was with 'em. I'd bet my life on it. You don't suppose that little brat would take them to the cabin and swipe our truck, do you?"

Ed panicked. "The keys are in it, too. I left them right in the ignition!"

Carl gave the boat more gas to gain speed. "I'll kill that kid when I catch up to him," Carl swore under his breath. Occasionally a wave hit them and water slopped over the side, so he had to back off on the throttle again.

"Maybe we should stop someplace and unload this stuff," Ed suggested.

"That'll take too long," Carl said. "We gotta get back to the cabin before that kid does, or we're gonna have big problems."

Chapter 44

Designed to carry a five thousand pound plane, the pontoons rode high in the water, allowing the raft to move through the water surprisingly fast, considering its size. "It's about another mile," Adam said, his forehead glistening with sweat.

"Whew! I'm getting tired of paddling," Matt said, sweat dripping from his face and his shirt soaked through.

"Keep at it Matty," Brandon said. "We can't take a chance on those guys catching up with us. If what Adam says is true, they'd probably shoot us. Let's switch sides so we can use our other arm and shoulder for a while." They switched and it felt a lot better paddling with a somewhat rested arm.

Adam kept glancing over his shoulder as he paddled, hoping he wouldn't see the boat coming after them. They covered the distance across the last channel closest to the cabin and when they rounded the tip of the island Adam shouted, "There it is and they're not there! The boat is gone! We made it!"

Brandon and Matt exchanged grins and they paddled even faster to cover the last few hundred yards. They realized that they were approaching the rickety dock too fast to stop. "Back paddle!" Brandon yelled, but it was too late. The whole structure tipped about a foot off center when the raft crashed into it. They paddled backwards until they were free from the dock, and then Adam paddled hard on the right side and turned the raft so they could push the nose up onto the bank.

Donald in his mouth, Kirby jumped off onto dry ground, ran to a tree and lifted his leg. Matt and Adam helped Brandon step off onto the grass, and then they both jumped off. They pulled the raft up onto the shore far enough so it wouldn't drift away. "We made it!"

They were all laughing and congratulating each other when Adam stopped and a look of worry came to his face. "Listen!" They all listened quietly, and Brandon and Matt heard the same sound. "An outboard!" Matt said.

"Coming this way. It's probably them," Adam said looking down the lake. Just then they saw the heavily loaded boat come around the last island headed straight for them. "Shit! Let's get out of here!"

Carl and Ed were plowing along through the water in their overloaded boat and were getting close to home. Just as they turned around the last island, Ed yelled, "There they are. There's three of them!" Carl saw Adam and two other young looking kids scrambling off the pontoons up onto the bank. The tallest kid seemed to be limping badly, moving much slower than the others. A big yellow dog was running with them.

"Now we're gonna kick some butt," Carl said.

The kids disappeared up the bank toward the cabin as they covered the last few yards and pulled up to the dock. Ed tied a rope from the bow to a dock post and they both jumped out. The dock began to shift under their weight, as if the posts that held it up were broken. "Hurry up, Ed! This thing is falling down! Those damn kids wrecked our dock too."

They had taken only a couple of steps when the dock collapsed, toppling them both into the lake. Carl held onto his rifle tightly as he went under water, and just as he hit the bottom, Ed's foot kicked his hand and the gun fell from his grip. When he came to the surface Ed was floundering up onto the bank. "Wait. I dropped the gun," he said and dove down to look for it. He groped around in the grass and mud until he felt the cold steel, grabbed the gun and kicked for the surface. "Give me a hand," he yelled. Ed stopped, reached out and helped him into shallow water.

Adam and Matt ran up the bank. Brandon had trouble keeping up with his broken ankle. His crutch had been left behind on the island and he had to hop on his one good foot. When Adam and Matt reached the truck, Adam looked back to see that Brandon had fallen far behind. "See if you can start the truck. I'll go back and help Brandon."

Just as Adam got to Brandon he saw Carl and Ed pulling up to the dock with the boat.

"We gotta hurry Brandon! They're here!" he shouted as he put Brandon's arm over his shoulder and helped him hobble up the road. Brandon lifted his lame foot and hopped as fast as he could, leaning on Adam for support.

"Hurry up!" Matt yelled as he gunned the pickup motor. "Kirby! Come!"

Kirby ran to his master. Matt jumped out of the cab and lowered the tailgate. Kirby hopped up into the truck box. "You stay," Matt said to the dog.

He saw Brandon and Adam coming as fast as Brandon could go, and beyond them, Carl and Ed pulled the boat up to the dock. Ed tied a rope to a post. The two heavy men jumped onto the dock and scurried toward the shore. When they were just about half way, the dock started to tip, the damaged posts broke off, and both men were dumped into the lake. They went under but quickly popped back to the surface and began thrashing, trying to get to shore. "Hurry!" Adam urged Brandon. "They fell in. Come on!"

Matt got back in the cab and looked at the shift lever. He felt scared. He had never driven a truck before, but he had seen them in movies and there was a racing game at the arcade that he played, so he had a good idea of what to do. He revved the motor and looked into the rearview mirror. Brandon and Adam were just a few feet behind the truck coming on a run.

Carl and Ed were covered with mud and sea weed, dripping wet, and rapidly gaining ground on Adam and Brandon. A look of murder was in their eyes.

Chapter 45

"Now I'm gonna take pleasure in beatin' those kids," Carl growled. "They busted our dock!"

They heard the truck revving as they topped the rise of the bank. "They're stealing the truck!" Ed yelled.

The two big men huffed and puffed as they ran up the road after Adam and the taller boy with the injured foot. "Shoot 'em!" Ed yelled.

They were gaining on the last two boys, about to overtake them in a few more steps. "No need to shoot them," Carl thought. "Beating them to death will be much more fun."

Adam heard Ed yell at Carl to shoot. He stopped and turned. He was ready to do whatever it took to give Brandon and Matt a chance to escape. "Run, Brandon! I'll hold them off!"

Just as Adam looked back, Ed plowed into him like a charging rhino and they fell to the ground. Ed's big beefy arms were cinched around Adam's chest, squeezing him so hard he could barely breathe. He managed to get one fist free and hit Ed's nose as hard as he could. Blood flooded from Ed's nose. "Aarrrrgh!" Ed yelled. He let go of Adam, clutching his bleeding nose.

Adam staggered to his feet and saw Carl bearing down on him. He prepared himself for the collision, and just as Carl was about to run into him he saw and heard a flash of snarling blonde hair as Kirby launched off the back of the truck and hit Carl at mid-chest. The impact knocked Carl on his back. The dog grabbed hold of the front of Carl's shirt, tearing and shaking him. "Help me! Get that dog off me!"

Kirby snarled ferociously, trying to get at Carl's throat. The big man screamed and thrashed, trying to get away from the enraged dog.

Brandon had the passenger side door open waiting for Adam. "Kirby! Come!" he yelled. Kirby released Carl, ran to the back of the truck, and jumped over the tailgate into the box. "Go! Go! Go!" Brandon yelled to Matt.

Matt already had the shift lever into low position, or at least he hoped he did. He let out the clutch and stomped down on the gas. They took off amid much spinning of tires, dirt and gravel showering Carl and Ed. They curled up into a ball to protect themselves from the flying debris.

They roared down the road with the engine screaming. "Shift, Matty!" Brandon yelled.

Matt grabbed the shift lever, pushed in the clutch and ground the gears a few times but finally managed to find second. He let out the clutch and the truck lurched forward. He glanced at Brandon and Adam. "Not bad, eh?"

They went another hundred yards, Matt shifted again, and they were flying down the road in third gear. Just as they came to the first corner they heard a gunshot. Adam looked out the back window. "Carl is shooting at us!" he said excitedly.

They made it around the corner where they were out of sight of the two uncles. "I'd say that was a pretty good getaway," Brandon said.

"Where did you learn to drive like that?" Adam asked Matt.

"This is the first time," Matt replied. "If I can fly an airplane, I guess I can drive a pickup."

He slowed down a little, feeling much safer now that they were out of sight of the two men. "Check Kirby," Matt said. "See if he has any holes in him." Brandon looked through the window. Kirby sat looking back down the road with Donald clutched in his mouth, his tail wagging.

"He looks pretty okay to me," Brandon said. "Jeez! Did you see him attack Carl? He's a killer! His tail is wagging like mad. He thinks this is a great game." They laughed about meek, mild Kirby and his bravery.

"How far to town?" Matt asked.

"I've only been on this road once... when they brought me here. It's about an hour drive. I'd guess about fifty miles or so."

Matt looked down at the fuel gauge and smiled. "How nice of them to fill it up for us."

Chapter 46

The truck was just rounding the first corner when Carl took a quick shot at it. "Damn. Those brats got away!" he yelled. Ed was wiping blood from his profusely bleeding nose.

"We gotta go after them," Ed said spitting blood. "If they get to town, our gooses are cooked."

"I'll get the four-wheeler!" Carl said. They ran back towards the cabin. Ed went inside and stuffed two big wads of toilet paper into his nose while Carl started the four-wheeler. "Hurry up! Get on!" Carl yelled.

Ed sat on the luggage rack on the back of the machine. Carl handed the gun to him, let out the clutch and off they went down the road. "If we get close enough, shoot at the tires," he yelled.

"If we get close enough, I'm gonna shoot them kids," Ed yelled.

They bounced and pitched down the rutted road, nearly flying off the track into the woods several times. "Slow this damn thing down," Ed yelled. "You're gonna kill us!"

Carl slowed a bit as they rounded a corner. The truck was no where to be seen. "They've got a pretty good lead on us," Carl yelled over his shoulder as they headed down the straight stretch of road.

They could see the truck a long way ahead of them as they came to the next rise. "There they are," Carl said. "They think they're safe." Ed grinned an evil grin and worked the lever action of the gun to be sure there was a shell in the chamber. "Just get me close," he said.

Carl gave the four-wheeler more gas and they sped down the road. They started to catch up to the boys in the truck. He almost lost control as they topped a little rise and hit a large boulder buried in the mud. But he regained control again and sped up, gaining more on the unsuspecting boys.

Chapter 47

The boys were feeling pretty good until Adam looked over his shoulder and saw his uncles rounding the corner on the four-wheeler. He knew they would shoot at them as soon as they got into range, and it was too dangerous to go much faster on that terrible road. "Guys! Carl and Ed are behind us on the four-wheeler!"

"Speed this thing up, Matty," Brandon said.

"We can't go much faster, or we'll wreck," Adam said. "This road is full of rocks and you never know when you'll come to a tree that's tipped over in the wind. There are fire roads cut into the forest along here. I remember seeing them on the way in. I have an idea. We can try to fool Carl and Ed. Get as far ahead as you can, so they can't see us, and when we see one of those fire roads, stop and back into it. Go back far enough so they can't see us. Can you do that?"

"Yeah. Just tell me where to go," Matt said giving the truck a little more gas, lengthening the lead they had over Carl and Ed. They were topping a small hill and the brothers were no longer in sight.

"Right there, Matt!" Adam said pointing to a side road. Matt slammed on the brakes and slid to a stop.

"Brand! Can you shift it to retreat?"

Brandon laughed. "Retreat it is, Matty." He reached over and moved the shift lever to the right and down. "Hey. You didn't make that grinding sound," Matt said.

He let out the clutch, backed into the side road just far enough that Ed and Carl wouldn't see them, shifted back to low and sat with the clutch pushed in.

"When they go by, pull out and follow them. That four-wheeler makes a lot of noise so they probably won't hear us until we're right behind them. Then get up close and give them a little push with the bumper," Adam said with an evil grin. "That four-wheeler is hard to steer, and if you push them, Carl won't be able to control it. You should be able to push them right off the road."

"Sounds like fun, but what good will that do?" Brandon asked.

"Check it out," Adam said. "There's a deep ditch to the right of the road, and at the bottom, there's a stream. The side of the ditch is pretty steep."

A wide grin spread across Matt's face. "The boys will get a little bath if we do this right."

Adam nodded and said: "It wouldn't hurt my feelings, either, if they broke their fool necks."

They could hear the four-wheeler getting closer coming down the road. Matt revved the motor a little, getting ready to pull out. When Ed and Carl roared past, Matt popped the clutch and spun out onto the road behind them. They were fifty feet behind, but it only took a few seconds to catch up. Matching their speed, Matt slowly crept up behind them. Carl was concentrating on the road, trying to miss the rocks and ruts, and Ed was craning his neck looking ahead for the boys in the truck. The two large gobs of blood soaked toilet paper sticking out of Ed's nose were flying back over the sides of his face, looking like streamers on a parade float.

Matt eased the truck up until the bumper banged into the four-wheeler luggage rack where Ed was sitting. When he felt the bump, Ed turned around. His eyes got about the size silver dollars. He tried to get the gun around so he could shoot, but things were happening too fast. In his haste, he hit Carl's head with the barrel and the gun fired. Carl nearly had a heart attack. He began skidding back and forth down the road. Matt goosed the truck a little and the four-wheeler skidded sideways as Carl worked furiously to regain control.

All it took was one more little nudge. The machine slid to the right and disappeared over the side of the road, down into the ditch. As they sped away, the boys could see branches and leaves flying through the air.

"Yahoo!" Matt said as he slowed down to a safe speed.

"Good work, Matt," Adam said. "Jeez. Did you see the look on Ed's face?" Adam was laughing hysterically.

"I bet he filled his pants," Brandon said, cheering their victory.

Matt turned to the others and grinned. "That'll teach 'em to mess with us."

"Let's get to town and find the sheriff," Brandon said. I'm sure he'll be interested to hear all of what we can tell him about our friends back there."

Adam just couldn't get the smile from his face.

Chapter 48

Forty minutes later they pulled into Baudette. "You know where the sheriff's office is?" Matt asked Adam.

"They never let me come to town, but it must be around here someplace. This isn't a very big town. We should be able to find it pretty easy."

They drove down the street and Brandon pointed to a squad car parked at a cafe. "Look there. Pull in, Matty!"

A deputy walked out of the cafe with a cup of take-out coffee in his hand just as Matt pulled the truck next to the squad car and shut off the engine. "Morning, sir. Could you tell us where the sheriff's office is?"

The deputy looked at the beat up old truck, and then at Matt. "How old are you, son?"

"I'm thirteen, sir."

"And what are you doing driving that truck? You don't have a driver's license."

"I had to drive. Brandon has a broken foot, and Adam was tackling Ed and bloodying his nose. I was the only one left to drive."

"Bloodying who's nose?"

"My Uncle Ed's nose," Adam said.

"Why were you doing that?"

"Because he was gonna shoot us," Brandon said.

"Why would he do that?"

"Well, most likely because we were gonna steal their truck," Matt said.

"I can understand their way of thinking. I wouldn't want you to steal my truck, either," the deputy said.

"We really had to do it, Sir," Matt said. "They were already really mad at Adam for stealing their boat. We figured they'd shoot us for sure if they caught us."

The deputy looked confused. "You guys get in the squad with me. We'll leave the truck here until we get this story straight."

"How about Kirby?" Matt asked.

"Who's Kirby?"

Kirby stuck his head around the side of the truck and barked.

"Oh, I see," the deputy said. "Get him in the back seat with you."

They all crammed into the back seat. Kirby sat on Adam's lap holding Donald in his mouth. "I'm glad we don't have very far to go," Adam said from behind Kirby's tail.

They stopped in front of the sheriff's office, got out of the car and walked in. The deputy told the boys to have a seat. He passed through a gate in a railing that separated the offices from the visitors' part of the room. He returned with an older man in uniform. "Boys, this is the sheriff. Suppose you tell him what's going on."

Matt and Brandon glanced toward Adam. He stepped forward. "Hello, sir," he said extending his hand. "My name is Adam Whitehorse Happalti, and I've been kind of a prisoner of Ed and Carl Whitehorse for the last eleven months." He nodded toward his companions. "This is Matt and Brandon. They crashed an airplane on an island on the lake, and we stole Carl and Ed's truck so we could get away from them."

The sheriff looked surprised *and* amused. "Carl and Ed had you prisoner? Are you Naomi's son?"

"Yes sir. When my mom and dad were killed in an auto accident about a year ago, the welfare people found Uncle Ed and Uncle Carl. Since they were my only living relatives, they gave them custody of me. Carl and Ed were supposed to sell our house and put the money in a trust fund for my college, and give me a place to live and see to it that I went to school. But they spent most of the money, and I haven't been in school for over a year. They made me do all the work and when they went someplace they locked me in the cabin with only a pail for a bathroom."

"Naomi is dead? I'm sorry to hear that. She and I were good friends. Why is it that you had to get away from Carl and Ed?"

"Because they beat me a lot and I was scared that they'd kill me sometime when they got drunk and angry."

"They beat you?"

Adam lifted his shirt and turned around, showing the sheriff the bruises on his back.

"So you've been living here for almost a year?"

"Yes sir... with Carl and Ed. They kept me as a servant, I guess. But they made me go with them when they broke into cabins and resorts in the winter and stole all the stuff from them."

"What?"

"We broke into cabins and resorts and stole all the stuff. Well, they did. I didn't have any choice. I'm skinny, so they used me to go in through a window that they usually broke. Then I'd open the door so they could get in. I didn't want to take other people's stuff, but if I complained, they slapped me."

The sheriff smiled. "So you can tell us all about those burglaries?"

"Sure can," Adam said. "And I can tell you all about their poaching, and their little deal with a guy named Tiny."

"Tiny! What do you know about him?"

"I think he's some auctioneer or something. He buys the stuff from Carl and Ed and puts it in when he is selling some estate, and pockets the extra money that he gets from the stolen stuff. Carl and Ed usually got drunk after they saw Tiny and they talked about it. They didn't know I was listening, I guess."

The sheriff turned to Brandon and Matt. "And you guys are the two they're searching for? Were you in a Beaver?"

"Yes sir," Brandon said. "We crashed several days ago in that big storm. Well, we really didn't crash so bad. We just drove the plane a long way up on an island and smacked it into a rock. The battery was destroyed so we couldn't call for help. But we figured they'd be looking for us, so we just waited. Adam came along and one thing led to another, and we escaped from the island. And I guess we made Carl and Ed pretty mad at us."

"No wonder they didn't find you... clear down this far south," the deputy said. "They thought you went down way up by Sioux Lookout or Kenora."

Matt grinned. "We were by Sioux Lookout before the storm blew us off course. I wondered why our dads were taking so long to find us."

"There are 14,000 islands on this big lake, boys," the sheriff said. "Rollie..." he said to the deputy. "Get on the radio and let the DNR and the Provincial Police know that the two missing kids are here."

"So, are you guys hurt any?"

"Brandon has a broken ankle, I think," Adam said. "But otherwise we're all okay. Lots better than Carl and Ed."

The sheriff eyed them inquisitively.

"Let's just say they had a little mishap with their four-wheeler," Matt added. "And the last we saw of them they were sailing out over a ravine." He gave an evil little grin.

The three boys broke into laughter. Kirby joined in, barking.

"We're going to have a long talk and get all the details," the sheriff said. "So... you think Carl and Ed might be hurt... or maybe dead?"

"I'm not sure," Adam said. "They took a bad spill on their four-wheeler... with a little help from Matt's driving. They went over the bank into that creek along the road to their cabin."

"Rollie... send a car out toward Carl and Ed's cabin. If they find those guys, tell 'em to slap on some cuffs and bring 'em in. If they find them dead, we'll send out the coroner."

Matt looked worried. "What'll happen if they're dead?"

The sheriff grinned. "We'll dig a hole and bury them, and that's that."

Chapter 49

The sheriff took the boys to the local emergency room to get them checked out. Adam and Matt were pronounced in fine shape. But when Brandon's ankle was X-rayed, they found the tip of the fibula broken. He was wearing a brand new cast on his foot in about an hour.

When the medical examinations were complete, the sheriff brought good news. "We've been in touch with your parents. They're flying down to Nestor Falls and they'll be here by morning. In the meantime, I've arranged for a room at the motel for you. I told them to feed you and take care of you."

"Thanks a lot, sheriff," the boys said.

"No thanks necessary, boys. If what you said is true, putting Carl and Ed in jail… or burying them… will make a lot of our problems go away."

The sheriff dropped them off at the motel and told them he'd be in touch in the morning. An hour later they had all showered and were lounging in their room in big white terry cloth bathrobes while their clothes were being washed. The lady at the front desk asked them what they wanted to eat. Their first choice was pizza, so they were treated to two large pizzas and a twelve pack of sodas to wash it down. They ate until they couldn't stuff another bite into their mouths. Kirby had gotten his share, and he was sleeping contentedly on one of the beds. "Whew," Matt said patting his belly. "I'm so full I don't think I'll ever eat again."

"Nothing wrong with our food at the island," Brandon said. "But there's something about a big pizza that's hard to beat. Of course, as clever as Adam is with food, I'd bet that if we'd been there a few more days, he'd have figured out how to make a pizza out there."

Adam grinned, happy with the compliment.

They watched television for a while, it being the first time in almost a year that Adam had seen any TV. "What will they do with you now, Adam?" Matt asked.

"I don't know. I was along with them when they burglarized all those places, and when they did their poaching. Maybe they'll put me in jail, too."

"But you were forced to go along."

"Yeah, but Carl and Ed will say that I wanted to. You just wait and see."

"I wouldn't worry, Adam. The sheriff looks like a fair guy to me."

There was a knock on the door. The motel housekeeper had their clothes cleaned and dried, so they put on their underwear and got ready for bed. "I'll sleep on the floor," Adam said. He grabbed a pillow and a blanket from the closet.

"Baloney! We can share," Matt said. "You don't have to sleep on the floor any more. This beds are big enough for a whole flock of kids."

They settled down, Adam and Matt in one bed, and Brandon and Kirby in the other. They had had a pretty full day, and they were all asleep in a little while.

Sunlight streamed in through the window. Matt was lying in bed going over the events of the past few days when he heard a knock on the door. He got up, unlocked and opened the door.

"Mathew!" His mother hugged and kissed him, and then his dad joined in as they both smothered him with hugs and kisses.

Brandon's parents were right behind them. Brandon bounded out of bed, clomped along on his new cast, and met them halfway across the room. They all embraced. "We were so worried," his mom said.

"We've been looking for you day and night," Brandon's dad said. "We never dreamed you'd be this far south."

Brandon's mom began worrying about his foot, and everyone was talking at once when Matt realized Adam was sitting in the bed with the covers pulled up to his chest, looking rather embarrassed. "Hey! Everybody, listen up! I want you to meet Adam. If it hadn't been for him, we wouldn't have been found even yet."

The dads shook Adam's hand at once, and the moms – being moms – hugged him and thanked him for his help. They didn't realize that he felt kind of foolish sitting there in his underwear in the midst of all these people he didn't know.

Matt tossed him his jeans. "Here," he said, "you wouldn't

offend anyone, but I know how I'd feel, undressed in a room full of strangers." Adam smiled, slipped on his jeans, and then got up from the bed.

"I've got an idea," Matt's dad said. "You guys get ready and we'll all go out for breakfast."

The adults filed out of the room and left the boys to wash up and get dressed. They put a rope on Kirby and met their parents in the lobby. In the dining room they pushed several tables together and put in their breakfast orders.

The waitress gave Kirby a sorrowful stare and said: "We don't allow animals in the dining room."

"You allow helper dogs, don't you?" Matt asked.

"Well, yes… ones for blind people and police dogs."

"Well, this is officer Kirby. He just finished a case where he apprehended two real bad guys. In fact, he hit one with a flying leap and saved several lives from a madman who was about to shoot them. The people were so thankful that they gave him that toy duck as a memento."

Kirby just sat there wagging his tail, holding Donald in his mouth. The lady grinned. "And what would officer Kirby like for breakfast?"

Everyone broke out in laughter. "I'll have a stack of pancakes, three eggs, sausage and a bowl of cereal," Matt said. "And maybe a couple of blueberry waffles, and a large glass of milk. Officer Kirby will share with me."

Brandon looked up and said: "Same for me."

"How about you, Adam?" Brandon's mom asked.

"If it's ok, I'll have the same, too, ma'am."

"Of course, it's okay, sweetie. You have whatever you want."

The adults ordered more traditional breakfasts, instead of one of everything like the boys. Forks clattered and everyone talked at once. The boys slipped Kirby bites under the table, and between them, he got a full breakfast, too.

"Adam," Matt's dad said. "We talked to the sheriff about your situation this morning."

"Are they gonna put me in jail?" Adam asked with fear in his voice.

"Oh, no, no. Nothing of the sort. They want you to testify against your uncles when they catch them, but you're not going to be charged."

Adam sighed relief.

"What we talked about," Matt's dad went on, "... is that you have no other relatives to live with. The sheriff called Child Welfare in Rochester, and they agreed to let you spend the summer with us at Clearwater Bay. Then, in the fall we'll see if they've found a foster home. So, if you want to come with us, we'd love to have you."

Matt and Brandon's faces lit up. "All right, Adam!"

Adam's eyes filled with tears; he nodded yes. "That would be great. I'd love to come with you," he said. He would finally be with someone who cared.

Chapter 50

After breakfast, they all piled into a large rented van and drove to the sheriff's office.

"Your uncles lit out for places unknown," the sheriff said.

"Did you find the four-wheeler?" Matt asked.

"Yeah. It was piled up in the creek at the bottom of the ravine. It wasn't damaged too badly, but there was no way Ed and Carl could get it out of there. And there's no sign of them. The boat is gone and the cabin is deserted. There was a pile of canned goods and other cargo that they threw up on the shore. Must be the stuff from your plane. We sent out a truck to pick it up. We found enough merchandise in the storage shed to convict them of burglary, and all the fresh moose… well, put it this way: when we find them, they'll be going away for a quite a while."

"Good. The longer the better," Matt said.

"Can you draw a map to the island where the plane is?" Brandon's dad asked Adam.

"Sure. No problem." Adam sat down with pen and paper.

"We'll fly the Otter back to Clearwater Bay. When we come back here, we'll bring a boat along, so when we meet the salvage people at Carl and Ed's cabin, we can tow the pontoons back to the plane. We'll put them back on, and then hope the big salvage boat can pull the plane back onto the lake. We'll tow it to Nestor Falls to make the repairs."

"It's not broke bad," Matt said. "Brandon did a good job until he smacked that big rock."

They all laughed and Brandon ruffled Matt's hair. "We were lucky, and you know it, Matty. You know what they say…"

"Any landing you can walk away from is a good one?"

They drove back to Nestor Falls and boarded the Otter. It was Adam's first time in a plane, so as they flew out over the lake toward Clearwater Bay, they let him sit up in the right seat while Brandon's dad piloted the Otter. Adam was fascinated by all the dials, switches, and pedals. Todd showed him how to handle the yoke and the rudder pedals. "Just put your feet on the pedals and your hands on the yoke and feel the plane," he said.

Adam carefully placed his hands and feet. He could feel the plane respond as Todd turned the yoke or moved the rudder. "See? It's not so hard," Todd said. Adam nodded.

Then, much to Adam's surprise, Todd released his grip on the yoke and took his feet off the pedals. "Just keep her heading just like she is. I'm going back to get some coffee."

"What? Are you kidding? Wait, wait!"

Everyone laughed, and then Adam laughed, too. "Maybe I'll just have someone hand me a coffee," Todd said. "You keep flying though. We'll consider this your first lesson."

Matt grinned as he watched Adam grip the yoke, recalling just a few days ago when he had done the same thing. Adam reminded him so much of Mark – about the same size, dark eyes and hair, although Adam's was much longer. Many of Adam's mannerisms were the same, too. He had Mark's sort of crooked grin and a way he tipped his head when he laughed. Matt smiled. "My new big brother," he said to himself.

Todd took over the controls as they saw Clearwater Bay Resort below them. Todd made a picture perfect landing and taxied up to a long dock that stuck out into the lake in front of the main lodge. "Wow! This place is great," Adam said.

"There are ten fishermen here now, and more coming next weekend," Mike explained. They understood that we couldn't spend a lot of time with them while we were searching for Matt and Brandon. But now we can get back to work and take care of our customers, and when we get the Beaver back in service, we'll be in good shape."

Todd pointed to a small cabin right next to the lake near the fishing docks. "That cabin is for you guys. It's up to you to keep it clean and everything working. You'll eat up in the lodge with us, but you'll have your privacy, too.

"What can I do for a job?" Adam asked.

"We didn't bring you here to work," Sandy said. "You're our guest."

"I'd rather work, too. I'm a pretty good cook. Could I help in the kitchen?"

"He's a mega good cook, Mom. He made stuff that was delicious from the supplies we had in the plane. I bet he could have made a meal out of stuff he found on the ground. He's pretty clever."

"Well," his mom laughed. "We have plenty of groceries. I don't think we'll need to serve our guests leaves and berries. But we could use some help in the kitchen, so that will work out just fine."

Adam beamed from ear to ear.

Some of Matt's and Brandon's clothes and shoes that their parents had brought were already in the cabin. Matt and Adam were close enough in size that they could share clothes. The boys cleaned up and change clothes, and then they spent the day settling in. The cabin was one large room with two single beds against the west wall. Matt and Adam carried in and set up a third.

Their parents lived in the main lodge, and that was where the guests met for meals, and told fish stories, and unwound after a day on the lake. The Great Room had high log ceilings with many mounted moose and elk heads, and a full sized bear. "A Grizzl bear," Matt said pointing to the snarling beast. Kirby looked at the bear and slunk back behind the couch. "I don't think Kirby is a Grizzl bear dog after all," Matt said laughing.

They had supper with the guests in the dining room and enthralled everyone with the story of their flight, and their escape from Carl and Ed. When it was time for bed, the boys retired to their cabin. They were still wide awake so they lit a fire in their fireplace and sat in front of it toasting their bare feet. "How long do you have to wear that cast?" Adam asked Brandon.

"The doc said six weeks."

"No swimming for six weeks?"

"Have you felt how cold that water is, Matty? I'll do my swimming in the bathtub with a plastic bag on my foot."

"Well, guys," Brandon said. "I think it's time for some rest. It's been a busy few days." He shut off the lights.

Moonlight beamed in through the windows. Adam lay there and listened to his two new friends as their breathing became slow and steady. He hadn't felt this safe in such a long time. Kirby jumped up and snuggled against his back. He scratched the dog's ears. "G'night, Kirby."

Chapter 51

Adam felt warm air blowing against his cheek. His mind was still fogged with the shadows of sleep. He tried to ignore the air and drift off again. Then he felt the bed wiggle. He opened his eyes. Kirby's chin rested on the bed, his eyes staring at him from a distance of about two inches. His tail wagged furiously, creating quite a windstorm. "Mornin,' Kirby," Adam said smiling at the dog. Kirby took that as an invitation, crawled up and lay on Adam's chest, and licked his face.

"He's woke me up like that for as long as I can remember," Matt said from the next bed. "I think he likes you better than he likes me now."

"I doubt that," Adam said. "He just thinks I'm an easier mark to get up and let him outside.

When Kirby heard the magic word – *outside* – he jumped up and down. Adam curled up in a ball trying to avoid being pummeled by dog feet.

"You'd better let him out or he'll pee on your bed," Brandon said laughing.

Adam jumped from his bed, trotted to the door, and Kirby bounded out. "It's a beautiful day," Adam said over his shoulder. "Not a cloud in the sky."

"Good," Brandon said as he swung his feet off the bed. "It'll be a good day to fly down and put the Beaver back together so we can tow her in."

"How's the ankle feeling, Brand?" Matt asked as he sat up in his bed.

"Not too bad. The cast itches a little but I think I'll be able to get around better. They put that rubber heel on the cast so I can walk on it."

Kirby barked at the door. Matt let him in. The boys washed up, dressed in shorts, tee shirts, and tennis shoes and went up to the main lodge. The smell of frying bacon floated through the air and the boys didn't waste any time filling their plates from the warming pans.

"How did you sleep in your little bungalow?" Mike asked.

"It was great," Matt said. "The fireplace was nice, and the beds are real comfortable. Of course, anything is comfortable when you've been sleeping on the floor of an airplane for a week."

"Well, do you guys want to come along to get the Beaver?" Todd asked.

"Sure," Brandon said. "Unless there's something we need to get done here."

"We're good, here. I thought you guys could come along and help get things squared away so the salvage guy can tow it to Nestor Falls. When it's repaired, one of us can fly down with Brandon and he can fly it back here."

"Uh, you do remember the last time Brandon flew the Beaver don't you?" Matt said grinning.

They all laughed. "I think he'll do better when there's not a huge storm front pounding on him," Mike said.

"How soon do we leave?" Adam asked.

"Let's make it about an hour. We'll meet you down at the dock by the Otter."

The boys sauntered out of the lodge. Brandon and Matt gave Adam a tour of the entire camp. They had been here before as guests so they knew their way around quite well. After the tour they went to the kitchen to say goodbye to their mothers. Sandy and Carol were busy getting things prepared ahead of time for the evening meal. Most of the guests had taken sack lunches out with them fishing.

"Boy! This is a nice kitchen," Adam said looking things over.

"You think you want to work in here with two old ladies?" Sandy asked.

"What two old ladies?" Adam said grinning. "I only see two hot chicks."

"*That*, young man, will get you a long way here," Carol said as she put her arms around Adam and hugged him.

Sandy did the same. "We're going to love working with such a handsome young guy in the kitchen, won't we Carol?"

"Mom! Jeez!" Matt said looking aghast.

The women laughed and hugged the boys. "We're just so glad to have you guys back and to have Adam with us, too," Sandy said.

"This is going to be a great summer for all of us."

Adam's smile was as wide as it could possibly be.

Chapter 52

Matt and Adam each took a handle of the large cooler filled with sandwiches and soft drinks, carried it down to the dock and stowed it in the Otter. Todd and Mike had secured a fourteen foot V bottom fishing boat with a 25 horsepower motor between the pontoons to take to the crash site.

"You can haul boats with this plane?" Adam asked.

"Yeah. You can with the Beaver, too. That's how we'll get them back to the remote camps," Brandon answered.

Todd and Mike joined them, and all except Matt climbed aboard the Otter. He waited to untie the ropes that held the plane to the dock. After Mike started the engine, he waved. Matt unhooked the ropes and climbed aboard.

"Hook Kirby's harness," Mike said over the motor noise. The boys nodded and hooked Kirby's harness into the seatbelt. The dog wagged happily. No one loved flying more than Kirby.

Mike taxied the plane out onto the lake and lined it up between two floating milk jugs anchored about fifty feet apart. "Here we go," he said. He throttled up the motor, and they skimmed over the lake surface heading toward two more milk jugs several hundred yards ahead. Adam cupped his hands over Matt's ear. "What happens if we don't take off before we get to those jugs?"

"We crash" Matt said stoically.

"What?"

Matt burst out laughing. "Nothing happens. They're just there to keep us away from some rocks out there," he said pointing to the left. "Don't worry. Dad and Todd have flown almost every kind of plane there is. They know what they're doing."

Adam smiled and gave Matt thumbs up.

High in the air they leveled off over the huge expanse of Lake of the Woods. "It's pretty darn big," Brandon said looking down.

"No wonder they didn't find us. Just look at all those islands," Matt shouted. "We'd be old men by the time they found us if Adam hadn't come along." They all laughed and high-fived with Adam.

After a forty-five minute flight they started to descend. The boys saw a large boat parked near an island that looked quite familiar. "There's our island, Brand," Matt shouted. Inland a ways the plane was just barely visible below the foliage of the trees.

Mike circled the island, losing altitude, and soon the pontoons touched down on the small waves running down the lake. He cut the power, and when the plane settled he dropped the water rudder and throttled the engine enough to move them along. They taxied near the large salvage boat and stopped. "Matt," Mike said. "Toss out the anchor through the cargo door and tie us up, please."

When the anchor hit lake bottom and the rope was tied to a pontoon strut, Matt and Adam climbed down into the fishing boat and untied the ropes. Then Brandon and Kirby climbed in, Matt started the motor and took them to shore. Then he returned to the plane and ferried the dads to shore.

They all hiked up the path to the Beaver. Mike and Todd looked it over and pronounced it salvageable. "She's not hurt too bad at all. You guys were lucky to come on shore where there weren't any big trees or rocks."

"It was just Brandon's good driving," Matt said punching Brandon's shoulder.

"Okay, here's what we'll do," Todd said. "Mike, Brandon, and I will go with the salvage boat to tow the pontoons back here." He turned to Matt and Adam "While we're gone, you two transfer what's left of the cargo to the Otter with the fishing boat... and don't overload the boat and sink it. It'll take you quite a few trips. We'll load the stuff that Carl and Ed stole on the salvage boat. If we all help, we can get the pontoons bolted back on, and then we can fly home while the salvage boat tows in the Beaver." He scanned all the faces. "Any questions?"

"Nope," Matt said. Adam shook his head.

"Okay. See you in a few hours."

Mike waved to the salvage boat crew, and they brought the craft to shore. Mike, Todd and Brandon went aboard. The big salvage boat was surprisingly fast with two one hundred horsepower motors.

"Well, I guess it's time for us to go to work," Matt said.

They went back to the plane and started carrying boxes from the cargo hold to the boat. In a short time the boat was full. They climbed in, motored the short distance to the Otter, and tied up to the pontoon struts. Matt climbed up into the plane and Adam handed him boxes. When the boat was unloaded, they headed back toward shore.

"Where's Kirby?" Adam asked. "He was right here on the shore when we left."

"He's probably out hunting for a KFC," Matt said. Adam laughed and nodded.

They began hauling more cargo out of the plane. Matt was handing boxes out to Adam when Adam heard Kirby barking. "I hear him. He's out in the woods," he said to Matt.

Matt stopped working and stuck his head out of the plane. Kirby was barking loudly from quite a long ways off. "Suppose he's hurt or something?" he said.

"He sounds excited. Maybe he found another skunk," Adam said. "I'll go find him. You keep unloading. I'll come right back and help you carry."

Matt agreed. Following one of the trails they had worn when they were on the island, Adam walked into the woods toward Kirby's frantic barking. He could tell that he was getting closer to the dog. "Kirby! Hey, Kirby! Come here!"

He waited, but Kirby kept barking and didn't come any closer. "What the heck is he up to?" Adam thought.

He started down the trail again, and just as he came to a large pine tree he saw movement in the corner of his left eye. Before he could make another move, Carl's huge right fist caught him on the left cheekbone. He heard a crack inside his head, and then everything went black.

Chapter 53

Everything was unloaded. Matt sat on the pontoon waiting for Adam when he noticed that Kirby had stopped barking. "He must've found him," he thought. "I hope he's not full of skunk stink."

He thought of carrying boxes to the boat when Kirby came running down the path from the woods. "Hey, Kirbo. Where's Adam?"

The dog was strangely frantic. He barked and ran back and forth from the plane to the edge of the woods. "Adam! Are you coming?" Matt yelled.

He waited. No Adam. Kirby wouldn't settle down. He kept barking and running back and forth. "You know where Adam is?" he said to the dog.

Kirby ran to the woods and kept on going. Now Matt was getting worried, so he followed Kirby down the path that cut across the island. "He's probably playing a trick on me," he thought as he walked. "Pretty soon he'll come out of the brush pretending to be a Grizzl bear." He smiled, expecting Adam to jump out at him at any second.

Matt was nearly across the island when he heard the sound of someone pulling on the starting cord of an outboard motor. He walked forward slowly, and when he neared the edge of the lake he stooped low and peered through the brush. "Oh, no!" he muttered under his breath.

"Kirby. Come!" he said just loud enough for the dog to hear. He held his collar to keep him near, moved a little closer, and looked through the brush again. Carl was starting the motor and Ed was just pushing their boat off the rocks. Carl backed the boat out into the channel. Adam was lying in the bottom of the boat, not moving.

Matt watched the boat increase speed and head toward the east. "They're not going back to their cabin. We gotta see where they go, Kirby." He struggled through the brush and trees, keeping out of sight, watching the boat as it moved down the lake. It was tough going, crawling over logs and going around brush and rocks, but he kept up with the men in the boat. As he ran across a little meadow of grass, a Spruce Hen flew up from under his feet and startled him. He jumped to the side, not knowing what it was, at first. Then he saw the bird flying, so he kept running.

In a short while he had reached the end of the island. The boat kept going across a wide expanse of water toward a bunch of islands two or three miles away. Matt climbed a tree and watched until the boat seemed to stop at one of the distant islands. It was a small island that appeared no more than a big rock with a few trees on it. He took a careful look to be sure he would know it again, and then he and Kirby ran back toward the Beaver as fast as they could go.

Matt climbed up into the plane and wrote "Gone to get Adam—Wait for us" on a piece of cardboard with a pen he found stuck into a map folder. He laid it in the doorway and put a rock on it. Then he and Kirby ran down to the boat. "Jump in, Kirby," Matt said, and the dog jumped over the gunwale and sat on the front seat. Matt pushed the boat out and jumped in. He lowered the motor, pulled the cord and the motor sprang to life. He turned the steering handle to point the boat toward the east end of the island, opened up the throttle and they sped down the lake. "We gotta find Adam. Those bastards have him," he said to himself.

Then Matt realized that Carl and Ed would see him coming if he just headed across the open water, so he turned behind some small islands and kept working his way to the east. Having to go around some of the islands took a long time since some of them were quite large. Motor noise carried a long way across the water. Carl and Ed would hear him coming if he went too fast, so he ran the motor fairly slow, so it didn't make a lot of noise.

He stopped and tied up along the shore of a small island about two hundred yards from the one where the other boat had stopped. He snuck to the end of the island, and from there he could see a small shack on rocky ridge on the other island. Smoke came from the chimney. Carl and Ed's boat was pulled up on the shore. "We'll have to wait here till dark, Kirby," he said. "Then I'm goin in there… and I'm getting Adam."

He lay back against the trunk of a big pine tree that had dropped a soft blanket of needles on the ground. The wind whistled softly through the needles of the tree, comforting and soothing. He closed his eyes and fell asleep. When he awoke, he was surprised that it was already dark. "Jeez, Kirby. We slept a long time." The dog woke up and yawned. Matt crept to the shore and peered toward the shack. He couldn't see any light, nor could he see anyone moving around. "Get in the boat, Kirby." Matt got in, put the oars in the oarlocks and began rowing toward the island. "We'll pull a sneak attack," he whispered.

Chapter 54

Matt pulled up next to Carl and Ed's boat on the shore. "Kirby, you wait here," he said to the dog. "Wait!" he said again and patted the boat seat. Kirby lay down on the seat. Matt got out, pulled the boat up and made sure it wouldn't drift away.

He snuck up through the rocks and brush to the edge of the clearing where the shack stood. He could see something on the ground in front of the shack next to a small tree, but there was no sign of Carl, Ed, or Adam.

He snuck closer and then he realized what was next to the tree. "Oh my God! It's Adam!" he thought. He hurried to the tree and knelt next to Adam. He felt sick to his stomach.

Adam was unconscious, hands tied behind the tree. His bare feet were covered with blood, and his long black hair was matted with dried blood, hanging over his face. Matt gently lifted his head. Adam's left eye was swelled shut, and his face, too, was covered with dried blood. His right shirt sleeve was torn off and his arm and shoulder were scraped and bruised. "Oh, Adam! What have they done to you?" Matt's eyes filled with tears. "Those dirty bastards!"

"I'm gonna save you, Adam. Just hold on, pal," he whispered. He got up and snuck up to the shack. There was a metal hasp and latch on the door. He found a sturdy stick, slid it through the hasp, locking the uncles inside. Then he knelt behind the tree and untied the rope from Adam's hands. The boy flopped forward as soon as his hands were free. He moaned and coughed.

"It's Matt," he whispered. "I'm gonna get you out of here."

"Matt?" Adam's voice, dry and raspy, he passed out again.

Matt got his shoulder under Adam, lifted him up and slowly carried him across the clearing to the boat. Adam wasn't real heavy but he was a little larger than Matt, so it was hard to keep his footing. He stumbled and fell once. Adam moaned when he hit the ground. Kirby was all agitated when he saw Adam. He whined. "Shhhh, Kirby. Quiet."

Matt waded into the water far enough so he could lay Adam over the side onto the bottom of the boat. He pulled himself over the side and sat down on the middle seat. He started to push off with the oars, but then he had a thought and stopped. He jumped out of the boat again and went to Carl and Ed's boat. He unhooked the gas tank from the hose and set it on the shore. Then he found wooden matches in the survival kit from his boat. With grim face he snuck back to the cabin carrying the gas can.

He took the cap off the can and dumped gas against the side of the cabin, soaking the wood. "Those stinkin' bastards. Beat up Adam like that," he said to himself. He set the empty gas can down and took out a match. He struck the match and just held it, staring at the gas-soaked cabin wall. Suddenly he felt his blood run cold. "Can I do this?" he thought. The match burned down, he blew it out, and tossed it into the clearing. He reached for another and then stopped. "If I do this, I'll have to live with it for the rest of my life." he thought. "Nobody deserves it more than they do, but..." He put the matches away and hurried back to the lake.

He untied Carl and Ed's boat and pushed it out into the dark lake, and then climbed over the bow of his boat and rowed over to it. He grabbed the rope at the bow of Carl and Ed's boat and tied it to a cleat on the back of his boat. Then he worked the oars until he was pointing out into the lake. He put the oars down inside the boat, climbed over Adam and sat on the back seat. "Hang on, Kirby. We're gonna rock and roll."

He started the motor and gave it gas. Soon they were making their way down the lake, towing Carl and Ed's boat behind. "I hope we don't crash into something," he thought. He wasn't absolutely sure how to get back to the island where the Beaver was, but he knew the general direction, and as long as it was ***away*** from Carl and Ed, he thought they would be okay.

"I just hope they don't hear the motor and somehow get out of that cabin… and start shooting at us," he said to Kirby. The dog was now on the floor next to Adam, licking his face and whining.

After some distance, Matt decided to pull up and wait for daylight. He was lost, and in the darkness he had no idea which way to go. He had been motoring along quite fast and had nearly collided with an island. Luckily he saw it in time to turn away. He tied up to a tree branch at the next island, shut off the motor, and knelt down next to Adam to look him over. He had been savagely beaten and Matt wasn't sure if he would even live. Adam was still unconscious and shivering. Matt told Kirby to lie against Adam, and Matt lay down next to him on the other side. Huddled together, their body heat helped warm Adam, and after a little while he stopped shivering.

"Are you my Knights in Shining Armor?" Adam said weakly.

Matt's eyes popped open and he saw Adam looking at him with his one good eye. "Adam! Oh, God. I was so scared you were gonna die," he said, his eyes filling with tears.

"Not yet, I don't think. But if you hadn't come along, I might have."

"You're hurt pretty bad."

"I've been better, Matty. My ribs are hurtin'... real bad. Carl kicked me in the chest... I think my ribs are broke."

"I'll get you back to the plane. Dad and Todd will fly you to the hospital."

There was enough light to see now. Matt tied Carl and Ed's boat to a tree, started his motor, and pulled out into the lake. He stopped, looking up and down the lake, trying to determine where to go. Adam pushed himself up on one elbow and looked back and forth a few times over the side of the boat. He pointed at a cut between two islands. "Take that cut and I think our island is just about a half mile on the other side," he said. He lay back down on the deck. Matt opened the throttle and followed Adam's directions. When he emerged from the cut he saw the Otter anchored next to their island. "You were right, Adam," he said. "Must be the Indian in you."

Adam smiled through his pain.

Chapter 55

Matt began yelling for his dad when he was still a hundred yards away from the shore. Mike and Todd came on a run, and when Matt pulled up to the shore, they were there. Brandon came limping just behind them. Mike saw Adam lying in the bottom of the boat covered with blood. "My God, Matt! What happened?"

"Carl and Ed must've been hiding here and they kidnapped Adam and beat him up," Matt said excitedly. "After you guys left, we started unloading the plane, and they must have lured Kirby away. He started barking and Adam went to look for him. Kirby came back but Adam didn't so I went looking for him. I saw Carl and Ed taking him away in their boat. I followed them to a cabin on another island. When they went to sleep I snuck up and found Adam tied to a tree, all beat up. I got him in the boat, but we had to wait for daylight so I could find my way back here. He's hurt bad, Dad! They hurt him bad."

Todd climbed in the boat and knelt next to Adam. Kirby hovered over the boy as if he wanted to protect him from them. "It's okay, Kirby. Let us help," Todd said quietly to the dog. Kirby lay down next to Adam and whined.

"Adam… can you hear me?" Todd asked quietly. There was no response.

"He was awake a while ago. He's got his ribs all broke. He said they kicked him in the chest," Matt said, anger in his voice.

"Mike," Todd said. "We have to get him to the hospital." He instructed Brandon to ride out to the Otter and help them get Adam into the plane. "Mike can take him to Nestor Falls and we'll wait here for the salvage boat to come back."

Brandon climbed in, Mike pushed them off, and Matt started the motor. He drove the boat the short distance to the Otter parked in deeper water. When they were alongside the pontoon, Matt and Brandon held the boat in place while Mike and Todd carefully lifted Adam out, first onto the pontoon, then opened the cargo bay door and lifted him into the plane.

They made Adam as comfortable as possible, and then Todd climbed down onto the pontoon. "Mike's going to take him in."

"I'm going too," Matt said, climbing out of the boat.

"There's nothing you can do," Todd said.

Matt glared at Todd. "I'm going. I told Adam I'd take care of him, and I'm going. " He climbed into the plane and closed the cargo door.

Todd boarded the boat and he and Brandon pulled away from the Otter. Mike started and warmed up the engine. He taxied out into the lake where he had a straight path into the wind, revved up the engine, and the big plane gained speed until the pontoons lifted out of the water and climbed effortlessly into the sky.

Todd and Brandon watched them go and then walked back toward the Beaver. "Jeez! That kid was beat up bad," Todd said.

"Do you think he'll be okay, Dad?"

"I hope so, Brandon. But he might have a punctured lung if they kicked him in the chest. That poor kid. How could those guys be so cold hearted? That's their own flesh and blood."

Brandon put his hand on his dad's shoulder. "I think we should pray for him, Dad. He needs all the help he can get."

Matt sat on the floor next to Adam. He watched carefully as Adam's chest rose and fell and he wanted to be sure it kept on doing just that. He put his hand on Adam's forehead and brushed the hair away from his eyes. "We'll take care of you, Adam," he said quietly. "Those guys won't ever get a chance to hurt you again." His eyes were full of tears as they sped through the air toward Nestor Falls and a waiting ambulance.

"How's he doing, Matt?"

"Okay, I think. Did you call ahead for an ambulance?"

"They'll have one waiting. I called the sheriff, too. Can you tell him how to get to that trapper's cabin?"

"I think so. I can remember it pretty well. Carl and Ed aren't going anywhere... unless they're really good swimmers. I don't know if they can even get out of the cabin. But if they do, they've got no way off the island. I made sure of that. I took their boat and it's tied up a long way from them."

Mike turned and smiled. "Pretty good thinking for a kid."

Matt grinned for the first time that day.

Chapter 56

Matt felt the plane descending. He looked out the window to see Nestor Falls below. His dad banked the plane around in a half circle, landing very near the dock where the ambulance was parked. Two uniformed men waited for them as they taxied up to the dock. Each of the men tossed a rope around struts on each end of the plane and pulled it steadily into the dock. By the time they had tied the ropes, Matt had the cargo door open.

The men pushed a stretcher over to the side of the plane, took a back board from the stretcher and climbed into the cargo hold.

"How's he doing?" one of them asked Matt.

"He hasn't been awake for a long time, but he's still breathing," Matt answered.

The medical tech listened to Adam's breathing with his stethoscope. "His right lung sounds bad. It might be punctured. He's in shock. We have to get him in and let the docs work on him. He's a sick boy, right now."

They strapped Adam to the board. Matt and Mike helped load him onto the stretcher. They pushed it down the dock to the waiting ambulance. Matt ran along with them, and when they got Adam into the ambulance, he climbed in, too. "You can't go, son. It's against the rules."

"I'm going! And if you won't let me ride, I'll run along behind… but I'm going!" Matt didn't move.

"Matt," Mike said. "Let the men do their jobs."

"I'm going, Dad. I have to go."

The driver shrugged his shoulders. "Let him ride along. We need to go."

"I'm going to fly back," Mike told his son. "As soon as we get the Beaver off the island, we'll all come back here."

"Tell the sheriff they're east of the island on a small rock with a little cabin on it."

"Okay," his dad replied. "Good luck."

Matt nodded and they closed the doors.

While Mike and Matt were talking, one of the ambulance techs started to work on Adam. He put an IV line in Adam's left arm and hooked up a bag of saline. "He's your buddy?" he asked Matt.

"Yeah. Is he gonna be okay?"

"Keep your fingers crossed. He's in bad shape, right now," the man said. "He's in shock, and other than that, it's hard to tell. If you pray, do it now."

Matt closed his eyes to fight back tears. "Please, God. Help Adam. Don't let him die like Mark did."

The ambulance backed up to the hospital emergency room and the back doors flew open. Three or four new people, all talking and scrambling around whisked Adam's stretcher away. Matt was left sitting in the back of the ambulance alone. He got out, walked into the emergency room, and found several doctors and nurses crowded around Adam. One nurse was cutting his clothes off and another was hooking up a machine to his chest. One doctor was looking in his eyes with a small flashlight and the other was shouting instructions to some other nurses. Matt stood against the wall, out of the way.

"He's going to need surgery. His right lung is punctured," one of the doctors said. "Call the O.R. Alert them that we're on the way up."

A nurse was taking Adam's blood pressure. The doctor looked at her questioningly. "86 over 50," she said.

The doctor shook his head. "We've got to move, people!"

The doctors and nurses removed Adam's clothes once they were cut loose. Then Matt could see just how badly he had been beaten. His whole body was bruised and scraped. One of the nurses came forward with a camera and took several pictures of the injuries. Then, just as quickly as they had wheeled him into the emergency room, they wheeled the gurney out another door.

The emergency room was quiet and deserted except for Matt, standing against the wall, wondering what he should do when suddenly a man came in wearing a janitor's uniform. "What are you doing in here?" he asked.

"I was with Adam, but they took him to some O.R., whatever that is."

"Adam… that kid that just came in?"

"Yeah. He's my friend. He's my… he's my… new brother,"

Matt said.

The man stared at Matt with compassion. "Come on, kid. I'll take you upstairs where you can wait for him," he said softly.

It was like living a nightmare, Matt thought. A few hours ago he and Kirby and Adam – his new brother – were having a great time, looking forward to a summer together filled with fun and adventure. And now, someone was cutting Adam open in an operating room, attempting to keep him from dying.

The janitor took Matt to a waiting room on the fifth floor and talked to a nurse at the nurse's station just down the hall. Then he waved good-bye to Matt and got in the elevator. The nurse, an older lady with gray hair, sat down next to Matt. "Are you okay?" she asked.

"You mean… am I hurt?"

"No, I can see you're not hurt. But are you okay?"

Matt's eyes filled with tears. "No, I'm not okay," he said. "Adam, my friend, is hurt real bad, and I'm scared he's gonna die."

The nurse put her arms around Matt and pulled him close to her. "It's okay. You just get it all out. Go ahead and have a good cry. Sally will take care of you, honey."

Sally rocked back and forth and Matt had his cry. When he had calmed a little, she let him go and smiled. "A good cry is sometimes just the thing, isn't it?"

Matt smiled back at her and nodded, his face wet with tears.

"Are you hungry? I've never seen a boy your age that isn't hungry," she said.

Now that she had mentioned it, Matt realized that he was starving. "I'll wait to see if Adam is okay," he said.

"Isn't anything you can do for Adam by starving yourself," she said. "Come on. I'll take you down to the cafeteria. We'll get you something to eat. I'll let the nurses know where we are. They'll page me if any news comes from the O.R."

Matt got to his feet. Sally put her arm around his shoulder and they walked down the hall. She stopped at the nurse's station and told the nurse where they'd be. Then she and Matt got into the elevator.

Matt piled his tray with food. His stomach growled once he smelled it. Sally got a cup of coffee and they sat down at a table. "Go ahead and eat," she said. "I'm too fat. I'm just having coffee."

Matt grinned. "You're not fat, Sally," he said.

Sally smiled. "You know just how to handle the ladies, don't you, little man?"

Matt smiled.

"So what happened to your friend? Was he in an accident?"

"His uncles beat him up," Matt said shaking his head. "Can you believe anybody could be so ugly? They beat up their own nephew."

"Honey, I've seen everything in this job in all the years I've been here. Every time I see something like this, it just makes me wonder what some people are capable of. I'm sure he's going to be okay. We have good doctors here." Sally reached for Matt's hand. She squeezed it gently and gave him a warm smile.

Chapter 57

Mike could see Brandon sitting in the small boat waiting as he circled with the Otter. He touched down and taxied toward the island. Once the motor was shut down, he opened the cargo door and climbed out onto the pontoon. He let the plane glide in a little closer and then tossed out the anchor. Brandon pulled up in the boat and he jumped in. "How's Adam doing?" Brandon asked.

"I don't know, Brandon. The ambulance was waiting for us and they took him right in. Matt went with him. He wouldn't take no for an answer."

Brandon smiled. "Matty is really fond of Adam. He thinks of him as a new big brother, and he's a stubborn kid when he wants to be."

Mike smiled and said, "If Matt gets something in his head, there's no changing him. I'm proud of him and how he rescued Adam. I doubt that the kid would have lived through this if Matt hadn't been so brave."

Just then they were at the shore. Mike jumped out and pulled the boat up. As Brandon stepped out they heard an outboard coming from the bay. The sheriff's boat was coming toward them.

The salvage boat was already anchored just a few feet from shore and the two salvage men and Todd were working on the Beaver. Mike and Brandon waited for the sheriff and the two deputies as they nudged their boat onto the shore. "So, you've got some problems with Carl and Ed again?" one of the deputies asked.

"Well, we're not the ones who had trouble," Mike said. "My son and Adam were here unloading the Beaver so we can tow it in, and apparently, they were waiting for them. They kidnapped Adam and beat him up severely. Matt followed them and rescued Adam after it got dark, and he took their boat. We were just about frantic wondering where they were. But we decided it would be better to wait for morning to look for them, and then they showed up back here. We flew Adam to the hospital at Nestor Falls. Matt stayed there with him."

"So did he say anything about where they had taken the boy?"

"Matt said he was at a little cabin due east of here about four miles. He said it was a real small island… just a big rock."

One of the deputies turned to the other. "Must be at Robinson's Rock," he said.

The other nodded. "Those trapper's cabins are all over the lake. In the old days any trapper who needed shelter could use them. There are still a few left, and I know, for sure, that Robinson's Rock still has one on it. I know right where it is. We'll see if they're still there."

"Matt stole their boat and tied it to an island just east of here, so watch for it," Mike said.

"Clever boy. That was a good idea to take their boat. I hope they tried to swim for it, and all we have to do is wait for their worthless carcasses to float up," the deputy said.

With that, they started the motor, backed the boat away from the shore and headed down the channel to the east. Brandon and Mike walked up the trail to the plane. They arrived just as the salvagers and Todd finished attaching the cables to the struts. "Well, the pontoons are all back on. Now we're ready to see if we can pull this old girl off this rock," Todd said. "We heard a boat. Was it the sheriff?"

"Yeah, and he knows right were to look for Carl and Ed."

"Good," Todd said. "I hope they resist arrest and they have to shoot the bastards."

The salvage men and Brandon drug the cable through the water with the small boat to their big boat. They attached the cable to cleats on the transom and started the twin hundred horse motors. "Stand back," one of the men said. "She's comin right through where you're standing."

Mike, Todd and Brandon moved aside. The boat's propellers churned up the water, and at first they didn't move. But, then slowly they started to move out into the lake, and the plane came sliding backward through the willows. It was soon sitting on the lake bobbing in the breeze.

"See?" Brandon said grinning. "They slide real easy over willows."

His dad smiled. "You guys were just full of dumb luck to find a place that wasn't all trees and rocks."

"Sometimes luck is better than sense," Brandon said.

The salvage men pulled up the excess cable and reattached the Beaver to their boat. They waved to the three on the shore. "See you in Nestor Falls," one of them yelled.

Mike, Todd and Brandon waved, climbed aboard the small boat and headed toward the Otter. They maneuvered the boat between the pontoons and secured it for the flight home. Brandon gazed toward the island as they taxied out into the lake for take off. "I can't say I'll miss this place, but we did have quite an adventure here," he said.

Chapter 58

Matt was just finishing his pie when Sally's beeper sounded. He stopped in mid-bite and waited while she looked at it. She smiled. "It says A-O-K."

Matt's heart leapt. "Does that mean he's alright?"

"Well, it means he's out of surgery, and that's a good thing. He wasn't in there very long, so they must've patched him up without too much trouble."

"Can we go see him?" Matt asked.

"He'll be sleeping, so there's no hurry. Finish your pie. Then we'll see how he's doing."

They rode the elevator back up to Sally's floor. Just as they came off the elevator, two surgical nurses pushed a gurney past with Adam lying on it. Matt hurried to catch up to them and walked alongside looking at Adam. He didn't look very good. "Is he gonna be okay?" he asked one of the nurses.

"He did real well in surgery. He's a strong young boy. He's going to be just fine," she said smiling at Matt. "He's banged up pretty bad, but it's nothing that time and lots of care won't heal."

Matt could hardly contain himself. He was so relieved.

They turned into a room and he stood by while Sally helped them move Adam to a bed and situate his IV's and the machines that monitored his condition. He had several tubes and wires stuck all over him. He looked like a bionic man. "Why does he have all those tubes and stuff?" Matt asked Sally.

"They're all there to help him, honey. Some are IV's that are giving him his breakfast, and others have pain medication, and one is a drain from the incision in his back where they fixed his lung. And one is a catheter."

Matt's eyes got big.

"You mean… they got a tube in…"

Sally nodded. Matt grimaced and Sally laughed. "It's not for very long – just till he gets a little stronger."

The two nurses left and Sally finished up with Adam. "Well, he's going to sleep for a while, so you should get some rest, too."

"I don't have anyplace to go. My dad left me here with Adam, and they won't be back here until they get the plane that Brandon and I crashed off the island."

"Well, I'll have the janitor bring in a nice chair and some magazines for you. We have sodas at the nurse's station and..." she said in a conspiratorial whisper, "we keep the donuts and cookies hidden. Just ask."

Sally left the room. Standing next to Adam's bed, Matt looked down at him. He was very pale and the entire left side of his face was a large black and purple bruise. Wearing only a hospital gown, Matt could see both arms were badly scraped and bruised. His legs were all banged up with black and blue marks and his feet, scraped and cut, as if he had been drug barefoot across rocks. Matt carefully brushed the hair from Adam's forehead. He smiled sadly at his friend. "You're a tough little Indian," he said. He carefully pulled a light blanket over Adam's lower half and then sat down on a chair next to the bed.

A little while later a janitor wheeled in a large reclining chair and set it next to Adam's bed. He returned with a box full of magazines and comic books. "Sally said to come and get some cookies and a pop if you want."

Matt walked down the hall to the nurse's station. Sally was waiting for him. "Here," she said handing Matt a plate full of cookies and a can of soda. "This will hold you over for a while."

"Thanks, Sally," Matt said.

Sally hugged him. "You go be with your friend. I'll check on you a little later. And don't you worry. Adam is going to be okay. We'll see to that."

He strolled back to the room, sat in the recliner, ate a few cookies, popped open the soda can and took a drink. He set the can down, laid his head back, pushed the chair to a reclining position, and a minute later, he was sound asleep.

Chapter 59

Matt heard voices and opened his eyes. A doctor was examining Adam and checking the machines hooked up to him. "Let's take a look at the drain and incision," he said to Sally.

"How's Adam doing?" Matt asked.

"Oh! Did we wake you? Sorry, Matt," Sally said. "He's doing just fine. Why don't you ask him yourself?"

Matt jumped up and stepped to the bed. Adam's right eye was open, and he smiled the best he could.

"Adam! Oh, man, am I glad to see you awake!"

Adam lifted his right hand and Matt clasped it in his. He couldn't talk with the tube in his throat, but Sally handed him a tablet and pencil. He wrote, "Thanks for saving me."

"Don't say that," Matt said grinning. "I just gave you a boat ride."

"We're going to remove his gown to check his drain," the doctor said. "Would you step out for a minute?"

"I'm staying with him until he is ready to come home," Matt said matter-of-factly.

The doctor shrugged. "That okay with you Adam?"

Adam faintly nodded. "I'm not shy," he wrote.

They removed the gown and Matt's jaw dropped open. Adam was one huge bruise from head to toe. The doctor carefully turned Adam to his side and checked the surgery incision and the drain in his back. Adam groaned a little when he was moved. A long cut just under his shoulder blade curved down to his side. It was held together with nine staples and covered with what looked like scotch tape. "Looks real good," the doctor said. "No seepage and no sign of infection." He laid Adam back down and continued the examination, top to bottom, pushing here and there and asking Adam to comment. "How's this?"

Adam grimaced.

"Here?"

He nodded yes.

"Well, you're about seventy percent bruises. They did a pretty good job on you. What did you do to them to deserve this?"

"I was their nephew," he wrote.

The doctor just shook his head.

"What did you do in his back?" Matt asked.

"One of his ribs was broken off and it had punctured his lung," the doctor explained. "We opened him up and sewed the hole in his lung shut."

"You stapled him?"

"Yeah. It's the newest way of doing it. It's lots faster and they come out much easier than stitches. He's got stitches inside holding his muscles together, but we just staple the outside."

"Cool," Matt said.

The doctor smiled. "Anything else you'd like to know?"

Matt thought for a minute. "No, I guess that's about it. If I think of anything else, I'll ask Sally."

The doctor and Sally broke out laughing. "Adam? I think you've got a guardian angel, here, looking out for you. I wouldn't worry about a thing."

They put a fresh gown on Adam, pulled the sheet up over him, and the doctor left. Sally checked the IVs. "Are you warm enough, Adam?" Sally asked. He nodded yes.

Adam wrote on the tablet: "I'm thirsty."

"I'll get a cup of ice chips," Sally said. "Matt, would you like to give them to him a few at a time?"

"Sure."

"Just take it slow. With that tube in his throat he can't swallow much at a time."

Sally returned in a minute with a cup of shaved ice and a plastic spoon. "Now remember, just a few at a time," she said. Then she turned a knob on a machine. "I'm turning down the oxygen in your throat tube, Adam. If it gets hard to breathe, let Matt know."

Adam nodded.

"If we can turn it down a little at a time for the next hour or so, and you can tolerate it, we can take that tube out of your throat."

Adam picked up the tablet and wrote: "GOOD!"

Sally laughed and walked from the room. Matt put a few ice chips between Adam's lips. He sucked them into his mouth. His expression turned to one of satisfaction. He smiled. "Yum." he wrote on the tablet.

Matt fed him the rest of the ice chips during the next hour. Sally came back in to reduce the oxygen flow again. "How's that? Are you having any trouble breathing?"

Adam shook his head no.

"Well, then, I think we can remove that tube," she said. She pulled the tape off the tube and then glanced at Matt. "You want to watch?"

Matt shook his head and walked away

"Breathe in and then let it out," Sally said, and when he did, she pulled the tube from his throat. Adam gagged a little and his eyes watered, but he smiled once the sensation of the tube coming up his throat was past. "Wow, that feels a lot better," he said hoarsely.

"Matt? It's all done," Sally said loudly.

Matt came back in the room and stood next to the bed. "Can you talk now?"

"Yeah, but my voice is kinda rusty."

"It'll be like that for a while," Sally said. "Do you feel like eating something?"

"Yeah. I'm starving."

"I'll bring up some *Jello*. You can try that first, and then we'll see about something a little more solid."

"I'm ready to try it," Adam said. "I've been looking at those cookies Matt is hoarding. They're making me hungry."

Sally laughed. "A typical boy. Food is their number one goal in life."

"Can I give him a cookie?" Matt asked.

"Wait till I leave. I'll bring you some milk to go with them, but don't tell the doctor I said that. Just tiny bites at first – okay?"

When Sally was gone Matt broke off a small piece of cookie and put it between Adam's lips. He pulled the cookie into his mouth and chewed. A smile spread across his face. "Yum! Got more?" Matt laughed out loud for the first time in a long while. He broke off another piece of cookie.

Sally came back with two glasses of milk, two bent straws, and Adam's *Jello.* "You can push that button if you need me, but I think you guys will be just fine for now," she said tousling Matt's hair. She walked out of the room.

"She's a nice lady," Matt said.

"So," Adam said. "How did you find me yesterday?"

Matt related the story of seeing Adam lying in the bottom of Carl and Ed's boat, and how he snuck up and locked them in the cabin, and about getting Adam away, and stealing Carl and Ed's boat. "I had to wait for you to wake up to tell me where to go."

"Really? I don't remember that. I told you where to go?"

Matt laughed. "We must have got lucky. You didn't even know I was there, or where to go, but you told me the right way."

After they had talked for an hour, Matt could tell that Adam was getting tired. "I think we should rest for a while. I've got a big comfortable chair here, and you look like you need a nap."

"Yeah. That's a good idea," Adam said. "But Matt, one more thing." Adam reached up and took Matt's hand. "Thanks for saving me."

Matt nodded and squeezed Adam's hand. "No problem, bro."

Chapter 60

"He looks like he's pretty comfortable." Matt's mind stirred and he realized someone was next to his recliner. He opened his eyes to see Brandon standing over him, smiling. "Hey, Matty. Tired?"

"Jeez! I was, but I'm good now. How long you been here?"

"We got to Nestor Falls about an hour ago. Dad and I and your dad and Kirby flew down in the Otter. They're downstairs talking to the doctor. Kirby's at the floatplane office."

"So, how'd everything go out at the island?"

"We got the Beaver off the island and the salvage boat is towing her in."

Matt noticed Adam awake and listening to the conversation. "How long you been awake?" he asked.

"Not long. I heard Brandon come in. I smelled food."

Brandon laughed and held up a bag of burgers and fries from a local fast food joint. "I figured you guys would be hungry. Is it okay to have food like this, Adam?"

Adam nodded his head and then whispered, "Close the door, just in case."

The three of them waded into the bag of food. It didn't take long for all of it to disappear. Adam had to eat carefully because of several IV lines in the back of his hands and one in his arm just below his elbow. Matt gathered up all the papers and tossed them in the trash can just as Sally came through the door. "Do I smell fast food?"

They all tried to appear as innocent as possible. Sally smiled. "I'm not angry that you had it, but you could have saved me a few fries."

"Sally," Matt said quickly to change the subject. "This is my friend, Brandon. He's the guy who I crashed the plane with."

Sally shook hands with Brandon. "You and your friends, here, have sure had your share of adventure this spring, haven't you?" She looked down at Brandon's cast. "Looks like you had some bad luck, too. Did young Doctor Matt take care of you, too?"

"As a matter of fact, he did take care of me when I was hurt in the crash, and now he's rescued Adam. He must be working on some kind of hero award."

They all had a good laugh, and then Sally took Adam's temperature and blood pressure, and checked the drain in his back. "You're coming along just fine, Adam. No fever, your pressure is real good and your drain is slowing down. That means you're not bleeding inside, so I think the doctor will be real pleased with your progress. It sounds like your voice is getting stronger, too."

"How long will he have to be here?" Brandon asked.

"Probably a few more days – three or four, I'd think. We want to be sure he's not getting any infections, and that his plumbing is working." She checked the urine bag at the side of the bed and it was dripping steadily. "This looks good. I think a few more days will do it. But, of course, then he'll have to take it easy for several weeks."

"We'll get him back to the lodge," Todd said as he walked through the door. "A couple of weeks of home cooking and sunshine will fix him right up." Mike was right there, too, and they both patted Adam on the shoulders. "You're looking a little better than the last time I saw you," Mike said. He carefully ruffled Adam's hair.

"Thanks for taking such good care of me," Adam said. "I'm sorry to be so much trouble."

"That's silly. You're family now. It's not any trouble."

They chatted a while and then it was time to head back to Clearwater Bay.

"Dad, I'm going to stay with Adam," Matt said.

"Are you sure it's okay?" Mike asked.

Sally nodded. "We'll get him a cot… and my son is about his size. I'll bring him some clean clothes. He can stay right here – we're getting kind of fond of him. We'll take good care of him for a few days."

"Well, okay. Let us know when Adam can come home. We'll come to pick them up."

"Call the airport," Todd said, handing Matt a business card with the number. "They'll radio us and we'll come as soon as Adam is released."

"See you in a few days," Brandon said. He gripped Matt's shoulder. "Get well, Adam," and with that said, Todd, Mike and

Brandon left the room.

"Did you hear that, Matt? Adam asked.

"Hear what?"

"Let us know when Adam can come *HOME!*"

Matt beamed.

Chapter 61

Over the next few days machines and IVs disappeared regularly. The doctor removed the drain from Adam's back and then the pain medicine IV was removed. The next day the bag of saline was gone, and then Sally came in with a grin on her face. "How would you like to get that tube out of you?" she asked.

Matt left the room when she removed the catheter. It wasn't because he was embarrassed to see Adam without clothes, he just wasn't sure he wanted to see how they took the catheter out. When he returned, Adam looked a little embarrassed. "How was it?" Matt asked.

"It didn't hurt, but it was kinda embarrassing having Sally… you know… there."

Matt giggled when he thought of Sally removing the catheter. "She's probably done it a million times. I'm sure she didn't even think about it."

"Yeah, I know, but…"

Just then Adam's doctor came in and greeted the boys. "Well, I've called your parents and they're going to be here in a couple of hours to pick you up. You're going home, Adam."

"No kidding? That's great! Thanks, doc."

"I'm glad we could help you. Those ribs will be sore for a long time, so you take it easy for a while. No football or horsing around," he said looking at Matt. Matt grinned.

Adam didn't have anything to take with him. His clothes were all cut up, so Sally brought a set of clothes in for him to wear home. "Just drop them off sometime when you're in town," she said.

Matt helped Adam dress, and put on his socks and shoes. He then helped him get into a wheelchair, and he pushed him out of the room. On the way to the front lobby, Adam and Matt stopped to say goodbye to Sally and the other nurses they had made friends with over the past few days. All of the ladies had to hug and kiss them good-bye. "You two stay out of trouble for the rest of the summer," Sally said as she hugged Adam. "I don't want to see you here again, at least not as patients."

Matt hugged her hard. "Thanks Sally. You're the best."

"Now go. Get out of here and stay out of trouble." Sally turned and left quickly, trying to keep her tears from showing.

The hospital provided a wheelchair for Adam to take with him until his feet and legs healed. He still had trouble walking very far, but he was moving better each day. He and Matt had taken little walks around the halls, stopping to let Adam rest every so often. The parents were just coming in the front door when they rolled out of the elevator. Mike and Todd and the two moms hovered over Adam and acted like he would break if he were jostled a bit. "Hey, it's okay," he said. "I'm not sick anymore. I'm fine."

"Take the extra pity while you can get it, Adam," Mike said. "Pretty soon you'll be all healed up and then you'll have to work like everyone else."

Adam climbed slowly into the Otter and they belted him in the seat opposite Matt. After an uneventful flight they landed at Clearwater Bay. Brandon sat on a chair near the dock with a cane next to him. Kirby waited at the end of the dock, and when he saw Adam, he jumped up and down and barked unceasingly until the boy was in his wheelchair on the dock. Kirby's front feet were in Adam's lap, and he vigorously licked his face. "I think Kirby missed me," Adam said laughing at the dog's antics.

They rolled him up to the main lodge. Brandon hobbled along with his cane. He had been taking it easy on his broken ankle, having done too much walking on it at first and making it sore. It was healing much better now that he had used it less for a few days.

Adam slowly walked up the steps into the lodge. Matt pulled the wheel chair up onto the porch, and Adam sat in it again. There were several guest fishermen at the lodge. Everyone was asking questions about the boys' adventure. Matt relayed all the stories about the plane crash, the stolen truck, and Adam's kidnapping. The guests had a good, entertaining evening with all the stories.

After dinner Matt pushed Adam's wheelchair down the hill to their cabin near the water. Brandon limped along with his cane. "Let's sit on the porch for a few minutes," Adam said.

Matt parked Adam out on the porch. He and Brandon sat next to him in deck chairs. "Well, Adam. It's good to see you home again," Brandon said.

"We only had one night together before you guys got into trouble... been kind of lonely here all alone with just Kirby for company. The dog lifted his head, sighed, and lay back on his paws again.

"Believe me, Brandon. I'd have much rather been here than with Carl and Ed."

"Oh! I bet everyone forgot to tell you! They found them in the cabin on Robinson Rock."

"Really?" Matt said. "They were still in there?"

Brandon laughed. "The sheriff said they had beaten everything to pieces trying to break the door open. There aren't any windows in that shack, so they hammered on the door until they were worn out... and sick, too. It seems that someone spilled gas all over the cabin and the smell was just about enough to make them puke. I think they were glad to be arrested, just to get out of that cabin."

Adam stared at Matt. "Gas?"

"Don't ask," Matt said.

"Where are they now?" Adam asked with a touch of fear in his voice.

"They're safely locked up in the Baudette jail."

Adam looked pleased. "I hope they stay there for a long time."

"Oh, don't worry about that. The sheriff said that now they have cause to charge them with kidnapping, unlawful imprisonment, assault on a minor and unlawful flight. Add those charges to the burglary and poaching, plus fraud for stealing all your money and they'll be looking at the inside of a cell for longer than they have left in this world."

"Couldn't happen to two nicer guys, too," Matt said.

"Well, time for bed. It's been a big day."

Matt rolled Adam into the cabin and helped him get undressed and into bed. When they were all in their beds and the light turned out, Kirby's toenails clicked across the wooden floor, and then the mattress creaked when he jumped up and lay down next to Adam.

Kirby snuggled up next to Adam, rested his head on the boy's shoulder and gave a big sigh. "Home sweet home," Adam said.

Chapter 62

When the boys rose the next morning, they all showered and got ready for breakfast. Adam was able to help himself, but he still needed a little assistance with his shoes and socks. Matt helped him and then he pushed him across the yard to the lodge where they joined their parents and the breakfast guests. Everyone was happy to see Matt and Adam again, and they all had a grand time telling tall tales. When they finished, Matt said he was going down to help the fishermen off in their boats, which was his job. Brandon and Mike were going to fly to Nestor Falls and pick up the Beaver, and Todd was going to fix some plumbing in one of the cabins.

"So what can I do to make myself useful?" Adam asked.

"You don't need to work your first day home, Adam," Carol said.

"I'd like to help. Don't you have any sit-down jobs in the kitchen?"

Sandy got behind his chair and pushed him out of the dining room toward the kitchen. "I think this chair will fit just right under the dish washing sink."

Adam grinned. He was soon wearing a white rubber apron and up to his elbows in soapy water washing the breakfast dishes. After the dishes were finished, Sandy brought in a big bag of potatoes and dumped them in the sink. Adam peeled twenty pounds of potatoes for the evening meal. They were having roast moose with mashed potatoes and gravy. At lunch time a few of the guests came in for a sandwich buffet, and then during the afternoon he and the two women made cookies and pies for supper, and sack lunches for the next day.

While Adam sat at the counter dropping cookie dough onto the pan, Sandy put her arm around his shoulder. "Matt wasn't kidding. You *are* good help in the kitchen."

"Thanks, ma'am."

"You can call me Ma Sandy, and call her Ma Carol. How about that?" Sandy gave him a kiss on the cheek.

Adam smiled. "That's great, Ma Sandy."

All repairs on The Beaver were completed. It was ready to fly. Brandon climbed into the cockpit, started the motor, and let it warm up. His dad radioed for him to follow, and then taxied down the lake. Brandon waited until his dad was in the air and then he taxied down into position. Mike circled the bay until Brandon was air born, and then they flew side by side up the lake toward the lodge. Brandon circled the bay while his dad landed the Otter. Then Brandon set the Beaver on the lake like a butterfly landing on a rose. He taxied to the second dock where Matt was waiting to tie him up. "Nice landing, Brand. I think it's easier when there aren't any rocks to aim for."

Brandon laughed. "And when I can see where I'm going, too. What's Adam been up to all day?"

"He's up in the kitchen cooking up a storm… been there all day. I went up for lunch and he was flour head to toe."

Brandon grinned. "I'll bet we have a good supper tonight."

He was right. The dinner was spectacular. Adam had offered some suggestions on seasoning the moose roasts, and the women had let him take over. "Carol! This is outstanding," one of the guests said as he took a second helping of moose and potatoes.

"Adam is responsible for that," Carol said. "He did the moose and made the gravy."

The guest raised his glass. "To the chef!" he said, and everyone raised their glasses in a toast to Adam.

Adam blushed to a bright red.

Later, Adam and Matt were washing dishes wile Brandon wiped. They chatted about their day and how nice it was to get back to normal again. "I haven't had a normal family for such a long time," Adam said. "I forgot what it was like to just be normal people."

"Well, I don't know how normal we are," Matt said. "But I guess it's a mite bit better than two drunken uncles."

"Just a mite bit," Adam chuckled.

Chapter 63

The rest of the week passed quickly and the boys all had their jobs to keep them busy. But every evening they found time to visit with the guests and the parents, or just sit in their little cottage and enjoy each other's company.

Adam's feet and legs had healed enough that he could walk back and forth from the cabin. When he worked in the kitchen he sat on a tall stool to keep from standing too long.

Departing guests all stopped at the lodge to say good-bye, and they always made a special point to see Adam. Each of them slipped him a tip for his fine cooking services. Matt got tips, too, from the fishermen for having clean boats ready for them every day. And Brandon did quite well with tips, flying guests to the outpost camps in the Beaver.

Everyone pitched in on Saturday afternoons, cleaning the cabins and getting things ready for the new guests that would arrive on Sunday. Brandon and his dad flew both planes to Nestor Falls and returned with loads of fresh faces and lots of fishing gear and luggage. Now they had a new bunch of people to take care of for the next week.

Everything was going along great. Brandon's foot had healed well enough that he seldom used the cane, and he had an appointment in Nestor Falls on the coming Wednesday to get the cast removed. Adam had scheduled a check-up for the same day so they didn't have to make two trips.

Adam's bruises had turned from black and purple to dark brown with yellow edges. Some were nearly gone, and the one on the left side of his face was almost faded away. The swelling had gone down in his eye, and now he had two good eyes.

Matt was cleaning up one of the boats when he heard someone walking down the dock. He looked up and his mouth dropped open. Adam came walking across the planks with a huge grin on his face.

"Holy shit! What happened to all your hair?" Matt asked.

Adam grinned sheepishly. "I thought I'd like to look like just a normal kid, and that long hair was kind of out of style anyway."

His hair was short like Matt and Brandon's, and it was even spiked up on top like theirs.

"Ma Sandy cut it."

Matt smiled and a chill tingled the middle of his back at the same time. With his new haircut, Adam looked so much like his brother, Mark. It was almost spooky.

"What's wrong? Don't you like it?" Adam asked.

"Yeah, it's cool. It's just that… you look so much like Mark now."

"Your mom had the same look on her face when she saw it," Adam said.

Just then Brandon came walking down the dock and stopped dead in his tracks when he saw Adam's new haircut.

"Looks like Mark, doesn't he?" Matt said.

"Jeez! I thought I was seeing things," Brandon said. He walked up for a closer look. "I like it. Makes you look real cool. The chicks will dig you," he said. "Well? You ready to go and let the docs check you over?"

"Yeah, I guess so. You coming, Matt?"

"No. You guys go. I've got a lot of stuff to do here. Say hi to Sally for me if you see her."

"Oh! That reminds me," Adam said. "I have those clothes she loaned us in the cabin. Just a second, Brandon. I'll run and get them." He turned and hurried off the dock toward their cabin.

"Wow!" Brandon said to Matt. "I almost fell off the dock when I saw him with his new haircut."

"Me too," Matt said. "He even acts like Mark, too. I mean the way he grins and stuff? Kind of like getting him back, isn't it?"

"Maybe crashing into that island was all meant to be," Brandon said. Just then Adam came walking down the dock carrying the sack of borrowed clothes.

"All ready."

Brandon and Adam headed off to the Beaver. Matt waited until the motor was running, untied the ropes, and pushed them off. He waved as they taxied out into the lake.

Chapter 64

When Brandon had the Beaver in the air and cruising, he turned to Adam. "Feel like flying it for a bit?"

"Do you think I can do it?"

"Sure. You know where to put your feet and hands. Get a feel for it and I'll give you control."

Adam put his feet on the pedals and took hold of the yoke.

"You have control," Brandon said. He took his hands off the yoke.

Adam felt the plane respond to his slightest movement and in a short time he started to relax. He enjoyed the idea of flying the big plane. "If you'd asked me three weeks ago if I thought I'd ever fly a plane, I would have told you that I doubted I'd ever see the inside of a plane, let alone, fly one," he said.

"Those days are over, Adam. Better days ahead."

They approached Nestor Falls. "Want to try a landing?"

"Oh, I don't think I should, Brandon."

"Matty did the first time I let him fly."

"Well, you'll be ready to take over if I screw up, won't you?"

"Don't worry. One crash landing is enough for me."

Brandon talked him through the descent procedure. As they neared the water Brandon said: "Now give it a little more flaps." Adam moved the flap lever up one more notch.

"Now ease her down, a little at a time. You have a lot of water ahead... no worry about running out of landing strip."

Adam moved the yoke forward a bit. He could feel the pontoons clipping the tops of the waves. "Just keep the nose up," Brandon instructed. "You don't want to spear a pontoon into the water." The plane settled a little lower, and the pontoons skimmed along the surface. "Now, cut your power," Brandon said. Adam cut back on the throttle and the plane settled down onto the lake.

"There. You've made your first water landing," Brandon said with a big, congratulatory smile.

Adam couldn't speak; he was too full of emotion.

"Now, pull that water rudder lever. That'll drop the rudder at the tail into the water. Using the rudder, we can steer easier."

Adam did as instructed. Just a few minutes later, they nudged the plane up against the tires hung over the side of the dock. Brandon jumped out onto the pontoon and tied up the plane. "Cut the engine, Adam."

Adam climbed down onto the dock. "That was fantastic, Brandon! Thanks a lot."

The two friends walked to the office and borrowed the airport manager's car to drive into town to the hospital.

They each saw their doctors, and both were pronounced fit. Adam took the elevator to the fifth floor and found Sally at a computer sorting through some records. "Hey, remember me?" he said.

Sally looked up and broke into a smile. "Adam! My goodness you're looking so good." She jumped up, came around the counter, and hugged him so hard it made his ribs ache a bit, but he didn't say a word. "A new haircut, too! My, you look handsome," she said. "Girls! Look who's here. Adam is back for a visit."

All of the nurses came to say hi and to give their approval of his new look. "Too bad I'm not about twenty years younger," one of them said. "I'd be takin' you into the break room, son!" All of the nurses laughed. Adam turned six shades of red. He handed the paper bag of borrowed clothes to Sally with his thanks.

He passed on Matt's greetings, and then he said good-bye. He promised to stop and see them the next time he came to town.

Brandon was waiting for him in the lobby. "How did it go?"

"Doc says I'm good to go. I don't have to come back unless something starts to bother me. How about you?"

Brandon held up his foot, a shoe replacing the missing cast. "All better. Looks like we're not patients anymore."

They went back to the airport, thanked their friend for the use of the car, and boarded the plane.

"Well," Brandon said as they taxied out onto the bay. "You might as well learn to take off now, too."

Adam got ready. He glanced at Brandon with a big grin. "Just give me the okay and we're off."

Brandon gave him instructions and they were soon soaring high above the lake and islands, heading for home.

Chapter 65

The weeks passed, and both Adam and Brandon were completely healed. Brandon's ankle was back to normal. All the black and blue had faded, and he walked on it easily without any pain. All but the most serious of Adam's bruises were completely gone.

They had settled into a normal routine and their lives at Clearwater Bay were fantastic. Adam had a wonderful time working in the kitchen with Ma Carol and Ma Sandy. Matt and Kirby charmed all the guests and took special care to have their boats ready just as they wanted them.

Brandon helped wherever he was needed, and did most of the flying between Nestor Falls and the lodge. He often took the Otter on weekends to pick up the new guests, who were usually a bit surprised to find their pilot an eighteen year old kid. During the week, he used the Beaver to haul small groups of fishermen to the outpost camps on six small, remote lakes.

Mike and Todd spent most of their time helping guests, and occasionally accompanied them on the lake, giving pointers to increase their fishing success. Whenever time allowed, they made repairs to the cabins and machinery that kept the place running. All in all, it was a great life, and all of them enjoyed it very much.

One evening after the guests had gone to their cabins, the two families were cleaning the dining room when Mike took Adam aside. "I got a radio call from the sheriff at Baudette today," he said. "Carl and Ed's trial will start next Tuesday."

"Do I have to testify?"

"Yes. You're the star witness. They want Matt to testify, too. He wants to be sure both of you will be there."

"How about Brandon? Doesn't he have to say anything?"

"He was with us when they kidnapped you. With you and Matt telling the story of them shooting at you, he thought that would be enough."

A chill tingled Adam's spine. "If I have to, I'll go," he said, and then, as if he needed some reassurance he added: "There's no chance they'll get out of this, is there? I mean... they can't be found not guilty and get turned loose?"

"The sheriff says the trial will go well. They have all the stolen goods; they have the statements that we all gave. The pictures they took of you in the hospital will convict them for sure. But he still wants you there so the jury will put a face on the victim."

Adam nodded. "Will you come with me?"

"Of course. Carol and I will be there with you."

The following Tuesday, Adam, Mike, Carol and Matt boarded the Beaver and took off for Nestor Falls. When they arrived, they rented a car and reached Baudette about an hour before the trial was to begin. They went to the District Attorney's office. Mr. Kress, the prosecutor met them. "Adam, Matt, when I call you to the witness stand, I want you to just tell us everything in your own words. Don't be afraid. Carl and Ed aren't going to hurt you ever again," he said looking at Adam. "I will see to that."

Adam and Matt sat on a bench outside and talked about small stuff, trying to take their minds off the ensuing trial. "Don't worry," Matt said as they were called inside. "You'll do good." He slapped Adam on the back.

As they walked into the courtroom, Adam felt like he had a stone in his stomach. He saw the back of his uncles' heads. They sat at a table next to a man he figured was their lawyer. As he took his seat, Ed turned and looked at him. He turned away, and then quickly turned back, suddenly recognizing Adam's different appearance.

Adam swallowed hard, and he didn't look away from his uncle. He wasn't going to give him the satisfaction of knowing he was scared. Then Ed smiled just a little, and nodded to Adam.

The court came to order and both the lawyers gave their opening statements. Matt was the first witness called. He approached the front of the courtroom, raised his right hand, swore to tell the truth, and then sat in the witness chair.

"How old are you Mathew?" the DA asked.

"I'm thirteen, sir. But only my mom calls me Mathew. Everybody else calls me Matt."

"Duly noted, Matt," the DA grinned and said. "Tell us how it is that you know the defendants?" He pointed to Carl and Ed.

"I first saw them near the island where my friend, Brandon,

and I had crash landed our plane. I was hunting, trying to catch a spruce grouse, and I heard them shooting. I snuck up to the edge of the island and I saw them shoot a moose that was swimming across the channel toward me."

"You crash landed a plane? How did that happen?"

Matt told the story of how he and Brandon had been caught in the storm, and how they were awaiting rescue from the island.

"What did they do when they shot the moose?"

"They drove their boat to where it went under the water. Then they made Adam dive into the water and tie a rope to the moose so they could pull it up to the shore."

"Will you please point out Adam?"

Matt pointed to Adam sitting in the gallery. "That's him. He's their nephew."

"Then what happened?"

"Adam swam to shore and climbed out of the water close to where I was hiding, but I didn't know he was Adam then. I just knew he was a kid with the poachers. I think he heard me telling Kirby to be quiet."

"And who is Kirby?"

"Oh, he's my dog. He was with me."

"Okay. Then what happened?"

"Well, Adam went back to the boat to get his clothes. He told them he had to poop and he came over by me again."

The courtroom broke out in giggles when Matt described Adam's ruse for getting a chance to meet him. Adam's face turned bright red.

The DA grinned. "Okay. So Adam came over to the woods to make a call to nature, and you talked?"

"Yeah. I told him we were crashed on the other side of the island, and he told me to be quiet, not to let the other guys hear me, and he would come back soon. I thought he was coming back with the boat to rescue us."

"I see. Then what happened?"

"They cut up the moose and they all left. I went back to the plane and told Brandon. We were pretty excited that maybe we would be rescued."

“The plane was damaged so it wouldn’t fly?”

“Yeah. The prop was smashed and the battery was toast. We were stuck there.”

“So then what happened?”

“The next day I was out with Kirby trying to find a grouse again. Adam met me in the woods. I was real glad ‘cause I thought he had a boat to take us out of there. But he had sent the boat out into the lake to fool his uncles into thinking he was drowned. He figured that if they thought he was dead, they’d just forget about him. He thought we had a way off the island, or a radio. He thought we were rescuing him, and we thought he was rescuing us.”

The DA smiled. “So then what happened?”

“Well, I took Adam to meet Brandon. We figured out a way to make a raft with the pontoons on the plane. Adam was sure his uncles would come looking for him, so we thought we’d lure them to the plane with a smoky signal fire, and while they were there stealing all our stuff from the plane, we’d take the raft to their cabin and take their pickup to find the sheriff in Baudette.”

“And is that what happened?”

“Yeah. The plan worked out pretty good, except that they caught up to us just as we got to the cabin. We crashed into the dock and broke it. We got off the raft and ran for the truck, but Brandon had a broken foot, so he was getting behind. So Adam ran back to help him while I got in the truck and started it.”

“Did you know how to drive?”

“Well, kinda. I never drove before, but it’s sort of like the race car game at the arcade.”

Another chuckle ran through the courtroom.

“Then Carl and Ed caught up to Adam and Brandon. Ed grabbed Adam, and Adam gave Ed a good punch in the nose and got loose. Brandon got into the truck, and just as Carl went for Adam again, Kirby jumped out of the truck and took Carl to the ground. Adam made it to the truck and we hollered for Kirby. He jumped in and we spun out of there.”

The DA looked amused. “So you got away?”

“Well, we thought we were okay, but they came after us with their four-wheeler. Ed was on the back and he shot at us. Then

Adam told me to duck into a fire road up ahead, so we went real fast and got ahead of them so they couldn't see us anymore. We backed into one of those roads and waited for them to go by. Then we pulled out. That four-wheeler made a lot of noise and they didn't hear us behind them. I bumped the back of it with the truck bumper. You should have seen Ed's face. I think he pooped himself."

The court broke out in laughter and even the judge was chuckling. He rapped his gavel and called for order, but with a grin on his face.

"Then Ed tried to get the gun around so he could shoot at us, but he bumped Carl in the head, and it went off. I suppose Carl has a deaf ear now, 'cause it went off right next to his right ear. When that happened, Carl swerved and almost tipped the four-wheeler over, but he managed to keep it on the road."

"Then I pushed them a little harder. Carl lost control and they went over a bank and down into a creek. It was really cool watching them fly through the air."

"And then you went to Baudette?"

"Yes, sir. We went to find the sheriff."

"And then your parents came and got you, and you went to your resort?"

"Yes, sir. Adam came with us. The sheriff contacted the welfare department in Rochester. They let Mom and Dad take custody of Adam for the summer, since he didn't have any other place to go, anyway."

"What happened next?"

"Well, the next day we flew the Otter down to get the Beaver off the island, so it could be towed in and repaired. Dad and Todd and Brandon went with the guys from the salvage boat to get the pontoons that were down at Carl and Ed's cabin. Adam and I were going to transfer the cargo that Carl and Ed hadn't taken from the Beaver into the Otter. Well, Kirby came up missing. We heard him barking so Adam went into the woods to find him, and a while later Kirby came back all upset and Adam was gone. I ran to the other side of the island and saw Carl and Ed taking him away in their boat. They had been there waiting for us to come back."

"Did Adam go with them willingly?"

"No. He was in the bottom of the boat… unconscious."

"And then?"

"I watched to see where they went, and then I got in our boat and snuck up on them after dark."

"What did you see there?"

Matt swallowed hard. He spoke softly and slowly. "I snuck up to the shack and found Adam on the ground next to a tree. He was covered with blood, and he was unconscious. His hands were tied with ropes behind his back. The dirty bastards had beat him till he was almost dead!" Matt's eye filled with tears.

The DA waited a few seconds. "Do you want to take a break?"

Matt shook his head no.

"What did you do then, Matt?"

"I untied Adam and carried him to the boat, and then I stole their boat so they couldn't get away. I went as far as I could go in the dark. Adam was hurt really bad and he was shivering, so Kirby and I laid next to him to keep him warm all night. I found Dad and Todd and Brandon in the morning, and we took him to the hospital."

"I have no further questions."

Carl and Ed's lawyer looked a little flummoxed. Apparently, he couldn't think of much to ask, so he just stood and said, "No questions, Your Honor."

"You may step down," the judge said smiling to Matt.

Matt walked past Carl and Ed and shot them a look that said: "Take that, you pukes!"

Chapter 66

When the DA called Adam to testify, his knees were shaking as he walked up to the witness chair. He raised a sweaty right hand and swore to tell the truth.

When he sat down, he glanced at Carl and saw murder on his face. "Don't look at him," the DA said quietly to Adam. "Just ignore him. Take a deep breath and don't be nervous."

Adam nodded and looked straight at the man. "How old are you, Adam?"

Adam looked questioningly for a second and then said, "What's the date today?"

"It's the twelfth."

"I'm fifteen today, sir."

There was a murmur in the courtroom. Several of the jurors smiled.

"Well, happy birthday."

"Thank you."

"So, how is it that you were living with the defendants?"

"They're my uncles. My mother was their sister. She and my dad were killed in a car crash a little over a year ago. The welfare people found Uncle Carl and Uncle Ed, and they took custody of me. We lived in Rochester, so I had never met them before."

"You had no other relatives?"

"No, sir. My dad was from Finland, no relatives here, and my mom's parents are dead. I had no one else."

"And the defendants agreed to take care of you?"

"Yes, sir. They agreed to sell my parent's house and belongings and put the money into a trust fund for my college education, and see to it that I went to school and had a place to live."

"And did they do that?"

"No, sir. They bought a new boat and motor, a four-wheeler and a snowmobile with the money. I don't know how much money there was, but they either spent the rest, or they have it hidden somewhere."

"But they did arrange for you to go to school?"

"No, sir. I haven't been to school for a year. I was supposed to be in ninth grade last year, but I never went."

"So, what did you do all that time?"

"Uncle Carl and Uncle Ed made me do all the work. I cooked, cleaned, washed the clothes and was pretty much a slave. If I didn't do something just right, they slapped me, so I tried to do things well… and tried to stay out of their way, especially when they were drunk."

"They beat you?"

"Yes, sir. Not every day… but a lot."

The DA turned and scowled at Carl and Ed. "So tell me about the burglaries."

"Well, once the lake was frozen, one of them drove the four-wheeler with a big sled behind it, and the other took the snowmobile. They went to cabins and lodges all over the lake and broke in and stole all the stuff they could sell."

"And you participated in this?"

"I didn't have much choice. If I said I didn't want to go, they beat me. And then I had to go anyway, so I just went along and helped, but I didn't want to."

"What did they do with all of this stolen property?"

"They have a big shed behind the house and it's full of stuff. About once a month, they'd take a load of it to town and meet Tiny. He's the guy that bought the stuff. I never saw him, but they talked about him and they probably didn't know I was listening. He's an auctioneer and he puts the stolen stuff in with regular stuff at an auction, and then pockets the extra money."

Just then an enormous man got up from the back of the courtroom and started for the door. The DA turned and motioned to the bailiff. The bailiff quickly met the man at the door, took him by the arm, and walked out with him. The DA winked at Adam. "That may be your Tiny," he said.

Adam was a little startled, but then he saw Carl's and Ed's expressions, and he knew the DA was right.

"So, tell us about the poaching?"

"Well, they just shot deer and moose whenever they needed some meat. They put out gill nets for fish whenever they wanted to. They didn't worry about licenses or seasons."

"And again? You participated?"

"I didn't have any choice. Help or get beaten."

"Can you tell us what happened on the day they kidnapped you from the island where you and Matt were unloading the plane?"

"Well, I don't remember too much, but I was trying to find Kirby. He was barking like crazy, and when I finally found him, he was tied to a small tree with a piece of rope. I couldn't figure out how he got tied up, so I started toward him. I walked past a big tree and the last thing I saw was Carl just before he punched me in the face. I remember them hitting me and kicking me, but by then, I was almost unconscious. I do remember them taking my shoes and socks so I couldn't run off. I don't remember Matt coming or the boat ride out of there, but Matt said I talked to him. The first real thing I remember afterward is waking up in the hospital with all sorts of tubes sticking out of me."

"But you have no doubt that it was Carl and Ed who did all this to you?"

"No, sir. It was them. Carl did most of it, I think."

"So, these men, your only blood relatives, took your inheritance, made you a slave and an accomplice to crime, and then nearly beat you to death?"

"Yes, sir. I guess so."

"No further questions."

Carl and Ed's lawyer had no questions, either.

"You may step down, son," the judge said.

Chapter 67

The DA called Adam's doctor to the stand. "Doctor, are you familiar with the last witness, Adam Happalti?"

"Yes. I treated him for severe beating injuries and performed the surgery to repair his punctured lung."

"And how do you know his injuries were caused by a beating?"

"I have photos, showing the bruising and footprints that were left by kicks to the back and stomach."

The DA asked for a slide projector to be set up. The doctor clicked the first slide. It showed Adam in the emergency room, his clothing cut off, his body covered with blood and bruises. Part of the image was blacked out to keep from showing Adam completely naked. "If you look here, you can clearly see a footprint on the side of the boy's chest. This kick was obviously made to break his ribs, which it did." The doctor clicked another slide and it showed more boot prints on Adam's back. They went through several more slides. The last one showed Adam in his hospital bed, with tubes connecting him to machines.

The lights were turned on again. Several of the women jurors had tears in their eyes. The men stared at Carl and Ed with anger and disgust.

"So, doctor. In your professional opinion, could Adam have survived if Matt had not rescued him? Could he have healed up from the beating on his own?"

"No. Adam would have died in twelve to twenty four hours had he not been brought into the emergency room. He was in shock. He had a punctured lung. Over seventy percent of his body was severely bruised. His blood pressure was dangerously low. He would not have survived."

"No further questions."

Carl an Ed's lawyer looked as if he were going to be sick. "No questions."

The judge recessed the court for lunch.

Mike and Carol took Matt and Adam to a cafe for a late lunch.

Adam suddenly realized he was famished. "My stomach was all knots before, but now it's empty as heck," he said.

"You did good up there, Adam," Matt said.

Adam grinned. "So did you, Matty. The jury liked you."

"If that doesn't convict them, there isn't any law," Mike said.

"Let's go home," Adam said after they had finished their lunch. "The sooner I'm away from those two, the better I'll feel."

They stopped at the DA's office first. "We'll be called back in this afternoon," he told them. "But only for the summaries. Then it goes to the jury. There's no need for you to stay."

"How do you think it will go?" Adam asked nervously. "They won't get off, will they?"

"They're going away for a long time, Adam. You'll never see them again."

When they were in the air, Mike let Adam fly the Beaver. "Brandon says you've been practicing with him," he said.

"Yeah, he let me do it a few times. I love flying. It's an amazing feeling to control such a huge piece of machinery."

They were approaching Clearwater Bay. Mike glanced over at Adam. "Want to land her?"

Adam nodded. The widest smile possible came on his face as he set the plane down on the lake like a feather falling from a passing duck.

He taxied to the dock. Matt jumped out and tied the ropes to the struts. Adam shut down the engine and sat back in the seat.

Mike put his arm over the boy's shoulder. "That was as perfect as they come, Adam. You've got the touch. I'm real proud of you."

Adam's eyes filled with tears. He threw his arms around Mike. "Thanks… thanks for everything."

Chapter 68

After the trial, everyone returned to a normal routine. A few days later Carol came to lunch with a big smile. "Well, I just got off the radio with the sheriff. The jury came in with a verdict this morning." Everyone stared expectantly. "They were found…"

"Come on, Ma! Quit fooling around," Matt said impatiently.

"Guilty, of course. Guilty on all counts." Everyone cheered and patted Adam on the back.

"So, how long are they going to be in jail?" he asked.

"They haven't set the sentence yet, but the sheriff expects that they will never get out. The kidnapping and assault charges will keep them in prison for the rest of their lives."

Finally, Adam felt safe from his uncles' terror.

"I think you guys should take a couple of days off and celebrate," Mike suggested.

"And do what?" Matt questioned.

"Why don't you take the Beaver into one of the outposts? Spend a day fishing. You guys have worked hard all summer. You've barely had any time for fishing."

"Yeah! That sounds like fun," Brandon said.

Carol and Sandy smiled conspiratorially. They went to the kitchen and came back with a birthday cake lit with fifteen candles. Everyone sang *Happy Birthday*. Adam blushed bright red.

"Sorry it's a little late," Carol said. "We didn't know about it until the trial."

"I forgot about it till then, too," Adam said smiling.

Brandon and Matt went to the kitchen and returned with an armful of presents. "Brandon did some shopping for us the last time he went to Nestor Falls," Mike said.

Adam's mouth dropped open. "You didn't have to do this," he said.

"Don't be stupid. Presents are good," Matt said handing him a long thin one.

Adam opened it and held up a brand new rod and reel for everyone to see. Among the others were a tackle box, lures, shirts, jeans, and new underwear.

"Model them!" Matt yelled. Adam was overwhelmed by all the attention as they all sat down to a great lunch.

The next day the three boys and Kirby boarded the Beaver and headed into one of the outpost camps. Adam did the flying. As they came in for a landing, Brandon told him to adjust the flaps.

"You know that lets us lose airspeed without stalling," Matt said from the back seat. Brandon grinned. Matt was now an instructor.

When the plane was secured, they loaded their fishing gear and lunch into one of the boats and took off to fish below the rapids of a small creek that ran into the lake. The fishing was great. They caught walleyes and northern pike, and they had a great time.

"You remember those guys who were in this camp last week?" Brandon asked.

"The two guys from Iowa?" Matt said.

"Yeah, those two. They stayed two nights. The first night, they cleaned their fish on the dock and left the heads and guts in a pail instead of dumping them out in the lake. Next morning the pail was gone. So the second day, they got rid of them like they should have done. That evening, just before they went to bed, they came down to the dock to look out over the lake. While they stood there, they felt the dock shaking. They turned around and saw a bear walking down the dock right toward them. Of course, they yelled, and the bear was so startled that it fell into the lake, scrambled up on the shore and ran off."

"Wow! A Grizzl bear?" Matt asked grinning.

"No, Matty. Just a black bear."

"S'pose he'll show up again?"

"Not unless he smells food," Brandon said. "So we're not going to leave any food out where he can smell it."

They spent the day fishing and eating tons of food that they had packed. Kirby loved the boat and spent the entire day looking over the side into the water. He went crazy every time one of them caught a fish, trying to catch it as it swam past the boat. That evening they ate their sandwiches and then sat on the dock, watching the stars. When it got too chilly, they went into the cabin and crawled into their sleeping bags. In a short time they were all asleep.

Matt woke up during the night and had to pee. He crawled out of his sleeping bag and tiptoed to the door in his underwear. He walked a little ways from the cabin and watered the bushes. Just as he finished, he heard a huffing sound. The moon was just bright enough to see fairly well through the darkness. He turned and his mouth dropped open. There, ambling up the path from the lake to the cabin was a bear heading right for him.

"Holy shit!" he yelled and took off for the cabin. The bear stopped dead in its tracks, turned, and ran the other way. Matt flew in the door and slammed it behind him, waking Brandon and Adam. "Grizzl Bear! Grizzl Bear!" he shouted.

Adam and Brandon jumped up to look out the window. The bear was at the dock sniffing through their gear, most likely searching for something to eat. "That's the blackest, smallest Grizzl bear in the whole world," Adam laughed. "Matty, you're something else."

"Well, it looked pretty big and scary when I was only a few feet from it," Matt said in his defense. The other two just laughed and climbed back into their beds. "G'night, Matty."

Matt piloted the Beaver on the way back to the lodge and made a perfect landing. "Looks like I might be out of a job next year if you two keep this up," Brandon said.

The last weeks of summer passed uneventfully. Guests came and went, and the boy each built up a nice little nest egg with their tips. Everything was about as perfect as it could be. As the last couple of weeks approached before the boys and their moms would leave for home and school, Adam thought about what would happen to him. He didn't want to bring it up, but he knew eventually he would return to Rochester and the welfare people would put him in another foster home.

A few days before they would be leaving for home, Mike and Carol took a day off to fly into Nestor Falls for some mysterious business that they kept secret from the boys. When they returned that evening they didn't say what they had been up to, and after dinner, when the lodge was empty of guests, they all gathered in the Great Room in front of the fireplace. Brandon, Matt and Adam sat together on the couch, the four adults in easy chairs, all chatting and laughing as usual.

Mike and Carol exchanged glances. She nodded and he stood. "Carol and I have something to tell you," he said. The boys stopped goofing around and gave their attention to Mike. "Actually, there are two things," he said pulling an envelope out of his back pocket.

"Adam? This is yours."

Adam opened the envelope. It contained a Certificate of Deposit. He looked at Mike with a frown.

"If you open that, you'll see a rather large number on it."

Adam opened the certificate, saw his name, and the amount. "Fifty-one thousand, two hundred and forty dollars? How did I get fifty-one thousand dollars?"

Matt grabbed the paper from Adam's hands. His eyes widened. "Holy shit! Adam, you're rich!"

"Mathew! Your mouth!" Carol scolded.

"Oops. Sorry, Mom," Matt said smiling.

"Your uncle Ed told the sheriff where they had stashed the remainder of the money they stole from you, Adam. When they sold your parents house in Rochester, they didn't put the money in a trust fund, but they bought all of that stuff instead. The sheriff confiscated all of that stuff, and sold it all at auction and that's part of this money. The rest Carl and Ed had hidden in a strong box under the floor. I think Ed was feeling guilty about how they treated you and was trying to make amends. Anyway, that's most of the money… plus a five thousand dollar reward offered by the Lodge Owner's Association for information leading to the arrest and conviction of the burglars was awarded to you, too. So the grand total is a little over fifty one thousand dollars. Plus, one of the stipulations of the jury was that everything Carl and Ed owned should be turned over to you, since they stole your money, so their cabin and the land where it sits are now yours, too. The other paper in that envelope is the deed to the cabin and land. They won't be using it, at least for one hundred and fifteen years. That's the sentence they both got."

"What am I going to do with the cabin?" Adam asked.

"Well, you can sell it or keep it as a summer cabin to use once you get out of school. It's up to you."

"What's it worth?"

"Well, I'd think that lake property is fairly valuable, and while the cabin itself isn't much, it's probably worth twenty-five or thirty thousand dollars. Why?"

"I don't have any good memories of that place. I don't want to keep it. I'd rather sell it and be done with that part of my life."

"I'll call a realtor tomorrow. He'll put it on the market."

"The money is going to be in an interest bearing fund," Carol said. "But you can't use it until you're eighteen. And then you can use it for a college education."

"I… I don't know what to say," Adam said.

Brandon and Matt both high-fived Adam and jostled him good naturedly. "Hey, buddy. How about a loan?" Matt said laughing.

"There is one more thing," Carol said squatting down in front of Adam. She took his hands in hers. "Adam, Mike and I have been corresponding with the welfare department in Rochester for several weeks. They have agreed to transfer your case to Milwaukee County." She paused and looked up at Mike. He smiled. "Now," Carol went on. "If you're agreeable to it, we would like to have you live with us in St. Francis as a foster child for the next six months. We've loved having you with us this summer, and we feel like you are already a part of our family. If, after the six months you feel you want to stay there, we want to adopt you and make you our son."

Silence stunned the room. The snapping and crackling of the fireplace was the only sound. Adam's eyes filled with tears as he glanced from Brandon to Matt. He saw tears in their eyes, too. He nodded. "Yes. Oh, yes!"

The quiet room was suddenly full of laughter and conversation. They all hugged in one big group. Adam noticed Kirby barking and trying to get into the middle of the pack. He knelt down next to the dog. "Kirby, I'm going to come and live with you. Is that okay?" Kirby licked his face.

After a while, when the celebration wound down, the boys said goodnight. They headed down the path to their cabin.

"I'm too excited to sleep yet," Adam said.

"Me too," Brandon said. "Let's sit on the porch."

There was a long silence while they sat in the padded deck chairs on the porch overlooking the lake. Then Matt said: "I'm really happy you're going to be my brother, Adam."

"Thanks, Matt. I couldn't ask for anything better."

"Mark's room has been empty for too long," Brandon said. "It'll be good to hear some laughter in there again."

Just then Adam noticed the Northern Lights dancing across the horizon. Flashes of bright light shot into the sky like searchlights. The colors pranced and swirled like clouds before a windstorm. "The Great Manitou must be happy tonight."

Brandon went into the cabin and returned with blankets for each of them. They covered up and snuggled down in the deck chairs. Kirby climbed up in Adam's chair, carefully put Donald down in Adam's arms, and then lay with his head on Adam's lap.

"You suppose your parents and Mark are up there watching us right now?" Matt asked.

Adam smiled as he stroked Kirby's head. "That's a nice thought, isn't it?"

"I'd bet they are," Brandon said. "And they're happy for the way things turned out."

They watched the Aurora's amazing light show quietly for the next fifteen minutes. Then Adam heard Brandon quietly snoring. He turned toward Matt. He was lying on his side sleeping, a little drool coming from the corner his open mouth. Adam grinned at his new brother. He reached over and pulled Matt's blanket up over his shoulders. "We'll be in the same class in school since I missed last year," he thought. "That'll be fun."

Kirby's feet twitched as he dreamed of whatever it is that dogs dream of. Adam patted his head and whispered to him until he settled down. Then he slid down in the chair with the dog's head next to his. He put his arm around him. "G'night, Kirby. Sweet dreams."

ABOUT THE AUTHOR:

Dan Bomkamp grew up along the Wisconsin River and has enjoyed hunting and fishing the hills and waters his entire life. He made his home in Muscoda after graduating from UW-La Crosse and has been involved in the sporting goods industry most of his life. He began his writing career in the 1980s with short stories and how-to articles for outdoor magazines. This led to a series of stories about his favorite character, Thunderfoot, and from that beginning he has written 6 books. He has hosted 26 foreign exchange students from 11 countries and has traveled to Europe to visit many of them in their home countries. Dan's books, written for adults, have been also very popular among kids. He enjoys visiting schools and talking to kids about reading and writing. He lives in Muscoda with his golden retrievers, Katy and Kirby.

You can contact him at: Dan Bomkamp, 403 Catherine St., Muscoda, WI 53573, or email him at amerdad@mwt.net, or visit his website and leave a message on the Guest Board. www.thunderfoot.wz.cz